It's bizarre—I've only seen Earth from space once, and I was busy trying not to die at the time. Now I'm looking down on a completely different planet, in person, in space, while flying a ship I stole.

I'm actually here. This is all I've ever wanted, though I didn't get it in the *way* I wanted.

And in a few painfully long minutes, I'll find out whether I get to live to see the other seven colony worlds one day, or if I get to die in a dramatic crash and kill all my new friends instead.

Fantastic.

ALSO BY
M. K. ENGLAND

Spellhacker

M. K. ENGLAND

An Imprint of HarperCollinsPublishers

Library of Congress Cataloging-in-Publication Data
Names: England, M. K., author.
Title: The disasters / M. K. England.
Description: First edition. | New York, NY : Harper, An Imprint of
    HarperCollins Publishers, [2018] | Summary: Nax and a handful
    of other space Academy washouts are the only surviving pilots
    after the school is hijacked by terrorists, but in order to spread the
    truth about the attack, Nax and his fellow failures must execute a
    dangerous heist.
Identifiers: LCCN 2017057327 | ISBN 9780062657688
Subjects: | CYAC: Science fiction.
Classification: LCC PZ7.1.E536 Di 2018 | DDC [Fic]—dc23
    LC record available at https://lccn.loc.gov/2017057327

Typography by Jenna Stempel-Lobell
19 20 21 22 23   PC/LSCH   10 9 8 7 6 5 4 3 2 1
❖
First paperback edition, 2019

To everyone who's ever felt like a disaster.
Here, have a spaceship!
Now fly.

ONE

Name: Nasir Alexander "Nax" Hall
Admission Status: Denied

I've been at Ellis Station Academy for exactly twenty-four hours. *Twenty-four hours*, and I've already washed out.

Honestly, I'm not even surprised.

I shove a wadded-up, still-clean pair of boxers into my travel bag, right next to the brand-new Academy T-shirt I just bought *yesterday*. May as well burn it now. Maybe I'll light it on fire and hoist it up the flagpole at Command once I'm back on Earth soil.

A cluster of guys sprawls across the back wall of the barracks, laughing as they pass their exam scores around. They're either too oblivious to know how loud they are or they just don't care, but I hear every word of their conversation.

"Why'd he even bother unpacking? He thought he was such hot shit in the cockpit, but y'all saw how *that* went."

My flight papers crumple in my hand, and I breathe in, slow and deep, barely resisting the urge to put my fist right in the asshole's face. Like I really need a reminder when my brain keeps up a constant lecture on how much of a screwup I am.

Only one other person from my high school made it to the Academy, and of *course* it had to be Tucker Fineman. Somehow this guy, who once got high in a cornfield on laughing gas stolen from his mother's dental practice, is worthy of being an Academy pilot. And I'm not.

I thought I hated him back home, but apparently his douchery hadn't yet achieved its greatest heights. He waltzed into the exam room this morning with a fake smile and a cheesy handshake, like some kind of wannabe politician. I held my breath through his whole entrance interview, waiting for him to spill all my dirt, tell the examiners every reason they should send me home.

He never did. Turns out I didn't need his help getting kicked out anyway.

But if asshats like Tucker are what they're looking for in future colonists, then it's no wonder they decided to pass on the cow-town failboat. Me.

I dump a pile of travel-sized toiletries on top of my packed clothes and tug at the zipper. It resists me, of course, because nothing would make this day better than missing the shuttle back to Earth because I'm too incompetent to even zip my bag. I yank it once, twice, and it closes bit by bit . . . until finally it breaks altogether.

I stare at the bag. The bag stares back.

Finally I pick up it up by the shoulder strap and storm out of the room, followed by snickering whispers and a trail of leaking mouthwash.

Left turn, then right turn, past staff-only doors and high-voltage-area warnings. Eyes up and forward. Don't meet anyone's gaze. Something hot and terrible burns in my chest every time an Academy student walks by with squared shoulders and straight back, laughing, the Academy logo prominent on their chest and sleeves. I count air vents in the ceiling and breathe.

Uniformed instructors and students slowly give way to working officers and plainclothes citizens as I cross from the Academy wing into the common area of Ellis Station. Behind me, new students settle in for their training— six months for civilians relocating to the colonies, and anywhere from one to four years for pilots and officers. Ahead of me, people who have completed their training prepare for their one-way trip out into the black, looking forward to their new lives.

I get neither option. I get awkward parental silences and overly formal politeness instead. Whoo.

The terminal for Earth-bound shuttles isn't far, but my ride is supposed to arrive any minute, so I break into

3

a light jog. My deodorant bounces out of my open bag and clatters to the floor behind me, but I've got no shits left to give for it. Honestly, if I miss this shuttle, I think I'd rather swim back to Earth without a vacuum suit than stay here for a second longer. The bright outline of Earth glows through the viewports like a taunt, casting eerie shadows over the craggy lunar terrain beyond. The silhouettes of the old cargo tunnels connecting the station to the abandoned first settlement slice through the light like something out of a nightmare. They seemed massive and beautiful when I arrived yesterday evening.

Now they're just ugly.

One more left turn, and I'm there. Through the enormous bay window, the arrival/departure board glows with a single flight status: mine, marked as ARRIVING SOON. I haven't missed it. I'd be thankful, but I was actually starting to look forward to that little vacuum walk. Probably better than showing my face back home after screwing up yet another thing.

My parents will be nice enough about it, like they always are, but "nice" and "disappointed in their loser son" aren't mutually exclusive. Nothing like a lecture about good life choices with a side of motherly weeping in the morning. Can't wait. They watched me play pilot while herding the goats out in the field behind the house from age five until embarrassingly recently. Now that future is impossible. Their pity will be excruciating.

At least the golden boy won't be there to witness my grand return and scold me like a child. Malik actually got *his* one-way ticket to life in the colonies. Of course. It's cool, I'll just live with my ammi and dad for the rest of my life, feeding the chickens and flying simulators.

The terminal door is blocked by a black guy about my age locked in conversation with none other than Dr. Herrera herself, the headmaster of the Academy. The guy stands straight and confident, his expression calm, with long English vowels smooth and reasonable on his tongue. His well-fitted polo shirt bears the crest of the School of Colonial Relations stitched over the right side.

Another wannabe politician type. Great.

"Surely there's something we can work out," he says, oozing charm, but apparently the conversation is already over. Dr. Herrera cuts him off with a sharp gesture.

"You made your choice, Rion. Now you have to live with it. Excuse me," she says, glancing at her watch as she dashes away. The guy's cool mask slides into a scowl, and he runs a hand through his dyed-red hair. I catch his eye and grin.

"Guess that means you're with me," I say with false cheer. "What'd *you* do to get kicked out?"

His lip curls. "Piss off, wanker."

Ooh, never been sworn at in an English accent before. Can't say I mind it.

Rion snatches his posh leather travel bag off the

ground and slaps the door control. A green light blinks as the system verifies the breathable atmosphere beyond, then it whooshes open in a rush of stale, recycled air tinged with engine fluids and exhaust. Mechanics and deckhands shout orders and off-color jokes to one another down on the flight deck, their voices echoing in the vast landing bay, mingling with the clanging of tools and the hiss of pressurizing airlocks.

Two girls are already seated at the small cluster of uncomfortable metal chairs bolted to the floor at the back of the bay, underneath the LANDING ZONE 6 sign. We get a special late-evening shuttle just for us, coming to whisk away the freaks and failures under the cover of dimmed hallways and lights-out orders. They may as well glue my feet to the ground once we're back planetside. This is the *only* space piloting program, and I can't reapply for five years. But why bother, only to fail out again? I'm done.

The two girls in the waiting area are a study in contrasts. The blond white girl compulsively bounces her right leg, constantly in motion, staring off into the distance. The other girl is utterly still, practically a statue, her face hidden behind warm brown hands and black semitextured hair come loose from its tie. Neither seems terribly open to conversation, which is fine by me. I'd rather sit and wallow in silence. I wish they had let us bring our tablets to the Academy; at least then I could play some Starhunters and ignore everyone. I walk up and drop my bag, and the darker-haired girl startles at the noise.

"Whoa, on edge much?" I ask, jumping up onto a chair and seating myself on top of the back.

"Oh, bite me." Now that she's looking up, I recognize her; someone in the flight school dorms pointed her out over lunch, said she was one of those college-at-fifteen prodigy types. Some kind of genius. Her accent is 90 percent New York City, 10 percent Spanish, much sharper than my mostly suppressed North Carolina drawl. Her eyes are sharp and intelligent, a beautiful hazel brown that I study for a moment too long, and framed by arched eyebrows that telegraph how completely unimpressed with me she is.

"You know your gear's covered in shaving cream?" she says with innocent sweetness.

I glance down. Sure enough, my shaving-cream can seems to have exploded on impact. Rion gives it a wide berth as he claims a chair for himself, setting his fancy bag down with much more care.

I scoop up a bit of the blue foam from my bag and flick it away. "It's just my Academy shirt, and it's not like I'll be needing that anymore. Why are you all still wearing yours?" I sneer. "If you're here, that means you failed out. Still clinging to the dream?"

As soon as the words are out, I wish I could call them back, but it's like I'm watching someone else be an unbearable asshole and I'm too far away to intervene. Genius Girl purses her lips and looks away, crossing her arms over the tech school's pointed logo on her shirt, but not before I catch the flash of hurt in her eyes. Rion glares up at me from behind long lashes, disapproving.

"Everyone's so uptight," I mutter, eyeing the guy up. He's broader than me—I'm more the long, lean soccer-player type—and he's clean-shaven, compared to my perpetual irritating stubble. His face is angular and handsome underneath his tight curls, with narrow eyes that I'd much rather see bright with humor than glaring at me.

Oops. Too late now.

At the far end of the seating area, the other girl finally looks our way. She shoves her blond hair back from her face, revealing bright streaks of blue at her temples and perfect eyeliner around gray-green eyes. Her toned legs say athlete, but she's wearing the red-and-white of the Academy Medical Corps. I shift in my seat under her level gaze.

"You're right, though," she says, her accented consonants pointed and precise. Russian or something. "There's no point in clinging. They told me right at the start of the entrance interview that I shouldn't have even made it through prescreening. Apparently the colonies are in desperate need of doctors, but not desperate enough to take *me*. It is what it is, right?"

Genius Girl knits her brows and frowns. "That's awful. Why'd they wash you out?"

Dr. Eyeliner shrugs.

"It's personal," she says with a wry smile. "Sorry. What about you?"

Genius Girl is quiet for a long moment.

"It's personal," she finally echoes, combing her fingers through the ends of her tied-back hair. Everyone watches her, waiting for her to elaborate, but all she says is "I just want to go home."

Rion snorts. "I want literally *anything* other than home."

Dr. Eyeliner reaches over for a silent fist bump of solidarity.

A low, soothing tone reverberates through the landing bay, and a wave of blinking red lights chases around the edge of the huge transparent doors holding the vacuum of space at bay. We all turn to watch as a boxy, blue-striped Earth Command shuttle maneuvers into place beyond the outer doors. A calm voice drones over the interior speakers: "Warning. External doors opening." The shuttle nudges forward, and the doors slide shut behind it, trapping it in the transfer airlock. A hissing sound, a warning klaxon, then the voice again: "Inner doors opening."

As the internal doors crack open to admit the shuttle, I close my eyes and breathe slowly through my nose, willing the burning in the corners of my eyes to ease. This is it. The official, final, irreversible end to the only thing I've ever really wanted. The only time I'll see the colonies for the rest of my life will be when I'm sprawled on the couch in my friend's basement, playing Settlement III and covered in Cheetos dust.

I steal a quick glance at my companions, the Fail Class of 2194. Genius Girl takes deep, calming breaths through her nose, her face twisted with pain. Rion's eyes are blank, locked on his folded hands. Eyeliner is on edge, though, her gaze suddenly sharp. She points toward the shuttle as it settles to the deck a hundred yards away from us and to the right. There's a weird splash of color out of place, something bright blue and green on the starboard side.

"What's that on—?"

The lights go out.

The all-station alarm shrieks, the sound reverberating through the vast landing bay in a piercing cacophony. I drop to the floor on pure instinct, crouching behind the row of metal chairs, my heart hammering against my rib cage.

"Communication system failure. Warning. Communication system fail—"

Static.

I poke my head above the chairs just in time to see shadowy figures spill from the newly arrived shuttle, bathed in the dim red glow of the emergency lights. My entire body goes stiff. There are at least six of them, clad in all-black combat-grade vacuum suits and moving in tight, precise formation. Four of them break off and head straight for the doors that lead to the station's main control room. They pause near the traffic controller's booth, and there's a sound like a tiny, faraway gunshot. A distant thud, and the figures continue on.

This is not right, *so* not right. My harsh breaths echo in my ears, and my stomach is singing a reprise of the evening's gravy potatoes. I look to Genius Girl, can just barely see the outline of her face in the dark. The whites of her eyes are wide as she grabs my sleeve.

"There are still two of them in here," she whispers, just as the two commandos pick off a group of mechanics with six quick shots. Genius Girl barely suppresses a scream when the bodies hit the deck.

"They stayed behind to guard their shuttle," Eyeliner says. I nearly jump out of my skin. She's crouched directly next to me; I didn't even hear her move.

The overhead speaker crackles again, but the voice is garbled. "Lifeboat access locked. Life support error in-in-in-in atmospherics. Estimated breathable air remaining: two—"

Silence, but for the distant hissing rush of air escaping into space.

"Two what?" Genius Girl snaps, her voice loud enough that I check for movement near the shuttle. "Two hours?

Two minutes? Two seconds?"

"One minute, forty-fi—" the speaker adds, and our eyes meet, all four of us.

"We have to get to the lifeboats," Rion says, but Genius Girl cuts him off.

"They're locked. Were you even listening? We have to—"

"The shuttle, now!" I snap.

I explode from my crouch and dash off into the darkness, not bothering to check if the others are behind me, my breath rasping harsh in my throat. There's no time for subtlety, so I run as fast as I can, cutting left and right at random, my long legs tearing up the hundred yards between us and the shuttle. If the intruders have a chance to aim, we're dead, but if it's death by shooting or death by asphyxiation, I'll eat a bullet any day. My heart leaps into my throat, but I have to keep it together, keep it together, run, don't lose it—

Eyeliner catches up easily and slaps my arm, interrupting my panic. "I have the guard on the left," she says, and breaks away, leaping over a discarded tool chest with powerful grace. Definitely an athlete.

Another tiny gunshot cracks from somewhere, and there's a disturbance in the air as the bullet whizzes by my ear. The adrenaline of the near miss hits me like a sledgehammer. No time to think, no time—

"One minute, thirty seconds breathable air rema—"

The speaker cuts off again.

We reach the ship.

I have half a second to process the gun barrel hovering a meter from my face, illuminated by the terminal's pale emergency track lighting. I drop, the gun goes off, and I ram my fist between my assailant's legs.

Shit.

No balls. I'm screwed.

A slight *oof* comes from above me, but then the pistol whips down and catches me on the shoulder. I'm about to kiss my ass good-bye when a boot swings out of nowhere and rams into the woman's kidney, quickly followed by a second boot to the head. The woman drops to the ground, motionless, and cool relief floods through me. Dr. Eyeliner to the rescue. Holy hell, this girl is a powerhouse.

"Come on!" Eyeliner urges, fumbling for my arm. Beyond her, Rion and Genius Girl charge up the narrow ramp and into the ship. I hope there are no more commandos up there to greet them.

"Go, I'm right behind you," I tell her as I relieve the passed-out woman of her gun. If action movies have taught me anything, it's never leave the gun behind.

I hit the controls for the docking ramp behind me, make sure it's set to lock, whirl around, and charge down the central corridor. The others are already crammed into the cockpit, strapped into the crew seats. Genius Girl sits in the navigator's seat, but the pilot's chair is empty.

"Tell me you have a flight permit," Genius Girl says as soon as I trip through the door. She's tapping furiously at the touchscreen display and doesn't look up, the light of the screen glowing over her face.

I wince, an instant jolt of fear stabbing into my heart. "Uh, not exactly."

Rion swears creatively. I hold up my hands, then realize I'm still holding the gun and flick on the safety. Whoops. My ammi the police officer would be horrified with me right now.

"Hey, I didn't say I couldn't fly!" I slide into the pilot's seat, set the gun down on a side console, and grab the control wheel with shaking hands. "Just not legally."

Flying is what I came to the Academy for, after all. Can't have a space permit until they say I can, and they've already made their feelings on *that* perfectly clear. Should I tell them I've never flown a real ship, just simulators? Should I tell them about—

Well. What would be the point of that? I'm our only option, apparently. Better to just get my shit together and do this.

Yeah. I can do this.

I adjust the seat until my feet fit comfortably on the rudder pedals, blow out a slow breath, then look over at Genius Girl. "Any chance we can get those bay doors open, or do we have to do this the explodey way?"

"I've almost got it," she snaps back. "Scans show four more ships on the edges of Academy space, by the way, 269 by 53 by 620. You should see them on your heads-up display once we're out of here."

I wipe my sweaty palms on my pant legs and grip the controls again, glancing up at the HUD. "Great. Fantastic. Anyone religious? Want to say some prayers, maybe sing a hymn or two?"

Dr. Eyeliner forces a smile when I peek back around my chair, but Rion only taps his fingers against his folded arms, eyes fixed on the viewport. No one's impressed by my attempt at levity, but it helps tame the writhing ball of nerves in my stomach all the same. Flying by myself? Fine. That would be fine. If I screw something up and get myself killed, that's my problem.

But all these other people in the ship with me?

I close my eyes to the vivid memory of flashing ambulance lights, twisted metal, and blood, my brother's voice and the sirens melding into a blaring alarm in my mind.

"Got it!" Genius Girl says. My eyes snap open, and true to her word, the inner bay doors creep apart. I take a deep breath, say bismillah in my head, and steady my hands.

I feed some power to the magnetic coils, and the ship lifts smoothly off the deck. Okay, good so far. I can do this. Slowly, carefully, I spin us around and ease the throttle open. The ship jerks forward, way too fast.

"Open the outer doors!" I shout as we careen past the first opening.

"I'm trying!" Genius Girl taps away. The doors stay stubbornly closed. I ease back on the controls and tip the ship up, bringing the magnetic coils to bear on the closed doors in front of us, which bounces us back the other way, toward the closing inner doors. This is the worst game of Pong *ever*.

Someone behind me makes that hissing inhale-between-the-teeth noise my ammi used to make when she was teaching me to fly. I'd floor it and go hurtling down Route 401, racing past the cornfields, and she'd make that sound as she held her hair out of her eyes with one hand and choked the life out of the oh-shit handle with the other.

I *hate* that sound.

The outer doors finally begin their slow parting, and as soon as the gap is large enough I push the throttle wide open. The sudden momentum slams me deeper into my chair, my favorite feeling in the world. Simulators never quite got it right—it's even better in a real ship. My stomach swoops as the shuttle's inertial dampener struggles to compensate, and three terrified screams replace the irritating hiss as we hurtle toward the still-opening doors.

Much better.

My timing is fine, though, of course it is, and we

rocket through the opening with several generous inches on either side of the stubby wings. The screams die out as we roar away from the moon's craggy surface, toward the gentle blue glow of the Rock.

I put the ship through a little barrel roll just because I can. I can't resist, even though my brain is half waiting for the ship to explode underneath me or careen out of control without warning. The controls feel different, somehow. More . . . physical, like I can feel the ship as an extension of my feet and hands. I pull a few more maneuvers to get it out of my system, grinning like little-kid me running through the field with his arms out like wings.

"Wait, wait, wait," Rion calls from behind me. "You! You're that asshole all the pilot trainees were bitching about, aren't you? The guy who showed up with a perfect score on the prescreening flight exam."

"Yeah, that was me." I grin, letting it cover up the hollow ache in my chest. It started so well, but obviously it didn't end that way.

"Seriously?" he says. "How in the hell did you manage to fail out?"

"Bigger problems, guys," Genius Girl cuts in. "Point us back toward the station so we can see, hotshot."

I do as she asks, and we swing around just in time to see the billowing clouds of escaping oxygen from the station taper off, then cease altogether. And all at once, the gravity of the situation hits.

"Did they manage to keep the last of the atmosphere from venting?"

I know the truth even as I ask.

No one stopped it. The station ran out of air.

"I'm only getting a handful of heat signatures from the entire station. They're all . . ." Genius Girl trails off, her voice thick with tears.

Tucker Fineman is dead. We went to high school together. I just saw him fifteen minutes ago.

The guy I passed who was cleaning out the vac-suit lockers . . . did he manage to get one on in time? Is he dead, too?

And it's not just the Academy, but all of Ellis Station. The emigration port. The warehouses. The laboratories. All of the air from the whole station, gone.

All of those people, gone.

My stomach is hollow.

I dial back the throttle and let us drift for a moment. The emptiness of space surrounds us, swallows us up in blackness. Stars fill the void beyond the curve of the moon's surface, beyond the reflected light of Earth, dotting the endless horizon with glittering points of brightness.

It's silent in the cockpit for a moment. Just four strangers breathing the same air. Being alive. Trying to process. Who would do this? *Why* would they do this?

Finally Eyeliner speaks. "Should we try to hail the

station? See if any of those heat signatures are survivors? Maybe they were able to—"

Then the comm crackles. "All ships, you are clear to approach along your assigned vectors. The station has been neutralized."

The speakers hiss, then a different voice takes over. "Acknowledged, lead. Should we expect resistance?"

"We cut communications before Earth could be alerted. Clean and quiet. Our insiders are adjusting the logs and flooding the station with fresh atmosphere. We'll be ready by the time you dock. Everything should look status quo from the surface."

Insiders? Someone on the station knew this was going to happen? And helped? My breath catches in my throat, and I turn to Genius Girl. "We have to tell someone."

She nods, mouth hard and eyes blazing. "I'll open a link with Command down on the planet. It'll give away our position, but the GCC shou— Break hard starboard!"

My hands and feet obey before my brain processes her words, and the ship flips up and to our right. A missile flashes past the viewport, and a new voice crackles from the comm, lean and assertive.

"Alpha, this is Tiger Five. Two Flight has located the rogue shuttle. Terminating now."

"Good hunting, Tiger Squadron."

I jam my foot down on the rudder pedal, banking hard as a stream of bullets flashes past. Two hard maneuvers in a row, in an unfamiliar ship, and I'm completely disoriented.

Gotta angle for Earth, shitshitshit, which way is . . .

I spend a precious two seconds studying my instruments, then swing us around to port and tip the nose of the shuttle back. Earth comes into view, a long arc of blue backlit by the sun. With my brain finally calibrated correctly, I open the throttle wide again, prepared this time for the feeling of my organs being squished against the back of my rib cage. Two hundred thirty-nine thousand miles from Ellis Station on the moon to Earth Command down on the surface. My heart pounds deafeningly loud in my ears. I can't screw this up, gotta keep us alive, we're the only ones who *know*.

A flash of color in front of us, two, and a hail of cracking gunfire. Our shields handle most of it, but a single ping of metal-on-metal sounds from the aft, sending a coughing vibration through the ship. Not good, not good . . .

"Damn bastards!" I yank back on the controls as the HUD blares a shrill warning. Missile lock. Again. One of the fighters is on our tail, and there are at least three others circling around, skilled and confident predators. I wasn't *actually* planning on dying today, and as much as I didn't want to be stuck back down on the Rock, I like this even less.

"Another flight incoming!" Genius Girl reports. "About thirty seconds out. They're cutting us off."

I blow out a breath. Steady my hands on the sweat-slick controls. Push down the panic clanging in my skull.

"Okay. Unless you'd like to go home with significantly more holes, I think we need a plan B here," I shout over the ship's groaning complaints and alarms. "All cards on the table, y'all, because there's no way we're gonna make it back to the Rock. This is a clunky-ass shuttle, not a fighter jet, and I can't keep these assholes dancing forever."

Rion leans forward, gets a hand on the back of my chair. "Let's fight back," he shouts in my ear, then loses his grip as I cut the throttle and pull a hard maneuver. A fighter goes sailing past. "I'm a good shot. We can do this!"

"Yeah, great idea! Only we'll have to hang you out the window and let you throw rocks at them, because, once again, this is a damned shuttle, not a fighter. We're toothless," I shoot back. A politician who's good with weapons? There's a scary thought. Where did the fourth fighter go? What I wouldn't give for a ship with weapons right now. . . .

"Call for reinforcements, then," Rion says.

The shields flicker for a brief moment.

"We're being jammed," Genius Girl yells in between bursts of gunfire. She flips a switch, and the cockpit speakers hiss with random garbled patterns.

"Well, fix it!" I jerk the controls hard, throwing

everyone against their restraints, just in time to avoid another missile.

"I can't find a clear frequency!"

I grit my teeth. The nearest fighter wing would have been stationed at the Academy anyway. The pilots are probably all dead. We'd be dust long before help arrived, either by the fighters or the orbital defense guns ready to shoot down anything without landing clearance. We're out of options.

My stomach sinks. I hesitate, gulp for air to calm my racing heart, but there's no time.

Say it.

"I think we have to jump for the colonies."

A beat of silence.

"Do it," Dr. Eyeliner says, precise and calm.

"You're cracked!" Genius shouts over the increasingly worrying noise from the engines. "What about the no-return rule? If we leave—"

"What choice do we have?" Rion shoots back. "If we'd made it through our time at the Academy, we wouldn't have been able to go back anyway. That was always the deal. I want to live. So we have to jump."

I don't bother adding to the commentary. The HUD is solid red, and between its screeching and the static over the speakers, my head is crowded and panicked. I'm definitely going to get us killed. I can't do this, I'm terrible, I've never even flown a real ship before, this is *impossible*. My hands slip on the controls, nervous sweat and trembling muscles making the job so much harder. One fumble, one wrong maneuver, and those fighters will have us.

I take one last look at the sun rising over Earth's jewel-tone arc, then swing the shuttle around and throw us into the black, out of the moon's gravity shadow. The bullets follow, slamming against hull instead of shield now.

"Does this thing even have an A-drive?" I think to ask at the last second.

But it must, because Genius Girl pulls up the nav chart and picks an illuminated destination at random. The whining from the engines ramps up, increasing in pitch and sending a horrific shudder through the pedals under my feet. Oh god, we're actually doing it, actually leaving Earth space, never coming back, never seeing our families again, and I knew it was coming, I *wanted* it, but not like this, not—

Stomach dropping, rib cage compressed, light bending in incomprehensible headache-inducing ways. Hold her steady, hit the mark, one last sudden acceleration . . . then the space in front of us scrunches. A tiny hole in the universe appears, just for us.

We're gone.

TWO

BA-CLANG, BUMP, BA-CLANG, BUMP. SCREE-eeeeeeeeeeeeeeeeee . . .

The noises as we pop back into normal space are *not* comforting. The ship's vibrations crawl up my legs, an intense itch, and the controls buck in time with every *CLANG* from the aft.

"Status report!" I snap, because it seems like the kind of thing someone should say in this situation. It comes out less like authority and more like a plea for reassurance.

Genius Girl looks over her shoulder to check on Rion and Eyeliner. "Everyone's okay," she says, her voice shaky. "We're in the A-jump arrival zone outside the colony world al-Rihla. Um . . ."

She trails off, and her tapping on the display is much slower than it was before the jump, her fingers shaking over the glowing screen. She closes her eyes for a second and bites her lip, breathing in for four counts and out for eight. I have to look away. Her expression is too close to the same cracking feeling inside my chest, the one threatening to steal the breath from my lungs; I'm going to break open right along with her if I don't get us moving again.

I open the throttle halfway to move us out of the arrival zone, just in case any more ships jump in behind us. Good first step. It would be embarrassing to escape a daring firefight in the skies over Earth's moon only to be obliterated by some arriving supply ship. Once we're safely away, I flop back in the pilot's seat.

"Well," I start, then swallow painfully. My throat is thick, my voice a ragged disaster. "So much for Earth."

The no-return rule is officially in effect. We can never set foot on Earth soil ever again. Rion and Dr. Eyeliner don't seem too bothered—both staring out the viewport with blank expressions—but Genius Girl makes a strangled sound and hides her face in her hands.

The enormity of it comes crashing down on me.

I never got to say good-bye to my parents. Not for real. We sat in the spaceport parking lot in near silence for almost ten minutes before I gave up and got out of the car, grabbed my bag, and just . . . left. I was supposed to be back in six months for the winter break. I was supposed to come home with a flight permit and a wing-leader insignia on my uniform, and they were supposed to cook me dinner and call my uncles and aunts to brag and forgive me for every mistake I've ever made.

And now it'll never happen, along with video games

at Mel's house and pickup soccer at the abandoned farm and climbing all over ancient crumbling barns with Riz. No more stuffing my face during endless Eid visits with my ammi's whole family, or Christmas cider and pecan pie with Grammy and Pa, and it's all gone, *gone*.

It's not even like I disagree with the no-return rule, really. The last thing the human race needs is some weird space virus that only affects the fruit-fly population but leads to a worldwide ecosystem collapse. They have proven decontamination procedures out in the colonies, but no one trusts them enough to risk the homeworld. A bit paranoid, maybe, but it only takes one space plague to bring ruin to the birthplace of humanity. Besides, we couldn't just go out into space, multiply, then let all those people come back to an Earth that's already bursting at the seams and just barely over its first energy crisis. Harsh, but necessary.

I always planned to end up out here permanently. My parents mostly supported me, and I knew I'd be leaving Earth forever after my four years at the Academy. But this . . . this is not what I imagined at all. So soon. And sudden.

My stomach roils with the weight of it. This would be such a bad time to vomit.

"Hey, everyone?" Rion asks, his voice deep and even. "Does that screeching sound like venting atmo to any-one else?" He says it with the cadence of a joke, but his knuckles are pale where they grip the back of my seat.

Genius Girl wipes her eyes and peers at her display.

"I would love to disagree with you," she says, breath still ragged, "but this blinking red screen in front of me seems to think you're right."

"Can we make it to al-Rihla before the air runs out?" Doc Eyeliner asks, straight to the point.

I thumb the throttle control slowly forward, easing more juice to the engines, but they only cough harder. I really have killed us all. Deep breath, Nax. "Looking less likely by the minute."

"The atmo is actually not our biggest problem," Genius Girl says. Rion's and Eyeliner's calm seems to have steadied her somewhat. These people have their shit surprisingly together when faced with imminent doom. How the hell did they end up as washouts?

Al-Rihla grows larger on the horizon, filling the starboard side of the viewport with its glowing red-and-blue arc, its two moons reflecting the light of the yellow sun. I gently turn the controls to the right to bring us more in line with the planet.

Nothing happens.

I test the roll using rudder pedals, and the wings tip up and over just fine; I push the controls in and pull out again to test the pitch, and the nose of the shuttle tips up and down. Finally I wiggle the controls left and right to test the yaw, with small motions at first, then larger, until

I'm wrenching it from one extreme to the other.

Nothing. No side-to-side motion. We can't *turn*.

"So, I'm guessing *this* is our biggest problem," I say, lying back against the headrest to look at Genius Girl. I'm hovering right on the sharp edge of panic, every muscle in my body tense, but I keep my words as even and chill as I can. If I give in to that shivery tingle of dread in my gut, they'll all panic, too, and they'll figure out that I *really* shouldn't be flying this ship and we'll definitely all die.

Genius Girl's jaw tightens, too caught up in her own fear to notice mine. "Yeah. The yaw control mechanism is out."

"Okay," I say, wiping my palms on my thighs and checking my grip on the controls. "I'm fine. This is fine."

The ironic thing is, my first reaction to stress has always been to go blow money on flight sim time. What am I supposed to do when the stress happens *while flying*?

I close my eyes and picture the HUD as a video game screen, then study it again. "Okay, from our current angle, we should still hit the planet. Not literally hit, I hope, but I mean . . . I should be able to land. I think."

Super-inspiring leadership there, Hall. "I'm pretty sure I won't screw this up! You're okay with that, right, y'all?" Asshat.

Rion unbuckles himself and leans forward to look out the front viewport, his hand pressing into my shoulder where he grips the back of the pilot's chair. I glance over at the other two; Genius Girl has gone pale, and Eyeliner is unconsciously bouncing her legs again. We need to refocus.

"Okay, I don't want to keep calling you Dr. Eyeliner and Genius Girl in my head," I say, my voice light. "Don't suppose I could get some real names before we try to not crash this thing?"

"Dr. Eyeliner is a terrible nickname," Eyeliner says.

Very helpful. I blow out a slow breath.

"Well, give me something else to work with, then."

Eyeliner studies me with those cool green eyes and stills her fidgeting, her mouth playing at a smile as if she gets what I'm trying to do. "Zinaida. Call me Zee," she says.

"Case," Genius Girl says without looking up from her display, the name offered like a bullet. I shrug and look up to meet Rion's eyes.

"And you I already know, I suppose."

"Do you, though?" he asks, a playful lilt to his voice. "Well, you have one up on me. Do I get to know your name?"

Hello, now we definitely have to live through this. I put on my most charming grin and offer him my hand, which he takes in a firm grip. "Nax Hall, at your service."

Rion squeezes once, a tiny quirk at the corner of his mouth, then releases my hand.

"So, yeah, nice to meet you all and everything," he

says, "but I'd still prefer to not die if at all possible. What can I do to help?"

The naming exercise has just the effect I'd hoped. The others look to me, and I nod to bolster my confidence.

"Okay, um, Case," I say, trying my best to cement "Genius Girl = Case" in my mind. "Do you think the manual yaw will still work, or was the entire mechanism blown off?"

She taps the screen a few times, then shakes her head. "I can't tell. The computer can't *see* the yaw control, so I don't know if it's because it's not there, or because the connection to the computer was damaged. We'll just have to try it."

"Right." I look over my shoulder. "Rion, the manual crank should be—"

"I got it, hotshot," he says, clapping me on the shoulder as he ducks out the door. Doc Eyeliner—Zee—unstraps herself too.

"I'm going to see about parachutes and medical supplies. Good luck, friends. You'll be fine," she says, and disappears after Rion, muttering something under her breath in Russian with a shake of her head.

"Did you catch that last part?" Case asks me, shaking out the tension in her hands.

"I think I get the general idea," I say, though Russian isn't one of my languages. Swear at me in Pashto, then we can talk.

We sit in silence while al-Rihla, the jewel of the colonies, gradually takes over more and more of the viewport. It looks exactly like it did on the pages of my textbooks, only so much more. I let my eyes linger for a moment, taking in green continents outlined in rich red sand and huge, intensely blue oceans that glitter below. I know we're in a life-or-death situation, but it's hard not to be overwhelmed by the view. I can see why all the anti-exploration crap went away once a few humans actually got out here. Who could look at all this and not want it? It's bizarre—I've only seen Earth from space once, and I was busy trying not to die at the time. Now I'm looking down on a completely different planet, in person, in space, while flying a ship I stole.

I'm actually here. This is all I've ever wanted, though I didn't get it in the *way* I wanted.

And in a few painfully long minutes, I'll find out whether I get to live to see the other seven colony worlds one day, or if I get to die in a dramatic crash and kill all my new friends instead.

Fantastic.

Case interrupts my thoughts with a harsh laugh out of nowhere.

"Crashing in slow motion is the worst," she says, the bright edge of panic tearing her sarcastic words to ragged pieces. "My brain really doesn't need more time to list every possible thing that could go wrong. When we're

31

doing stuff, it's fine, but now it's like, are you sure you rerouted the power correctly? Better check again. Okay, back to the main screen. But are you *sure* it was okay? Better check again. *God*."

I almost chuckle, though she probably wouldn't appreciate that, because I know exactly what she means. Those obsessive thoughts—Don't screw it up, you're gonna screw it up, just wait until you screw it up. It's torture. Her hands twist and writhe in her lap, and her breath is getting worryingly labored. Maybe I should intervene.

"The slow motion thing, *yes*. It's like, hey! Wanna know if there's a fiery crash in your future? Well, you'll just have to wait and see. In the meantime, please enjoy an in-flight beverage. The latest SkyMall catalog has been uploaded to your tab."

A surprised laugh bursts out of her, the sort that's already halfway to a sob. I look over and catch her gaze, her dark eyes wet and lovely and defiant.

"Hey." I hold out my hand to her. "We got this."

She holds my gaze for a beat too long, her expression unreadable, then reaches out and gently squeezes my hand. "We got this," she echoes.

And she smiles, just a little bit, but it makes her hand in mine feel suddenly intense. I run my thumb over her knuckles, once, twice.

She's quiet for a moment, then squeezes my hand once more and drops it. She goes back to tapping on the display like nothing happened, swiping a map over to my screen with a quick gesture. "It looks like our present course will take us over the beach right outside the founding city, Saleem. No casualties on the ground if we can manage to aim there. Just a little help from the manual yaw should do it."

"I can think of worse places to crash than the most beautiful beach on the best of the colony worlds. Assuming we don't overshoot and land in the ocean, I mean, but it'll be a nice view on the way down." Silver lining, right? Maybe we'll get really lucky and they'll bury us here.

Case hums her agreement. "My moms always wanted to retire on al-Rihla, actually. They were planning to pack up and move as soon as I graduated the Academy. They'll be pissed I saw it first."

Then the comm crackles to life. "Unidentified shuttle, you have entered al-Rihla airspace. Flight is restricted to those who have filed an approved flight plan with the Air and Space Travel Control Commission. Please state your affiliation, cargo, and intentions immediately."

Case's gaze snaps to mine, her eyes wide. My mouth hangs half open, but my brain hasn't supplied it with any words to speak. A high-pitched warning tone pierces my skull, and I check the HUD: surface-to-air missiles locked on.

Shit.

I yank the controls sharp to the left, then remember.

No yaw. We won't be avoiding any missiles unless their aim is incredibly terrible. Gotta do something, gotta . . .

"Say something!" I hiss to Case.

"Uhhhh . . ." She looks all around the cockpit as if it might provide a magic solution. The comm crackles again: "Unidentified shuttle, we have a missile lock on your vessel and will fire in fifteen seconds if you do not identify yourself. Now."

Case slaps the control and shouts through a burst of static. "Mayday, mayday, mayday, our yaw control mechanism has been damaged and we are coming in for a hard landing. Please clear our approach vector. We're aiming for undeveloped terrain and will avoid collateral damage as much as possible."

"Negative, shuttle, break off and maintain orbit. We will send a transport up to—"

"Sorry, control, but we can't do that. We're leaking atmosphere, and asphyxiation is a really terrible way to go," Case says, and I snort. It wasn't funny, not really, but as the ship enters the outer atmosphere and begins to shake apart, I find it hard to keep a grip on myself—or the controls. My eyes burn with welling tears, but my breath keeps hitching like I'm about to bust out in hysterical laughter or start sobbing. Gotta pull it together. Gotta keep them safe. No fancy piloting, no sudden maneuvers. Do. Not. Mess. This. Up.

The nose of the ship glows a dull orange as we hit the

atmosphere in earnest, and the ship gives a violent shudder beneath us. There's an awful creaking sound, slow, then faster, faster until the metal shrieks, and *clangclangclang, fwing*!

"What the hell did we just lose?" I shout, my arms shaking with the effort of holding the ship steady.

"You don't want to know. We need that yaw control now if we're going to avoid taking a bunch of people out with us, though!"

"RION!" I throw my weight forward onto the controls to keep the nose of the ship from tipping backward. The atmospheric drag desperately wants to send us tumbling end over end, burn us alive, and rain our ashes over the kindly people of Saleem. "Rion, I need yaw to starboard, fifteen degrees!"

"Aye!" Rion calls back, and slowly, *slowly*, the nose of the shuttle eases to my right.

The rudder pedals are fighting me, so I stand up, bringing my full weight down on the right one as we careen into the mountainous region bordering the shoreline. Dark smudges of lush green foliage and riverside agricultural settlements whip past as the ship kicks onto its side just enough to slip between two peaks, but then the nose drifts, drifts. . . .

"Stop yawing!" I shout back to Rion, not even slightly sure that yawing is an actual word, but also not giving a flying, crashing fuck. The ground rushes up to meet us, a hard-packed wall of beach sand that may as well be steel at the speed we're going. At least we're going to miss the city. No civilian deaths on my conscience today. Who the hell decided I should be the pilot for this party of losers? Did we seriously survive the slaughter of the entire Academy only to die on the most beautiful colony world without ever getting to see it?

The ship gives a violent shudder as the landing gear snaps into place below us, but it won't do much for us on our makeshift landing zone. We're coming in way too hot.

This is going to hurt. Oh, it's going to hurt so bad. If I'd flown better once we left the station, we wouldn't be this damaged, we wouldn't be crashing at all, and this is *my* fault—but maybe I can at least give us a fighting chance.

"Strap yourselves down to something!" I call out, give them a count of five to comply, then haul back on the wheel, bringing the nose of the shuttle up. The viewport is all red-orange sand now, racing up to punch me in the face, and I have a sudden thought.

Red sand.

At the last second before impact, I thumb on the magnetic coils, and then *CRASH, CRUNCH!* The nose of the shuttle rushes back toward the cockpit in the second right before the impact cushions deploy with a deafening *POP*, blocking the viewport. The shuttle tips sickeningly, screams fill the cabin, and shattering glass tinkles like tiny bells. Then we're bouncing once, twice, then smaller bounces, over and over until finally, with one last scraping crunch, the ship skids to a stop.

Silence. I lie with my head pillowed on the inflated airbag, sprawled at an angle that wouldn't work if gravity were in the usual place. A slip-slide on my cheek—am I crying? I lift one shaky hand, and it feels like someone else's flesh as it presses to my cheek, gathers the wetness. I pull back, holding the hand in front of my half-lidded eyes.

The hand—*my* hand—is red.

THREE

THE FIRST FIVE MINUTES AFTER the crash are a blur. A few distant sounds clang and thump their way into my skull, but it's all so far away. Muted. Like the sound of the goats bleating at mealtimes, the volume cut by my closed bedroom window. Is it my turn to feed them? Make Malik do it. There's something glorious simmering in the kitchen, the air heavy with the warmth of sautéed onions and chiles and garam masala. But the taste—it's gritty, not spicy, and the peppery smell mingles with sweat and the rough pressure of strong arms wrapped around my waist, hauling me up—

Light bursts into my skull, and I stumble back. The scent of spices disappears. My heels sink into the ground and my arms pinwheel at my sides, but I fall anyway, my ass landing in a puff of red sand. Rion steps into my field of vision and holds out a hand, grinning.

"You all right, mate?"

His hand blurs into two for a moment, but I reach out

and manage to take it, my head spinning as he pulls me back to my feet.

"You know," he says, grabbing my shoulder to steady me, "I can't tell if it's the height of captainly self-sacrifice or absolute bloody stupidity to tell everyone to strap in and not do it yourself."

"My vote is stupidity," Zee says from somewhere behind me, but I don't feel quite steady enough to turn around and look.

"Case?" I ask. A shooting pain lances through my skull when I talk, so strong I feel it in my teeth. I lean into Rion until the pain recedes, hoping he won't mind my grip on his bicep.

Zee sets a bag down in the sand and leans in to inspect my face. She must have found the shuttle's first-aid kit. Lucky me.

"Case is fine, too," Zee says, dabbing a stinging antiseptic wipe over my forehead with cool confidence, utterly unfazed by the blood staining the cloth. "You're the only casualty."

My head goes light again, and Zee catches me by the shoulders as I sway. She keeps up a steady stream of chatter as she sprays the gash with liquid bandage to stop the bleeding, but her voice is as vague and wavering as the heat rising off the beach around us.

They're all okay. I didn't get them killed. It was a near

39

thing, though, and the giant weight on my chest won't quite let up.

"Is it going to scar?" I ask Zee, gesturing weakly at my forehead.

She smirks and strips off her glove. "Never fear, hotshot; it takes a pretty deep cut to leave a scar these days."

My vision finally begins to clear, and I'm glad it does, because this place is *gorgeous*. It was horrifying when it was rushing up through the viewport of the shuttle, but now that my feet are on the ground, the contrast between the red sand beach and the crystalline blue water in the near distance is stunning. Saleem sits bright and golden just a bit downshore, right up against the water only a mile or two away. The rhythmic rush of the waves drifts on the breeze, along with a sweet sort of perfumy smell that's probably coming from the flowering scrubby bushes we crushed with our ship. A ship that's making an ominous ticking sound. Hopefully just the engines cooling down. Yeah. That's it.

Case emerges from the shuttle with a cargo duffel looped over her shoulder and a focused, determined expression. "I grabbed the shuttle's emergency supply stash and pulled the flight recorder from the nav console," she says, setting the bag down and dropping to the ground beside it. "The data evidence, right? Of what we saw. All the comm recordings, nav data . . ."

She trails off, and everyone falls silent at the reminder

of the station, of the lives lost. In all the excitement of nearly dying, I'd almost forgotten. I can't help but be impressed, though, that she both thought to grab the recorder and knew how to take apart the console to get it. Glad someone here has a brain.

She continues, subdued. "The Earth Embassy should be our first stop. We tell them what we know, get a message onto one of the Earth-bound courier ships, and beg forgiveness for ignoring their traffic control. These are extenuating circumstances, right? Maybe they can waive the no-return rule or something."

Zee raises an eyebrow with a cool expression. "You can do what you want, good girl, but I'd actually rather not go back. Leave me out of it."

"Excuse me, *Dr. Eyeliner*, who're you calling 'good girl'?" Case snaps.

"I'm *not* going back," Rion says with finality, cutting off Zee's retort. "Besides, there were insiders at the Academy who helped the attack happen, remember? Everyone who wasn't born on this planet is an Academy graduate. Who's to say some of them aren't somehow in on it, too?"

Case rolls her eyes. "Bit paranoid, don't you think? Besides, I don't think we'll have much of a choice. We can't just decide we suddenly have colonial citizenship. What are you going to do, hide in the sewers for the next ten years?"

They both have good points. I take a few cautious,

experimental steps on my own, stretching my legs while Zee aggressively repacks the medbag.

"Maybe we should lie low for a bit," I say, choosing my words with care. "Get to town, find a place to stay, and see if a courier ship has jumped in-system with a news update. I know these murdering assholes tried to cover it up, but do you really think they could kill off that many people and keep it quiet? Then, if it looks safe, we can get the flight recorder to the authorities and try to negotiate over visas—whether for staying or going, as we each choose. And we'll try to get a warning back to Earth no matter what. Fair?"

Rion's fists unknot at that, and his face smooths into a neutral expression. "Fair. Once we know more, we can make a real decision."

"Assuming they don't arrest us the second we set foot inside the city limits," I add. "I'm guessing they won't be wild about us landing-slash-crashing illegally in their desert. They might be flying out here to arrest us right now, for all we know."

Case wraps a hand around her tied-back hair and pulls, her face drawn tight. She bites her lip, then shakes her head.

"We're only going to make it worse for ourselves if we don't come clean right away."

Zee hoists the medbag back onto her shoulder and stands, adjusting her somehow-still-perfect blue-and-blond hair. "You know, as much as I hate to say it, maybe she's right. There's nothing I want less than to finally get away from Earth, only to spend my first few years in jail."

I scrub a hand through my hair and look toward the buildings rising on the horizon. "Look, we don't even know where anything is. Let's just start walking toward the city. We can't keep standing next to this shuttle that could explode at any second. And if they *are* coming out to investigate the wreck, I'd rather not be here when they arrive."

The others turn to look at the shuttle as one, but I can't. The sight of the twisted metal, flaking blue paint, and shattered acrylic makes my stomach turn. We survived *that*.

Together, we set off toward civilization, shuffling along through the sand and scrub in silence while my brain plays on infinite loop. I could have killed us all. My first time at the controls outside of a simulator. I was responsible for their lives, and I almost blew them all to pieces. We were lucky as hell.

"I . . ."

Damn. I clear my throat.

"I'm sorry about the rough landing. I'm glad no one else was hurt."

Rion chuckles and peeks at me out of the corner of his eye. "The rest of us have half a brain and buckled up. Of all the stuff that broke on that ship, we were lucky

43

the safety systems stayed with us. The impact cushioning kept us all alive." He bumps his shoulder into mine. "That, and the last-second bit of fancy you pulled."

Even Case thaws a bit at that. "Yeah, what made you think to cut in the mag coils before we hit?"

A small smile pulls at the corner of my mouth, the weight of mortality easing a bit.

"At the last second, I thought, 'The sand is red. Red means high in iron. Worth a try.' My parents' farm has lots of red clay soil, so I guess it stuck in my brain somewhere. I'm surprised it worked. I didn't think there'd be enough unoxidized metal content to really give any magnetic pushback. The shuttle must've had really sensitive mag coils." I shrug. "It was just a hunch."

"Well, I like your hunches," Zee says, kicking up a sandy cloud. "I'm even tempted to call it genius, but I know what pilot egos are like."

She smiles to soften the teasing, and a little thrill of pride bursts in my chest at being called "pilot" . . . immediately drowned by a powerful wave of shame. I don't deserve that. We barely survived. Every time I get behind the controls, something goes wrong. Do they suspect?

"Well, you know, I do what I can." I swallow hard. "I guess some of us are just good like that."

Case rolls her eyes and snorts, but I catch her trying to suppress a smile, too. Cute.

Zee spins around and somehow manages to walk

backward through the sand as she talks. "You know what this day really needs? A *soundtrack*."

"*Yes*." I seize the neutral topic like it's a life raft. Distract me, *please*. "Tell me Bright and Burning isn't the absolute perfect background music for a walk along the most gorgeous beach you've ever seen after epically surviving a shuttle crash."

"*Yes!*" Zee claps her hands for emphasis, but Rion makes a disgusted sound. I roll my eyes.

"What, is Bright and Burning too *common* for your refined tastes? I suppose you and your *mates* take tea at the symphony?"

Rion flips me two fingers. "I hate the lead singer, actually. The rest of their sound is top."

Zee gasps, scandalized and more animated than I've seen her thus far. "You hate Ella Rider's voice? Never speak to me again, you heathen."

"Agreed. You've been voted off the crew. Have a nice life." I toss him a wink, and Rion chuckles, shaking his head.

I glance over at Case to see if I can draw her into the conversation, but she's lost in her head, her mouth tense and downturned. Maybe best to leave her alone for a bit.

We crest a particularly large dune, and the city is suddenly before us, spreading out over the beach like a glittering spiderweb of glass and steel. Just like the suburbs back on the Rock, the outskirts of this city are quiet and sparse, with only a few buildings placed intermittently along paved pathways. Al-Rihla is one of the oldest colonies, founded a hundred years ago, and Saleem is its oldest city. It's fairly well developed by colonial standards, with three generations of expansion piled atop the core infrastructure they laid out upon arrival. Still small when measured against Earth cities, but beautiful and fascinating all the same.

My mind is still reeling from everything that's happened in the past hour—thousands dead, getting shot at, crashing a shuttle, *stop it*—but even still, a part of me bounces with childlike excitement at actually standing on another planet, hiking toward a city I grew up learning about in history class. And not just any colony, but the *first* one, the site of so many important political conflicts in the early anti-colonization days. This is where I wanted to be. This is where I was meant to be. I always thought I'd be doing this with my brother along for the ride, but things change, I guess. Sometimes drastically.

We head toward the outermost roads. After falling out of the sky, my feet are eager to feel solid pavement beneath them, though a piece of my heart is still out there looking down on a new planet for the first time. The rolling beach dunes level out the closer we get to the city, the sand increasingly dotted with tiny shells and chips of rock. Empty construction sites line the outskirts of the city, signs of a thriving colony with reason to grow, though it must be a rest day because the workers are all absent.

We walk past half-finished buildings and windows with no glass until the structures come more and more frequently. As we move toward the center of the city, they shift from temporary portable dwellings to more permanent structures. After a few minutes we're surrounded on all sides by row houses, neighborhood markets, and coffee shops that smell divine even though I don't drink the stuff. A few people walk the streets, wearing everything from salwar kameez to jeans and T-shirts to business suits, sometimes with a hijab or other cover. We definitely stick out a bit, being a bit roughed up from the crash. We're just . . . farmers. Yeah. Who look like we've been rolling around in our own goat pens. It's fine.

Most people don't spare us even a cursory glance as we weave our way into the street traffic. I catch a few words of conversation here and there in several languages; some English, some Arabic, some Spanish, and I catch a few familiar words in Pashto and Urdu. But there's more that I can't even identify, all tangling together in a current of melodic speech that provides a steady background hum for the everyday clamor of city life. The building styles change as we move through the layers of the city, like a look back through its growth over the last hundred years: still-functioning pop-up shelters, sleek ultramodern towers, metal and poured concrete, treated wood and local quarried stone. Over it all, the planet's sun burns, bigger in the sky than Earth's own star without being oppressively hot.

More and more people press in around us as we near the center of the city, and the salty scent of ocean air is slowly overwhelmed by movie-theater popcorn, restaurants, fancy bakeries, and beauty shops. It's so busy here, so different from small-town Nowhere, North Carolina, packed with bodies and noise and constant motion. I hold up one hand and slow my pace. We should probably figure out where we're going before we get too absorbed into the crowd. Zee clears her throat, speeding her steps until she's at my side.

"Case is getting jittery back here," she says, low, with her chin near my shoulder. "We need to figure out where we're going before she bolts."

"Yeah," I breathe, barely a whisper. "I have no idea where we are, though. The signs aren't exactly helpful."

"As much as I'd love to visit the Arts District and Restaurant Row, I don't think they're going to help us right now," she says.

"There's got to be a map around here somewhere. Maybe we can—"

"We have a great visitor's center a few blocks away," a small, cheerful voice says, "but I'd be happy to show you around myself!"

My heart leaps into my throat. I nearly elbow the poor

kid in the nose when I whirl to face him. He can't be more than ten or eleven years old, but he wears a big grin on his face and an expensive-looking tablet link over one ear. He's dressed in fine clothes, and together with the earpiece it makes him look like a tiny businessman, the picture of respectability. I twist around to look at Rion and Case. They both shrug. Great. If this blows up in our faces, guess it's all on me.

"Okay, kid. We're looking for the Earth Embassy and a place to stay. And we need to schedule a message to be sent back to Earth on the next courier ship, too." Also, if you rat us out, I'll ask Zee to use her superior kicking skills on you; I don't care how old you are. And then I'll take that earpiece, because *awesome*.

"No problem, Earther, I know just the place. Follow, please!"

He sets off on a street perpendicular to our previous path, and the crowd parts for him with fond smiles and pats on the head. I struggle to keep up, though his legs are much shorter than mine. He leads us farther into the busy center of town, which makes me both more and less nervous—more bodies to hide our presence, but more eyes to follow our movements.

The architecture takes another turn when we reach Old Saleem, the heart of the original settlement. It's a complete mishmash; the original manufactured buildings that were shipped along with the first wave of settlers, heavily modified by this point, form the basis of the neighborhood. Saleem's first and grandest masjid is the focal point, built soon after the city's founding and the first structure to be constructed from local materials. Its grand dome and soaring minaret glitter white and gold as they catch the early evening sunlight.

This whole city reminds me a bit of my ammi's home in Pakistan. The enormous skyscrapers, the lights, though thankfully not the traffic. My heart gives a sharp pang, and a stab of homesickness knocks the breath from my chest for a moment. Those trips to visit my ammi's family in the years after peace settled in the region were some of the biggest highlights of my childhood. And I'll never see any of it ever again.

I nearly trip over two boys playing tag in the busy street, and the sight tugs at the deepest part of me, the part that remembers summers split between the farm in North Carolina and a high-rise apartment building in Karachi. That was me and Malik when we were that age, before he became perfect and I became an utter mess. Just two kids chasing each other around and annoying the hell out of everyone around us, inseparable best friends and ultimate rivals. Before everything got complicated.

I shove it all away and jog to catch up with our guide. We have bigger problems right now.

"Hey, wait!" I call, drawing level with him. "How far is it to the embassy? Will it take long to get there?"

"Only about ten more minutes on foot," he says, sketching a tiny bow to an older man who crosses in front of us. "It's out of the way. There's a hotel in the same neighborhood that will work for you. They are . . . quiet, there. You'll like it. Just what you need."

"Sounds good," I say, relaxing a bit. "But we don't have any money to tip you. Maybe you can show us to a secure bank on the way?"

"No need, sir. The shop and hotel owners pay me for each customer I bring to them. My services are free for you."

"Oh." Lucky break.

Zee steps to the boy's opposite side, giving the crowd a discreet once-over.

"So," she begins in a kind voice, "what can you tell us about this city? Did you grow up here?"

It's fascinating—one second she's ready to kick a guy in the head, and the next she's everyone's favorite aunt. The boy instantly warms to her.

"No, miss, I was born back on Earth, but I moved here when I was five. I know every street in this city, though. You'll see. It was founded by the 30:22 Explorers, so we have a large Muslim population with people from almost every country on Earth. Some of the smaller Muslim-owned shops will close for ten or fifteen minutes at prayer times, but many others will stay open. If you follow another religion, the multicultural center next to city hall can tell you where to go for your needs. Much of the food in Saleem is halal, and it is easy to find vegetarian options if you need. Umm . . ."

The boy sticks his tongue out as he thinks. "Most laws are the same as GCC standard, but there are a few differences. Mostly business related, boring money things. The embassy has an excellent guide to share with visitors that explains in detail. You'll be fine until then. I'll tell you if it looks like you're doing anything illegal," he says with a mischievous grin. "Any other questions, miss?"

Zee looks back to us and raises her eyebrows.

Rion shrugs. "That about covers the essentials, I think. You're an excellent guide, little guy."

The boy turns to smile at us, his gap-toothed grin infectious. "Just doing my good for the community. Happy to help."

Just then, I'm yanked to a stop by a hand on my elbow. I whirl around to find a girl in a bright turquoise hijab, her hand twisted in my jacket, eyes blazing.

"There you are, Nax!" She lets go as soon as she has my attention. "I've been looking all over for you. I've already made us all hotel reservations, but they'll give away our rooms if we don't get there soon."

I stare. I've never seen this girl before in my life, but she does something with her head that says, "Come on, ask questions later." She darts her eyes over to the little boy, then back to me, and that's interesting: our young guide is standing with his arms crossed and feet planted, brows deeply furrowed, with a glare far too intense for such a young kid. My gut gives a pang of warning, so I step closer and lower my voice.

"How do you know my name?" I ask, watching her eyes carefully.

"That boy is leading you straight to the police station," she hisses between her teeth. She scans the crowd over my shoulder, then snaps her gaze back to me. "He's after your reward money. I'll tell you whatever you want, but we need to go. Now."

I glance over at our guide, and sure enough, the boy is speaking in rapid-fire Bengali with two fingers pressed to his tablet interface. Shit.

"I'm sorry," I say to the girl, loud enough for the others to hear. "We tried to comm you but the call wouldn't go through."

"No problem, so long as we hurry." Her eyebrows are definitely *significant* as she says it, and she flicks a small coin to our young guide. "For your trouble, Khoka."

"Hey, but—" the boy starts, but our new guide grabs my sleeve again and drags me down an alley before I can catch the rest of his protest. I manage to look over my shoulder to make sure the others are following and toss them a smile I hope comes off as reassuring. After all, I may have just killed us by placing my trust in the wrong person.

For several blocks, we walk in silence, our quickened footsteps drowned out by the noise of the crowd going about their daily business. We duck down increasingly narrow alleys, and the crowd thins until we turn one final corner and find ourselves alone, pressed between the back door of a hobby-farm supply shop and the trash bins for the apartment building across from it. The layered scents of manure, sweet hay, and slimy vegetables threaten to overwhelm my poor nose, and I swear I hear quacking from behind one of the doors.

As soon as all five of us are there, the girl in the bright blue hijab rounds on me. She pulls a tablet from the back pocket of her jeans and taps for a moment, and her face . . . changes. The pointed nose blinks away to reveal one more narrow and rounded, her chin becomes less square, her lips thinner. I'd swear I was looking at a different person, one with weird little electronic things on her cheeks, forehead, and jaw.

"Are you completely cracked?" she snaps, waving a hand in my face. "That boy was leading you straight to the security station to turn you in! You were a block away from being arrested when I caught up with you, genius."

My mouth falls open. I want to defend myself, ask how I was supposed to know any better, ask what the hell happened to her face, but all that comes out is: "Do I know you?"

She rolls her eyes. They're nice eyes, rich and dark

against the warm golden brown of her skin, and highlighted with a thin black line of makeup. "Of course you don't know me, you've only just landed. I know you, though—from your wanted notice. Figured it would take all of ten minutes for someone to try to turn you in. You're either really brave or really oblivious, walking around town completely undisguised. Lucky I took it upon myself to save you sorry lot."

I turn to the others, and at least Zee is with me in looking sheepish. Case is halfway to panicked, though, revving up more every second. I've barely known her for an hour, but I can already tell when she's spiraling in her own head.

"Thank you for stepping in," Rion says, polite and formal, before Case can start the cross-examination. "Can you maybe elaborate on the whole 'wanted' part?"

The new girl shakes her head at us, pitying. "The last message courier jumped in-system right after you crashed. Ellis Station Academy posted an all-systems bulletin for the four of you. They don't waste any time—every GCC-sanctioned colony will know about you by the end of the day. They claim you were all denied entry into the Academy's program and are holding a grudge. Grand theft of an Academy shuttle, assault, defamation, and treason. You're to be detained on sight and shipped back to the station for prosecution."

"What?" I shake my head, then shake it again when

once doesn't seem like enough. Oh no, when my parents hear this, they'll have no trouble believing . . .

"But that's not even . . . the station was attacked! We barely survived! Does no one know? Does everyone really think everything on the station is just business as usual or something? How did they not notice the venting atmo, and the ships coming in, and . . ." I trail off, my wide eyes looking to the others for some kind of explanation.

The new girl looks startled. "That's definitely not what they said happened."

Rion's brows are drawn tight, and I'm sure I look the same; I feel like all the blood has drained out of my body, and my back is itchy, like there are a thousand eyes tracking my every move. Zee's face has gone even paler than usual, but Case looks about ready to boil over with anger, all traces of panic gone.

"All those people," she says, then chokes off, shakes her head and tries again. "No one noticed a damned thing? There were thousands of students there! And teachers, and people working in the rest of the station. I know those murdering assholes snuck in and kept it quiet, but I thought someone must have figured it out by now. What are they going to do, just step over all the bodies and carry on like normal forever?"

"If they had highly ranked help on the inside, it would have been easy," Zee says, matter-of-fact. "There's no other way. The people who make the hourly reports—they must have been in on it, gotten themselves to safety or worn vacuum suits before the attack."

"And they could have hidden people in the old abandoned station up there, the original one," Rion adds. "People waiting to move in and get the station running again as fast as possible."

"Why, though?" Case demands, drifting closer until our shoulders touch. I lean in, letting the contact comfort me while she talks. "Why the station? Why did they have to . . . ?"

"We have to get a message back to Earth," Rion says. "We don't know who those people are or what their plan is, but it can't be good if they're keeping it hush from Earth and they're willing to kill thousands to make it happen. I can think of tons of groups who might want to control the only sanctioned way off the Rock. They could be anyone. I still don't want to go back to Earth, but getting the word out should be our first priority."

"Yes!" I say, seizing the idea with a thrill of hope. "If we send them the footage from the flight recorder—"

"They've cut off courier service to Earth," the new girl interjects, and just like that, all my half-formed hopes of being a hero come crashing down. I slump back against the rough brick wall behind me, stunned.

"Completely?" I ask after a moment, through a mouth that feels like it's full of cotton. "There's no way around it?"

The girl shakes her head and peeks over her shoulder.

"They aren't just restricting who can get a message onto the ships. The ships aren't *running*. The one carrying your wanted notice was the last one for the next few days. I'll show you the notice once we're not crammed in an alley around the corner from the *police station*. So unless you've invented some magical supertransmitter that can send messages across the galaxy . . ."

No contact with Earth at all. We can't warn anyone. Even if we stole a ship right now and jumped back to Earth space, we'd be shot down long before we made it close enough to the planet to beam down a message. I can't even send a note to my parents to say, "Hey, I know I've fucked up a lot, but this time it really wasn't me and I swear I'd never do those things." They're just going to sit there together on their twenty-year-old couch and think the worst of me. Again.

I cover my eyes for a moment, then let my hand flop back to my side. "What can we do?"

"Well . . . you can live, for now," the new girl says. The lines of her eyes are stern, but they have a sparkle to them, and there's a little quirk at the corner of her lips. "Everything you want to accomplish, all your thrilling heroics, save the Earth, you can only do it if you're alive and free."

Case's eyes narrow, and she finally says what's been bugging me the whole time. "What's in this for you? Why are you helping wanted criminals?"

Zee nods, her stance widening. Is she getting ready

to kick again? "I'm wondering the same. Why should we trust you?"

I'm glad these two are on my side. Between Case's fierce intelligence and Zee's cool efficiency (and kicking prowess), I feel like the two of them could have me dead in a dumpster and move on with their lives in a hot second.

The new girl sighs and looks over her shoulder, then back at us with impatience. "Because I can make it happen. I know a way we can get off this planet and slip under the noses of enforcement, but it's not possible with only one person." She pauses, takes a deep breath. "And I've been trying to find people who can help me pull it off who aren't creepy old convicts or murderers. When I saw your wanted notice, I thought it might be you. A mutually beneficial arrangement. You get what you need, and I get a way off this planet and away from some family issues I'd like to be rid of."

She takes a step back and looks each of us in the eye. "This is all contingent upon a thorough background check, of course. Just a fair warning, I'll be hacking every available file on you all to make sure you're not going to kill me in my sleep. No offense."

The noise of the crowd on the next block over surges suddenly. Shouts, running feet, a rush of frenzied gossiping. That can't be good. I make a quick decision. "Look, we're way low on sleep and I don't think a dark alley is the place to be making a choice like this. Can we rest some-where and talk privately?"

"Of course," she says, cocking her head to listen to the crowd noise. A burst of shouts echoes from around the corner, and our young guide from earlier darts into view. He looks both ways and spots us immediately.

"They're over here!" he calls over his shoulder, waving forward what turns out to be a group of uniformed enforcement officers. Can we please catch a break?

The girl in the hijab rolls her eyes and yanks the edge of her scarf so it falls slightly more in front of her face while she scrambles for her tablet again.

"Follow me!" she says, and sprints down a branching back alley with a quick backward glance to make sure we're following.

I hesitate for the barest moment before charging after her, the others hot on my heels. She'd better know some sort of secret route, because enforcement is calling for backup as they chase us. Nothing seems to slow them down, not the trash bins, not the lines of freshly laundered sheets flapping behind an apartment building or the farm shop's pen of geese we piss off on our way around the corner.

The ominous clank of a gun cocking echoes through the narrow alleyway behind us. Don't think about bullets flying past you for the third time in as many hours. Just run.

"You know," Zee calls after us, sounding perfectly

calm and not even slightly out of breath, "if we're going to trust you, a name would really help."

The girl spares me a quick glance as I run beside her, and she smiles without slowing, the first non-glaring look she's given me. It's a lovely thing, briefly glimpsed; no teeth, just an upturning of red lips, like a secret. She taps her tab, and her face flickers again into a new, unrecognizable mask.

"You can call me Asra. You're safe with me. I promise."

As the sun begins to dip toward the horizon, Asra leads us deeper and deeper into the shadowy parts of the city, away from both our pursuit and the clean, glittering buildings of Old Saleem.

Hopefully it's not another trap.

FOUR

IT TAKES AN HOUR OF sneaking through back alleys and hiding behind dumpsters to lose the enforcers. By the time we arrive at Asra's tiny one-bedroom flat, we're exhausted, starving, and so thoroughly screwed I can hardly comprehend the situation.

We all sit huddled around the low coffee table on the floor, scraping our bowls of rice and chickpeas clean while a soccer game plays on the main screen. It's an old game, one that aired on Earth before I left for the Academy. Rather than watching the Carolina Racers get annihilated again, I take in the far better entertainment of Rion and Zee arguing over Premier League teams and trash-talking on FIFA.

Zee has lost all traces of her calm, even softness in the face of football politics, her cheeks flushed with the passion of her argument. Rion, for his part, manages to distract her with smooth talk and cutting jokes at FIFA's expense, then goes in for the kill once she's laughing too hard to fight back right away.

Across the table, Asra has managed to lure Case into a low-voiced discussion about some old classic book series I've never read, something about griffin doors and wizards. Case is the most relaxed I've seen her so far, her eyes bright as she geeks out over some character with a weird last name. She looks younger without all the anxiety pinching the corners of her eyes, like she's fifteen instead of nearly nineteen. Asra gestures to one of the dozens of pieces of dazzling paper crafts around the apartment, apparently one themed after the book, and Case brightens. Asra must be quite the crafting queen.

I have nothing to contribute to either discussion, so I stand and stretch, casting a nervous glance at the windows. Asra catches the look and shoots me a reassuring smile as she takes her bowl to the sink.

"You'll be safe here for now, so long as you don't show your face in the window or out on the street without a disguise. No one in this neighborhood is a snitch, especially not Nani."

The glorious savory smells of Nani's cooking drift up through the floorboards of the living room as she gets the restaurant ready for the dinner service. Every surface in the flat is coated with a thin layer of cooking oils, though Asra doesn't seem to mind.

"She's my mum-away-from-mum. I can't say a single bad thing about her," she says, wiping down her place at the dingy table with a damp rag. "Nani lets me stay here for free, and I do some work for her in return. She has an iron tongue; no one will get a word out of her about you."

Zee smiles with a bit of a wistful, unfocused look. Lost in a memory? She shakes her head and asks, "What kind of work do you do for her? Are you a server at the restaurant?"

"Hacking, mostly," Asra says, matter-of-fact. "A little net security work here and there. She's a feisty one. Don't want to get on the wrong side of her politics, that's for certain."

Case cocks her head, a shadow of a grin forming. "I bet the same could be said for you."

Asra smirks. "I bet it could."

I hate to break the chill we have going, especially with my eyes begging to fall shut, but we really need to figure out what the plan is here before I pass out on the floor. I catch Asra's eye, and she nods and pulls out a tablet. She takes a moment to connect to the citywide public Wi-Fi and sync with the wall screen, then looks up.

"Are you ready to see this?" she asks, her finger hovering over the local news app.

I glance over the rim of my bowl at the others. Rion is unreadable, staring blankly at the nothing on the screen. Case shreds her napkin into tiny pieces, collecting them neatly in her bowl. Zee is the only one who meets my eyes, passing me a fresh cup of tea as she does. I didn't even notice mine was empty, but the steam and scent of honey ground me in exactly the way I need right now. I smile at Zee, take a sip, then nod to Asra.

"No use putting it off. Let's see it."

As soon as the app loads, the screen fills with red blinking pop-ups: wanted notices, satellite and amateur video of our shuttle crash, and images of our footprints in the sand. There's even a crystal-clear picture of the backs of our heads, accompanied by the time and location of the sighting and a call to all citizens of al-Rihla to report any knowledge of our whereabouts in exchange for a hefty reward.

Cold horror floods through my veins; next to me, Case sucks in a sharp breath and grips the edge of the table.

Worst of all is the video notice that autoplays as soon as it's loaded. The face of the speaker is instantly familiar—Dr. Maia Herrera, the headmaster of Ellis Station Academy, who sat in on all of our entrance interviews and signed the paperwork that officially kicked us out, who Rion spoke with right before the attack. She looks . . . utterly normal. Uniform neatly pressed. Not a hair out of place. Calm. Collected. Not at all like thousands of people just died on her watch. Her voice is even and soothing as she speaks.

"This message was recorded on 10-08-2194, 22:13 Universal Time, for distribution to all Global Colonization Commission worlds on the first available courier ship."

Minutes after the attack. How?

"This is Headmaster M. Herrera, reporting from Ellis Station Academy. On behalf of the Academy and all Ellis Station personnel, I want to apologize for any concern our brief disruption in communication may have caused. Late this evening, our station was attacked on two fronts."

My breath catches in my throat. Case goes absolutely still.

The message continues. "One attack was internal. Four young students who were refused final entry to the Academy stole a shuttle and fled Earth-controlled space, causing damage to the station's primary transmitter and killing several personnel in the process. Information and images of the alleged thieves, along with the treason and lesser charges being brought against them, are attached to this notice. After an analysis of their flight path and cockpit footage of our engagement with their shuttle, we have determined that they have likely crash-landed on the colony world of al-Rihla."

On my other side, Rion's expression crumples. "What? That complete and utter . . . She, of all people . . . I was talking to her right before we left. I thought she looked distracted. Guess now I know why."

A man steps into the frame next to Dr. Herrera, wearing the crisp uniform of a captain in the GCC military division. She nods to him, then turns back to the camera. "Captain Thomas will be leading the pursuit of these suspects with his air-and-ground tactical unit, Tiger Squadron. All colony governments are asked to give Captain Thomas and his team full cooperation in the recovery of the fugitives."

The name of the squadron sends an immediate jolt of pure adrenaline to my system, and suddenly, instead of sitting calmly around a table, I'm wrestling with the controls of the ship, dodging bullets and cringing away from the piercing shriek of the missile lock warning.

I suck in a ragged breath. "That's the squadron that nearly shot us down right after we left."

Case clutches my forearm, her eyes steely and her nails digging into my skin. Across from us, Zee folds both hands over her mouth and watches intently. All the shock has left Rion's expression; instead, the blank mask is back, hiding anything he might be feeling. The message continues.

"—believe this unplanned assault provided a convenient distraction that enabled the secondary threat we're facing: a coordinated attack on our servers. A new primary transmitter cannot be installed until the hacking threat has been eliminated and our digital security specialists have implemented the appropriate countermeasures."

Dr. Herrera purses her lips. "I regret to announce that until we have the matter firmly in hand, all nonessential travel and communication to and from Earth-controlled space has been suspended. Courier ships will continue to run between colonies, but none will be sent or received at Ellis Station. Anyone attempting to approach the station or Earth will be detained."

Asra was right. It's true.

No couriers. No messages. We can't tell our parents we're alive, can't tell the truth about what happened.

We can't warn Earth.

My heart gives a painful throb, and I cover Case's hand with my own. She squeezes back and scoots closer, every line of her body tense.

"We expect full communication and travel to be restored in approximately four days. This message and the attached warrants stand until newer ones are issued. Thank you."

The headmaster's image crossfades into a room filled with reporters and photographers crowded before a long, curved desk on a raised platform. The wall behind the desk bears the seal of the city, and the subtitles label the room as the city council chambers. There are nine seats at the desk, each filled by a city councillor representing one of Saleem's nine wards. At a podium at the front, an umber-skinned woman gestures for silence, her sheer dupatta catching the light. The subtitles label her as Sabira Bahmani, mayor of Saleem.

Asra utterly transforms at the appearance of the new setting; she sucks in a breath, eyes narrowed, her mouth twisting into something ugly and harsh.

"This part is new," she spits, and glares at the screen.

The mayor folds her hands on the podium and speaks.

"By now you've all heard the news of the fugitives in our midst. Saleem enforcement will be fully cooperating with GCC and Academy personnel in the efforts to apprehend these four suspects," she says. "We appreciate any help the public can give and will be offering rewards for any information that leads to an arrest. Our head of enforcement, Raheem Ahmed, will be teaming up with Captain Thomas and Tiger Squadron to lead the investigation. Junior Councillor Jace Pearson of the fifth ward has more information to share with you before we take questions."

She steps aside, and the lone white guy on the council stands to take her place. He's stylishly dressed and approachable in a fine gray suit, his light skin washed even paler by the podium spotlight. He takes a moment to compose himself, then speaks.

"The suspects were last seen in the company of this girl." A picture of Asra's face fills the screen, half hidden by her bright blue hijab. "Her current whereabouts are unknown, and we believe the suspects may have taken her hostage to act as their guide while in our city."

The man looks away from the camera for a moment, swallows hard, then begins again. "The girl is Mazneen

Haque, my stepdaughter, and as both a city councilman and her father, I beg you to call the enforcement office with any information you may have. We thank you for your cooperation and hope to have this matter resolved quickly."

The low coffee table bangs sharply against my knees as I lurch to my feet and stumble back, away from Asra, my pulse thudding in my ears. She's his *stepdaughter*. I've lead us straight into a trap. I've screwed up *again*. Enforcement is probably already on their way here. I back straight into Rion, who grips my shoulders and directs me forward, toward the door.

"Wait!" Asra pleads, throwing herself in our path. "I kept you from getting arrested earlier, and you've been with me for almost two hours already. Don't you think I would have already called enforcement if I were going to?"

I stumble to a halt right in front of her, and Rion crashes into my back, bracing himself on my waist to steady his balance. His hands linger there, strong and thoroughly distracting, as I regard Asra with a cool stare. Out of my peripheral vision, I catch Case and Zee edging toward the door, making sure we have access to our escape route if necessary.

"Mazneen?" I ask, still primed to bolt if I don't like her answer.

She makes a face at my question. "Mazneen is my formal name and I hate it. Please don't call me that."

Her fingers linger on her cheek for a moment, then she punches the air with a sudden burst of ferocity. "Ugh, I hate that they got a look at my face. Couldn't avoid it, I guess. I didn't want to introduce myself to you with the facechanger active. Kind of sketchy, you know? Jace and my brother don't know about this flat, though, so we should be okay for a little while."

She meets my gaze dead on, and her eyes are pure liquid fire. "I haven't seen my stepfather in eight months. He plays the whole upstanding citizen thing, but he runs the entire criminal network of this colony, and everyone knows it. My ammu didn't, back when we first moved here after my abbu died. You saw how he is. He puts on a good act. Donates to charity, runs a local business, sits on the council, but when Ammu found out about the rest, she lost it on him. She got my sister away from him and off-world, but I got caught."

She sucks in a deep, calming breath through her nose. "He should have let me go, because Nani and I have been working to bring him down ever since. He's laundering money for someone, but I haven't figured out who yet. And at this point, I don't really care. I can't stand to share a planet with him anymore, which is why I came looking for you all. I want out of here, and I have a plan that will screw over his operation along the way. But I can't do it alone. I was going to tell you about him, I swear."

I glance over at Zee, who has relaxed somewhat

during Asra's explanation. Case, on the other hand, is like a porcupine about to shoot quills.

"What do y'all think?" I ask, looking over my shoulder to include Rion in the question.

"If she were going to sell us out, she would have done it by now," Rion says after a moment, looking Asra over with a calculating gaze.

Case fiddles with the ring on her thumb and presses her lips into a fine line, then shakes her head. "No, sorry, but this is bullshit. We need to get out of here, Nax, right now."

She's right, I know she's right, but I can hardly think over my brain's constant chant of Stupid, stupid, you'll get them all killed, way to go, asshole. Zee's cooler head prevails, though; she steps forward with her hands out in a calming gesture.

"Maybe we can at least hear her out. See what this plan is. But in full detail, yes? No more surprises."

Rion voices his agreement. Yes. Okay, that sounds reasonable. I can live with that. I step over to Case and nudge her hand with mine.

"Hey," I murmur, "I feel you on this, but do you think we can at least get some more info before we decide for sure?"

Her eyes slide back to the door, then down to our hands. I brush a thumb over her knuckles, and it seems to help.

"Fine."

I give her a little smile, then fold my arms over my chest and draw myself up to my full five-foot-ten height to look down at Asra. It makes me *feel* more confident, at least.

"Well, let's hear it, then. Better make it good."

Asra smiles. "Oh, it'll be good. I can promise you that. How do you feel about taking a ride in a Honda Breakbolt Mark III?"

My ass hits the couch in an instant.

"I'm listening."

FIVE

THE HONDA BREAKBOLT MARK III is the sexiest piece of machinery ever to grace this universe, and I'd do a *lot* to get behind that control stick. I don't know how Asra sensed this about me, but her lips twitch with suppressed laughter. She brings her tablet back to the main screen, logs off, then boots it up again with a completely different operating system, somehow managing to type accurately while talking at lightning speed.

"If anything, I think you'll be even more on board for this plan after seeing those wanted notices. They know you're in Saleem, so you'll need to get off-world before you can do anything to help your situation or the Academy."

Case purses her lips and looks away, but doesn't speak up.

After a minute, Asra flips the tablet around and sets it down in the center of the table, which we crowd around, pressed shoulder to shoulder. The tab's tiny projector fills the air between us with a three-dimensional rotating image of a ship. She's a *gorgeous* piece of work. All long lines and sleek rounded wings and powerful engines that are nearly boner inspiring. The thought of getting behind the controls of a ship like that is *hot*.

Asra grabs the image and pulls to zoom in. "This is the RSS *Manizeh*. She's barely a year old, with expanded cargo bays and upgraded living quarters. She's the classiest, most luxurious transport ship on the market, by far the most beautiful ship in Jace's smuggling fleet, and if you're up for a bit of crime, she can be ours."

Every cell of my body says, "Oh god, yes! Crime? I can do some crime!" I want this ship like I've never wanted anything in my life. I had a poster of the first-ever Breakbolt model on my bedroom wall when I was nine. It's like a manifestation of every dream I've ever had, everything I've ever wanted for myself: a piloting license, a beautiful ship under me, and stars out the viewport. Child Nax says, "Do it, do the crime!"

Rion leans his shoulder into mine with a raised eyebrow, and Zee shakes her head at me with a small smile, as if reading my thoughts. They're not feeling it, I guess. Case's brows draw together, though, and she thumbs at her lower lip in a thoroughly distracting way. Her eyes darken—looks like her fuse is starting to burn.

"Okay, I'm not getting it. Besides the fact that this is completely illegal and wrong and only adds to the charges against us, how is stealing a ship going to help us keep a low profile and avoid enforcement?" she asks, and I wince. She's obviously not let the ship get into her pants the way I have. Am I aerosexual or something?

"It won't," Asra says frankly. "But it's a sweet ship, and stealing it will get us off this planet and buy us time to figure out what to do. It'll also make Jace very unhappy, which I personally find hilarious."

I shouldn't even be considering this, but I have to ask anyway. "I get that your stepdad—"

"Jace," she snaps.

O-*kay.* "I get that *Jace* is some kind of big criminal boss, but are you sure you really want to steal a ship from him? How does you going all outlaw fix what he's done?"

Asra's lip curls, and she scowls at the table in front of her like it's personally wronged her. "He's more than just a criminal. He's got his hands in every terrible thing on this planet, and some others, too. He screws up families, cooks up drugs and smuggles them to other planets using this ship, he . . ."

She swallows hard and looks away. "Nothing would make me happier than taking away his favorite toy, and putting a dent in his drug-running business can only be a good thing, right?"

Zee pours another cup of tea and passes it to Asra. I hide a grin behind my hand. Something's wrong? Drink more tea. My ammi is the same way.

Zee smoothly changes the subject, giving Asra time to pull herself together. "The Academy's story, about the attacks and the disabled transmitter. It's a very neat lie. Gives the insurgents plenty of time to do . . . whatever it is they want to do without being bothered."

Rion leans back, resting against the front of the couch with his bottom lip between his teeth. "I wonder why they'd give a timeframe at all. In four days, everyone on the station will still be dead. There's no way they can cover that up forever. What happens when that time is up?"

A chill runs down my spine at the implications. Case says exactly what I'm thinking: "Unless it won't matter in four days. Unless they only need four days to accomplish whatever objective they have set."

Zee gives a thoughtful hum. "It makes people feel better, I think, having a specific date in mind. It's not time to *really* worry about the station until those four days are up. It keeps everyone away for a while without causing panic."

"Do you think they're planning something against Earth?" Asra asks, holding the steaming teacup under her nose. She takes a cautious sip, then sets it back down. "I don't know what else it could be."

"It *could* be anything." Case pulls her bag toward her and takes out the flight recorder from our crashed shuttle, turning it over and over in her hands. "There's no way to know for sure. The station is the hub for all emigration, trade, and communication between Earth and the colonies. They could be targeting Earth, but it's just as likely to be against any one of the colony worlds."

"And in the meantime, we're all boned," I say. "They've framed us for an attack and charged us with treason, and it's only a matter of time before someone calls enforcement on us. Considering those notices got blasted to every single citizen's tablet, comm, and toilet this morning, and the whole four-day timeline thing, I think whatever we decide to do, we need to do it soon."

I'm about to ask another question when a musical voice begins to call outside, the sound drifting through the town and into the open window. The lilting melody carries the familiar words calling the faithful to the Maghrib prayer. Asra stands and looks to the window, the warm colors of sunset glowing through the curtains.

"I'll be back in about ten minutes. I'm sure you all have brain whiplash right now, so take some time and figure out what you want to do. I don't expect you to take my word automatically, and I won't be offended if you don't trust me, but we need to decide quickly. Just let me know what I can do to help, okay?"

She grabs a small rolled-up rug and disappears into the back bedroom, closing the door behind her. The sound of running water comes a few seconds later as she begins her ablutions, so I turn back to my newfound partners in crime. Rion has a giant smirk on his face, and he shakes his head.

"What?" I ask.

He chuckles. "I just find it funny, is all. She's saying we don't have to trust her, but—no offense, mates, but I don't even know you lot! We met, what, a few hours ago? Am I the only one who finds it a little weird that in less than a day we've gone from strangers to co-conspirators in a grand theft aero plot?"

Truth. I haul myself up off the floor and plop down on the couch, clapping Rion on the shoulder. "I would seriously question your judgment if you immediately trusted the madman who crashed a shuttle with you in it. But here's the way I see it: we all washed out of the Academy, which gives us something in common—for whatever reason, we don't fit their mold. Honestly, after the short time I spent there, I'm thinking that's a compliment."

Case crosses her arms over her chest, as if protecting the Academy crest still displayed there. "Speak for yourself. I would have been top of my class if they'd let me in."

She's spitting mad, but underneath it is an all-too-familiar open wound. I don't blame her for it. If she's anything like me, the Academy was her dream for years. For me, it was escape from my too-small hometown and the chance to be my own person. An opportunity to rebuild myself from scratch: a crack pilot and captain of my own ship, not a screwup who's only good for video games, chicken feeding, and making the local news for all the wrong reasons. Malik got his dream—a life on one of the new colony worlds, a good job, friends, money to support his expensive taste in *everything*.

It was supposed to be my turn. The Academy was my way out.

The grin fades from my face with the memory of the venting atmosphere, the cold voice saying the station had been "neutralized."

Silence settles over the group for a few long moments. I pick at a loose thread on the hem of my shirt, letting the faint clatter of pans in the restaurant below carry me back to my parents' kitchen at home, Malik and me bickering at the table, my parents sneaking a kiss behind the freezer door while they tuned it all out. A surge of homesickness lurches in my stomach, and that does it—suddenly there's hot pressure behind my eyes, and it takes everything in me to hold it back. It wasn't supposed to happen yet. It was too fast and sudden, no time to really think about what we were doing. I'll never set foot on Earth again, and my last-ever time with my parents was spent in the horrible awkward silence of our parked aircar at the spaceport.

My throat hurts too much to swallow. I sneak a hand over to Case, the feel of her shoulder under my fingers a small comfort. Some of the stiff tension bleeds out of her at the touch, her shoulder sagging with a shaky exhale. I suck in a deep breath through my nose and push it all away.

"Look. At the end of the day, we're stranded together.

The no-return rule is in effect for us. The station runs the courier shuttles, so we can't send a message back to Earth. We can't go to the police here if they're allied with the Academy. We can't stay here without a visa. We're essentially all screwed—but together, right?" I look around, meeting each person's eyes. "That makes us natural allies. And hey, it's not like I'm a space murderer or something. I prefer to think of myself as an ambitious up-and-coming pilot in need of a ship. I promise not to kill you in your sleep."

Rion knocks his knuckles against my shoulder with a laugh. "Glad to know you aren't a space murderer. Warms my heart. How about the rest of you lot?"

Zee nods, toasting with her cup of tea.

"Also not a space murderer," she says, dry as the desert.

Case clears her throat. Her mouth is pressed in a hard line, and her eyes are flint and steel, ready to spark. Is *she* a space murderer? She might be soon, the way this is going.

"This is completely ridiculous," she says. "You all are really considering stealing this ship, aren't you?"

"Well, yeah," Rion says, looking from side to side like he's missed something. "I don't really see another option, do you?"

Case barks a harsh laugh.

"Are you kidding me?" She holds up the flight recorder again. "We have evidence, right here. We haven't done

81

anything wrong, nothing that wasn't in self-defense. There is zero reason why we can't just go to the embassy, turn over the data, and plead our case. I've never heard of the no-return rule being overturned, but we have to try."

"No," Zee says, just as Rion laughs out a pointed "Sod that!" He shrugs at Zee as if to say, "Can you believe her?"

"That'll never work," he says. "They'll ship you back to Ellis Station, all right, but you'll be executed in quarantine for your treason and grand theft and all that rot without ever setting foot on the Rock. At least this way we can warn all the rest of the colonies. Maybe *they* can mobilize and do something."

Case slides the flight recorder back into her bag, leaving her hands free for angry gestures in Rion's direction. "So the obvious solution is to add some *real* crimes to our list of fake ones? No, look, I have a friend of the family who works for the embassy, pretty high up in the ranks. She'll help us get in, help us be heard by the right people—"

"No," Zee says again. "I don't *want* to go back to Earth. Ever." She pauses, thinks for a moment. "Let me rephrase: I'm *not* going back. If you decide to do this embassy plan, you can leave me out of it. I won't beg to go back to someplace I couldn't wait to leave."

"Too right," Rion agrees.

Case throws her hands in the air and lurches to her feet, pacing the short length of the room. "What about you, Nax? You on board this train wreck, too? You been awfully quiet over there."

I feel her crosshairs settle on me, prepping for a head shot.

"Actually . . . I'm not so sure."

Zee and Rion both look at me in surprise. I close my eyes to block them out and push past the vision of the Breakbolt's sleek lines. Tempting, but . . .

"Look, there's no way I can get a piloting license without going through the Academy. Without a license, I can't be a pilot. And if I can't be a pilot, I don't see much point in being separated from my family on Earth for the rest of my life." Especially not with the way I left things off. I have to fix it. "If there's a chance I can go back to them, I should take it."

The bedroom door clicks open and Asra pads out, quietly rejoining the circle next to Zee. "Sorry for eavesdropping," she says, "but that's actually not true. I made fake IDs and ship registration documents for my ammu and sister when they left al-Rihla. I can do it for you, too."

She pulls her knees up to her chest and rests her chin on them. "Not to brag or anything, but I'm pretty great at it. It'll stand up to the highest scrutiny, I guarantee it."

"Still illegal," Case says, though it sounds like *obviously*. "Still an actual crime instead of a falsely accused one."

83

I hate this. Every option sucks in some way. There's no clear right or wrong, no way to make everyone happy, to get everyone on the same side. I close my eyes and tune everything out; decision time. What do *I* feel is the right thing to do?

I bite my lip, glance at Zee and Rion, then meet Case's expectant stare.

"I'm with Case on this one," I finally say, wincing at Zee's tut. "I don't think it's going to work, but I think we at least have to try doing the legal thing here. And if it doesn't work out, we'll consider option B."

"Not doing it," Rion says, pulling away from me and storming across the room. "My dad knows by now that I faked his signature on the age waiver. If I set foot back on Earth, that'll be it."

"You aren't eighteen yet?" I ask. I thought I was the only one.

Rion shakes his head. "He has my whole life planned out for me. It'll be more internships, and political science in uni, and suits and lies and bullshit. I'm not doing it."

"Me either," Zee says. "You two can do what you want, but at least give us a head start to get away. After all we've been through together, you can give us that much, can't you?"

"Wait, wait, wait," I sputter, mentally slamming on the breaks. What are we going to tell them at the embassy? We can't sell out Zee and Rion and Asra. I *won't*. We just pretend we don't know where they are? I hate this. I scrub my hands down my face and through my hair, tugging at the roots.

"Look, we can only do this once. We haven't slept in forever, and I'm basically dead right now. Can we please just sleep and make our decision in the morning?"

Case, Rion, and Zee can apparently agree on one thing, at least; they all fix me with their nastiest glares, as if I've personally betrayed each one of them. I mean it, though. My thoughts are a jumbled, foggy mess, and my brain can barely process two plus two right now. This is no time to be making life-altering decisions.

Asra stands, shooting me a wry smile. "Well, if you all are done tearing each other's throats out for now, there are a few extra pillows and blankets in the closet by the couch." She picks up her tablet from the table, swipes it off, and stores it in the back pocket of her jeans. "You could fight over those too, if you like. I'll be in my room if you need me."

The long sleeves of her kurta flutter as she gives us a little wave good night, a bright splash of gold-stitched white against the encroaching darkness. I try to find a hint of malice or deceit in her eyes or the quirk of her mouth, but it's all joyful intellect and a spark of sympathy. She retreats to her room, and the sound of a sitcom laugh track bleeds faintly through the thin walls a moment later.

The others grumble, grudgingly accepting the terms. We manage to distribute the three pillows and two and a half blankets roughly equally, and Zee wins the rock-paper-scissors match for the couch, damn her. Rion curls up against the far wall, Case by the door, and me underneath the room's lone window, folding the pillow in half to keep my head off the hard floor. The silence is tense and angry, and I can't help but feel it's all aimed at me.

It's bullshit. I heard everyone out, I tried to compromise, and now I'm the bad guy?

Whatever.

I turn my back to the room and glare at the wall.

I can't move.

My feet are like grav boots cranked to max setting, pinning me in place as Case and Rion whisper their arguments in my ears.

"Do the right thing, Nax," Case hisses, her nails digging into my arm. "Do you want more filth on your record? Your parents will hate you even more."

"Her plan is suicide," Rion says, his voice smooth and even, reasonable, his lips brushing my cheek and jaw as he speaks. "We can't fight for all those people who died if we're dead, too."

A projection of the Honda Breakbolt Mark III appears, rotating slowly in time with their whispers as Asra lists its features and improvements. Then it's suddenly two-dimensional, a poster pulled from Piloting *magazine, stuck fast to the floor as Asra twirls over it.*

Zee steps forward and hands me a cup of blazing hot tea, too hot to hold. I drop it, and it crashes to the ground. She tuts her disapproval and hands me another, and another, and another, until a drip of blood blinds my right eye. My forehead is bleeding. She tuts again and presses a stinging wipe to the gash.

"You have to be more careful," she says, but it's Malik's voice instead of hers, harsh and accusatory. "You're going to get someone killed one day, pulling shit like this. Remember what happened last time?"

Without warning, Zee pushes harder on the gash, sending a shot of pain through my skull, then draws her leg back and—

I jerk awake, my hand wrapping protectively around my upper thigh. The pain followed me from the dream, somehow. I blink blearily, then look up. Zee stands over me, her arms folded.

"You kicked me!" I whine, my voice still thick with sleep.

Zee grabs me by the arm and hauls me to my feet. "Case is gone, and she took the flight recorder with her."

The words are like a bucket of ice down the back of my shirt. I break away from Zee and scramble for my boots, though I don't know what I'm getting dressed for yet. What are we supposed to do? Wander around town, hoping we don't get seen, while we search who knows where for Case?

"That utter harpy," Rion spits, tugging on his jeans with force. "She's going to get us *all* arrested. I can't believe this."

Zee paces back and forth, her fingers threaded through her hair. "We should have seen this coming. She had that recorder in her hands last night before bed, and she was upset. What if she tells them where we all are?"

Asra strides into the room with her tablet and turns on the main screen on the wall. "If she's been caught, it'll be on the news feed. You all are the hottest story on the planet right now."

She flips through the channels until she lands on the news. And my stomach drops.

There's Case, her face twisted with anger as she shouts at someone off-screen while they haul her away. Her hair flies everywhere, sticking to her face, getting in her mouth as she snarls at them, though they don't play the audio, of course. What she has to say could be damning. Over the images, a voice-over reports.

"The suspect, Casandra Hwang-Torres, was taken into custody shortly after five a.m., when she entered the Earth Embassy building, claiming to have information for the authorities. She was arrested on the spot for treason, both for her part in the attack on Ellis Station Academy and for attempting to spread further misinformation about the attacks and the Global Colonization Commission. She will face charges in quarantine at Ellis Station, where she will likely receive the death sentence if convicted. She is currently held without bail at the Earth Embassy, awaiting transport off-world. No word on the whereabouts of her three accomplices or the kidnapped stepdaughter of Saleem city councilman Jace Pearson. Stay tuned for more details on the other suspects and analysis by our in-house experts."

Asra turns the main screen off, thankfully sparing us from the "expert" opinions on how utterly fucked we are. I turn back to the others, helplessness written all over my face. The others look back, like I'm somehow supposed to have the answer. I have no idea what to say. We have to do something. But what?

"What's everyone thinking?" I finally say to break the silence. We need to move, need to do something, but what?

"We should get out of here in case she's told them our location," Rion says, his face slipping into blank, neutral mode.

Zee nods in agreement. "Yes. We leave, head to the embassy. We have to try to get her out."

"What? No way!" Rion protests, looking at Zee like she's suggested they throw a party for the local cops. "She did this to herself. It's her problem."

"So you want her to die?"

"Of course not! But there's still a chance that she'll be acquitted on trial."

Zee cuts him off with a sharp wave of her hand. "You really think they're going to give her a fair trial, with this cover-up going on?

"If we try to go to the—"

"They'll probably execute her the second she—"

"I know, I know, I'm sorry, okay?" Rion shouts. "I know all that. I know we have to go after her. I couldn't forgive myself if she got executed. I just . . . I'm pissed, and if this ends up in me getting sent back to Earth, I'll throw myself out a bloody airlock."

Rion covers his eyes with one hand, hiding the shattered remains of his false coldness from view.

"If it helps at all, we really don't have a choice," I offer as a truce. "The Breakbolt needs a two-person flight team. Unless anyone else here knows ship systems the way Case does, we have to have her back."

I look to Asra, who's stayed out of the whole thing to this point. "I know this isn't exactly your problem, but we could use your help here. Any ideas?"

"Plenty. And for those ideas, we'll need supplies. Finish getting dressed," she says, gesturing to Rion, then smiles.

"It's time for you all to meet Nani."

SIX

NANI, AS IT TURNS OUT, is exactly what she sounds like: an old woman with a thin, wrinkled face, wispy silver hair, and stern brown eyes. She also happens to have arms like a sailor, along with a secret bunker full of weapons and illegal tech. Definitely not someone to mess with.

Asra embraces her as soon as she answers the door joining the woman's apartment to the restaurant below Asra's. They speak in rapid Bengali as Nani leads the way into the restaurant's kitchen and opens the giant walk-in freezer. The woman gestures at me, Rion, and Zee to shift enormous unlabeled crates from one side of the freezer to the other, which slowly reveals a five-foot-high hatch in the back wall. Nani snatches the tablet from Asra's hand, syncs it to the lock on the compartment, and with a series of surprisingly dexterous keystrokes, enters a complex string that unlocks the door. Zee, Rion, and I exchange a look, then follow them inside.

Nani slaps an old-fashioned light panel, and a cheerful

glow fills the room, illuminating three hundred and sixty degrees of guns, ammo, and tools neatly arranged on slat-wall displays. My spine goes stiff, and Rion breathes a low "whoa" next to me. Zee takes a hesitant step back, like she expects the room to explode. I grew up out in the country with a police officer for a mother, so I know my way around a gun, but the sheer size and power of this arsenal makes my skin prickle with discomfort. Nani beckons us forward as Asra translates her words.

"She says you all can stop looking like scared puppies. Nothing in here is going to kill you unless you mess with her, which I don't recommend, and she's only giving us nonlethal weapons because she doesn't want us to hurt ourselves. It's actually all nonlethal, but she likes to rile people up. We're a small grassroots group working to undermine Jace, not a militia."

That's a relief, actually; if my ammi taught me anything during our times at the shooting range, it's to have respect for the danger and responsibility that comes with a weapon. Between that and the horror stories she'd come home from her shifts with, I have no desire to carry a real gun.

Asra spins on her heel, the solid black kurta she chose for our covert operation swirling around her body, and removes five thin rectangular objects from a low shelf. She hands one to each of us, keeping two for herself, and slides back the outer casing of hers to reveal a foam insert cradling seven tiny metal circles.

"These are facechangers," she says. "Very illegal, but they'll keep us from being recognized by casual observers. One projector each on your forehead and chin, one on the tip of your nose, one on each cheekbone, and one on each side of your jaw."

Zee hums with interest. "This is what you were using when we first met you, right?"

Asra nods. "I rarely leave the house without one these days. Keeps Jace and my brother off my back."

She spins again, and turns back around with three tablets. "These are synced to the projectors and already have the app to run them. I'll help you get them calibrated. I'm just going to say this once, though."

She directs a frown at me. "No data presence whatsoever. No social accounts, no location tracking, no messaging. Basic functions only. The tabs are already locked down and net stealthed, but it would be easy enough for you to factory reset and do something to screw it up. Don't get us all arrested because you couldn't stand not putting a message on the next inter-colony courier for your ex."

I snort. No danger of that happening. None of my exes emigrated to the colonies, but even if they had, my last girlfriend hates my guts, and my boyfriend before her was an asshole I'd rather not talk to anyway. My ammi was never too thrilled about me dating, but when that guy broke up with me, she offered to go arrest him. I love my mother. If the couriers to Earth were still running, I'd be seriously tempted to ignore Asra's warning, to let her know what happened. I'm sure she and Dad hate my guts right now, but if I could at least apologize for how I left things, tell them this isn't what it looks like . . .

Well. It probably wouldn't do me any good anyway.

The glow of the tab screen as I boot it up is like the first ray of sunshine after a hurricane. Having to leave my tablet on Earth was horrible, and I've been without for over a day. It's probably a bad thing that I feel like I've just had my arm reattached, but Zee and Rion look as enraptured as I am, so at least I'm not alone. Considering we're about to break into a highly secure facility and probably die, though, I need to rein myself in and focus.

I slip the tablet into my pocket and start to open the small silver case with the facechanger projectors, but Nani shoves a gun into my hand before I have the chance. Training and muscle memory kick in the second the cold metal touches my skin, keeping the business end pointed away from everyone else. Nani hands a cautious Rion and hesitant Zee their own firearms.

"Chem guns," Asra says. "Sleep chem, specifically. It'll knock out any human on contact with bare skin, so don't get it on yourself, obviously."

"Obviously," Rion mutters, testing the gun's weight in his hand and sighting down the barrel at the opposite wall. Zee holds hers with two fingers as though it's a pair of three-day-old underwear and places it gently on the nearest countertop. She's got her own natural weapons, anyway, if she can get close enough to kick. Nani laughs in her face and produces a holster to hide the gun at the small of Zee's back, then slides the gun inside and pushes the hem of Zee's shirt up to put it on. Guess it's better to have it and not use it than to need it and not have it.

Asra's gun disappears into the folds of her clothing, and she pops the facechanger projectors onto her skin with practiced ease. "So. City hall and the Earth Embassy share a building. I say we use Jace's city-council access codes to gain entry and wing it from there. I've got some friends ready to cause havoc down the street from the embassy if things go truly wrong, but inside, we're on our own. Anyone have any better ideas? Useful diversion tactics?"

"I've been told I'm a hell of a dancer," Rion says. "You find me a table, I'll create a diversion you won't forget."

I bark a laugh. This is going to go *so* well.

But also, yes, the table dancing. Let's make that happen.

Unsurprisingly, walking around in public with a highly illegal piece of technology stuck to your face is a weird experience. I'm already sweating through the back of my borrowed shirt and twitchy as hell from strolling through the streets as a wanted criminal. The facechangers we wear should make me less apprehensive instead of more, considering the whole point is that they *change our faces* so we won't be recognized. Tell that to my paranoid brain, though.

The tech was a nice thought to start with: something to allow accident victims to wear their old faces over their scars. Took the government all of five seconds to realize it was a terrible idea. They can regulate all they want, but everything eventually ends up on the black market. But Nani hooked us up, so here I am, wearing an unfamiliar face in a crowd of unfamiliar faces.

The streets are surprisingly busy at six thirty in the morning local time. Al-Rihla is a fairly diverse place, with people of every size, shape, and skin color, though the 30:22 Explorers were mostly South Asian or African, and al-Rihla still reflects that majority. We all blend into the crowd without too much trouble, facechangers active and senses on high alert.

Asra has traded in her bright blue hijab for a simple black one to match her top, and with her facechanger active, it's hard to keep track of her as she leads us down endless streets: glittering steel arches over concrete and glass, low walls lining decorative pavers in the Arts District, reeking trash cans atop sharp gravel in the alleys behind the shops.

The tiny nodes of the facechanger itch like crawling

ants where they stick to my skin, but I manage to avoid scratching them off long enough for us to reach our destination: a glittering building with long, sweeping curves and a blend of metal and natural wood beams. The crowd around me breaks like a cresting wave, spilling us onto the pavement directly in front of the structure, but Asra swiftly leads us away from the main entrance and around the back to a tucked-away alcove with a single plain black door.

"Are we ready?" I ask.

Zee nods and gives me a reassuring pat on the shoulder, her legs coiled and ready to spring. Rion hefts his chem gun with a wry smile.

"Let's be bad guys," he says with a wink that makes my face go hot. I huff a laugh and nod to Asra, who runs the lock codes with a swift tap on her tablet. The door whirs, then clicks, and we're in.

The long hallway immediately past the door is deserted. It's early enough that most people won't have arrived for their shifts yet, and the quiet hangs heavy around us. We slip past walls plastered with labor law posters and inspiring messages from supervisors, our strides long and silent, with Asra and I guiding the way up front and Rion and Zee covering our backs. The rough *clang* of the air conditioner kicking on startles me so bad that I nearly twitch a shot of chem at Asra. Fortunately my ammi's gun-safety drills sank in enough that I didn't have my finger on the trigger at the time.

We come up on an intersection, my rattled nerves jangling, ears straining for any tiny noise. Asra taps my shoulder and points to the right, but before we can make our move, a faint click echoes from the left branch of the hallway. Asra drops to a crouch and I follow her lead, my lungs burning with the effort to hold my breath. Footsteps, barely audible but quick—but another door opens a few seconds later, and silence falls again.

Asra taps my shoulder again, then hurries down the hallways to the right, leading us through a series of twists and turns down seemingly random side hallways. Eventually we slip through a door into what looks like a maintenance area to access a hidden set of stairs. Zee and I have no trouble with them, quietly racing to the top (Zee wins) while Asra and Rion glare behind us. Finally Asra brings us to a halt in front of an unmarked door several floors up from where we started.

"This is the maintenance access for the floor where embassy security is housed," she says, projecting a tiny map from her tab. "Once we're through here, we need to make for this far corner, where the cells are."

I nod and take a deep breath. Case is counting on us. We can do this.

"Okay. I'll cover you while you work on the security system. Rion and Zee, I assume you can manage a diversion of some kind?"

They look at each other with an eyebrow raised each. "We'll manage," Zee says.

Rion smirks. I'm going to be really pissed if there's table dancing and I miss it.

I check my chem gun for the hundredth time and hold it at the ready. "Whenever you're set, Asra."

Rion and Zee fall in on either side of me, Rion with his gun aimed at the door, Zee ready to spring at the first sign of trouble. Asra looks back at us, then gives a silent countdown.

Three . . . two . . . one . . .

Asra slaps the control, and the door slides back with a hum—

Someone's on the other side.

Asra stumbles backward, bumps into me, trips again as she gestures for us to go back the way we came. It's too late though, no time—I raise my gun and move my finger to the trigger. . . .

Wait.

Case?

Her eyes go wide and fearful, and she stumbles back a step, then hesitates. Her eyes dart from one person to the next, looking us over from head to toe.

Oh, right, the facechangers.

"It's us," I whisper. "We came to break you out. Are you okay?"

"What the hell are you all doing here?" she hisses,

shoving me back toward the staircase we came from, one hand clutching a stolen tablet. "They know I'm gone and they're right behind me! And holy shit, who gave *you* a gun?"

"How did you get out?" Rion cuts in, instantly suspicious, and I can't blame him. It's too weird, and she's already screwed us once.

Case groans in frustration and shoves past us, taking the lead down the stairs. "Did you really think I'd walk in here without an exit strategy in case things went bad? I'm not *totally* cracked."

I huff a near-silent laugh. "Should have known Genius Girl would have a plan."

She's in hyper-focus mode, though, practically vibrating with adrenaline, and takes the next flight of stairs at a run.

At the bottom, Asra takes over and guides us back to the employee entrance. We race down the hall, motivational posters fluttering in our wake, and make it into the alley behind the building without encountering anyone. Asra immediately pulls a box of facechanger projectors from an inner pocket and gets right up in Case's personal space, sticking them to her cheeks without waiting for permission. Case jerks back at first, then holds still, apparently getting the idea. Asra cycles the facechanger until it projects a face that looks natural on her, then shoves the tablet into Case's hands and looks over her shoulder.

"I think we should split up and get back to the apartment," she said. "The second they get a look at that security cam footage, they'll be searching for a group of five wandering around together."

Rion nods. "We should get some new faces, too. They have these ones on camera now."

Zee takes a moment to inspect Case, checking over her minor injuries, before cycling her facechanger with the rest of us. I'm about to start breaking us into groups for the walk back home when farther down the alley, the employee entrance to the embassy bangs open.

"They're out here!" someone shouts.

Shit.

"Split up!" I say, and slap Rion's arm to get him to follow me.

We break off from the others, ducking down a side street with crumbling facades and barred windows, leaping over discarded boxes and stray cats. A shout goes up behind us, followed by thudding footsteps and crashes.

Well. Hopefully if they're following us, they're leaving the others alone.

No time for subtlety now. Down a narrow alley first, need to break their line of sight, throw some variables into the mix. Don't think too hard about left or right, just pick one and go, and again, and again, just like evasive maneuvers in a flight sim. I know they're still back there; I can hear their footfalls, hear them calling for backup over the comm, shouting our names. If that backup gets here, we're so screwed. Another left turn, and a dusty, familiar scent fills my nose.

Goats. A whole herd of them, just across the street in a paddock connected to an outlying pasture. Enormous, smelly, shaggy, crotchety goats. The closest one fixes me with a challenging stare. I stare right back.

"Rion," I say, grabbing for his hand. "Please forgive me for what I'm about to do."

SEVEN

WE'RE UP TO OUR NECKS in goats when Rion finally says what I've been thinking all along.

"You are, without a doubt, the absolute. Worst. Captain. Ever. Damn you *and* the horse you rode in on, Hall."

He's half laughing as he says it, but I actually agree with him. The black despair threatens to swallow me whole, so I scramble for something to fill the silence.

"Technically the horse is already pretty damned. Considering we crashed it. The ship. And by we, I mean I. That was on me." I wince and continue, quieter. "And I'm no one's captain, damn it."

I hold my breath and shove my tongue hard against the roof of my mouth, trying to hold in the dusty sneeze that's been crawling around in my nose for the past three minutes. I never thought anything could be worse than mucking out the goat pens back home, but . . . yep, this is worse.

The goats shuffle around us, their hooves scuffing up yet more dust, their eyes rolling with anxiety. They don't seem too pleased to have us cowering between their shaggy flanks, creeping with long, knee-killing crouch strides and breathing through our mouths as quietly as we can.

The embassy building recedes around the distant corner of the block ever so slowly, and we continue our crouch waddle until we run out of goats to hide behind, which happens far too quickly. I hold up a hand to Rion, then inch my head out from the forest of goat legs. The street looks clear. No sign of our pursuit. Doesn't mean they aren't there, though.

There's a field of high, dry grass beyond the fenced goat pen, but I've played hide and seek with my brother in enough wheat fields over the years to know it would give away our movements instantly. Better to make a run for the dark alley across the road. If we can get over there without being seen, we can easily lose ourselves in the back alleys and find our way back to Asra's flat. Now the hard part: checking the street back in the direction we came from. No way to do that but to look over the goats and hope no one notices.

My thighs and calves burn with the strain of the past thirty minutes as they push me into a standing crouch, just high enough to peek my eyes over the goats' sloped backs. I catch a brief whiff of fresh, salty beach air, and it's a beautiful thing, having spent the last fifteen olfactorally drowning in the dry, earthy scent of goat fur and the moist, inexplicably fishy scent of goat breath. I scan the horizon once, quickly, for immediate danger, then slower for more subtle threats.

Nothing.

The streets are empty and quiet, and the scariest thing in view is an alarmingly large pile of goat shit at the edge of the pasture. No shouts. No movement. I'm reluctant to leave the fresh(er) air, but I take one long last sniff and drop back to my aching knees.

"I think we're clear to get out of here. There's an alley right across the street we can run for, and from there we should have plenty of routes back to the apartment."

Rion levels me with a frank stare. "This bastard over here ate some of my hair. I don't even want to look at my boots."

I snort, and the goat next to me snorts back. "Still think they're cute?"

The look he gives me is haunted. "I've seen things," it says. Then the corner of his mouth twitches, and he falls into me, clutching my arms tight and smothering his laughter into my shoulder. It sets me off too, until I'm breathing a shuddering *shhh!* into his ear, broken up by totally uncontrollable chuckles.

"This is *ridiculous*," Rion says between gasps.

"You're going to get us caught!"

He shakes his head against my shoulder and pulls back, wiping tears from his eyes. "Nah, mate, we've got the ultimate in goat protection here. We'll be fine."

I pat the flank of a big tawny male goat with something like affection and nostalgia. "You guys are a lot nicer than my parents' goats. Thanks for not trampling us. Or eating my toys. Or spitting." God, the spitting . . .

"Are you done getting sentimental over these filthy shit factories?" Rion asks, and pokes his head out over the goats. I do the same. When he turns around, our eyes meet. I try to hold it together, I really do, but the corner of his mouth twitches again, and I'm gone. We break down and duck back into the forest of goat legs with hands over our mouths.

"These filthy shit factories saved our lives. I think they deserve your respect and admiration," I say in a shaky whisper.

Rion lets me know what he thinks of that in no uncertain terms, spitting out mouthfuls of dust as we crawl to the far corner of the pen, nearest the street. I guess not everyone can appreciate a good rescue by goat.

At the edge of the pen, we check for pursuit one last time, then bolt for the alley across the street, leaving a fading trail of literally shitty footprints behind. Crushed against the building wall, pressed together into the shadows from shoulder to hip, a moment of harsh breathing, listening—any boots on pavement? Any shouts of alarm, crunching gravel?

Nothing. Just our own rasping breath. We lock eyes for a brief, charged moment, then slip into the shade of the narrow alley. The relative darkness draws us into the maze of the warehouse district of Saleem. Hidden. Safe.

We make most of the journey back to the apartment in silence, navigating as best we can by barely familiar landmarks and glancing over our shoulders every five seconds. We really shouldn't—it screams *suspicious*—but it's hard not to imagine every tiny noise as an enforcement officer drawing a gun.

Rion holds his hands slightly away from his body as we walk, like it'll somehow keep him from smearing the filth around even more. Bit late for that. Wouldn't have taken him for the overly fussy type, but he *is* a rich city boy, so I guess it's not all that surprising. The air shimmers with waves of morning heat, and my shirt is soaked through in several places. I'm not exactly feeling fresh. Ugh.

As we draw closer to Asra's neighborhood, the adrenaline ebbs enough that I can loosen up, and Rion stops walking quite as stiffly. When a turn onto a side street presents a lull in the crowds, he glances my way with a raised eyebrow and a smirk.

"So what's with you and goats? Your parents had them, you said?"

Oh, here we go. Time to play city boy, country boy.

"Yeah. We lived on a bit of land in North Carolina and had a small hobby farm. Nothing huge, just some chickens, a few goats, a biggish veggie garden."

Rion doesn't laugh, thankfully, though his smile

widens like he wants to. "Did you have to feed them and clean up their shit?"

"Yeah, I cleaned up their shit. Someone had to, and my brother always managed to get out of it, somehow." I bite my lip, then glance at Rion out of the corner of my eye—and catch him looking back. I purse my lips against a smile. "I liked them, actually. The animals. I think if I'd ended up stuck on Earth, I probably would have taken over my parents' farm when they retired. What about you? No goats back home?"

He grimaces. "God, no. My dad and I lived in a tiny apartment in central London, and I went to boarding school most of the year. Any animal in our care would have died a horrible death from neglect in about a week."

"Boarding school? Really?"

"Whatever you're thinking, it's probably . . . exactly like that, yeah." He sneaks another glance at me, one that turns into a long moment of extended eye contact, then turns back to the road. "Uniforms, rich boys, laddish banter, latent homoeroticism, and lots of panicked studying so we could all grow up to be Oxbridge wankers and not disappoint our families."

Oh. Interesting. I clear my throat and work to keep my voice casual. "Latent homoeroticism is the backbone of the British education system, is it?"

"A long-standing public school tradition, if you ask the media. Some of us take it more seriously than others," he says, and tosses me a wink.

My face *burns*. That answers that question. Nice. Play it cool.

"So, what, no Oxbridge for you?" Whatever that is. Totally casual question, right?

"Hell no, mate. My dad was a Cambridge man. I wouldn't be caught dead following in his footsteps, and *he'd* rather be dead than see me at Oxford. Takes the rivalry way too seriously, that guy. I do miss London, though. Don't get me wrong, actually seeing the sun is great, but London is just . . . something else. But it's not worth the price." He shakes his head, his mouth tight. He really must hate his father.

"Do you have another parent who sucks less to balance him out?" I ask, hoping to shift the conversation in more pleasant directions, bring back a bit of that lopsided smile.

"I did." He pauses. "Mum died when I was ten. She was always traveling for work, for the World Health Organization. I got to go with her sometimes. It was great, the best times in my life. She's the one who made me want to go into colonial relations, actually. I wanted to be a settlement officer, help people build their new lives out here."

I wince. Way to go, bringing up the dead mother and wrecked life goals. Not great, Hall.

We check around another corner, wait for a small pack of children to rush past, then continue on.

Rion shoves his hands in his pockets (finally accepting

the filth, I guess) and heaves a sigh. "Look, I hate to be the downer here, but I think we need to talk about Case before we get there. What are we going to do with her?"

I shrug, but my heart pangs with sympathy for Case. I get why she did it. It's hard, accepting that we've done nothing wrong and somehow came out looking like the bad ones. We're raised to believe that if we do all the right things, the law will protect us. Reality is much harsher, apparently. How many times have I heard my ammi come home, frustrated over some case where a guilty criminal went free because of technicalities, or politics, or money? I, of all people, should have known the opposite must be true sometimes too. Can't help but hope, though.

"I dunno. I think we can chill, you know? We kind of *have* to go along with Asra's plan at this point, including Case. We don't have the evidence anymore, and this proved exactly what will happen if we try to go to the police. What choice do we have?"

His eyes linger on me for a moment, considering. "I think we all have different opinions on what's an option in this mess. And I've met *plenty* of people who can smile and say all the right things while still lying straight to your face. I'm not saying I think she's one of those, but I can't rule it out. I didn't see it coming, you know? Her taking off like that."

"I didn't either. But we don't really know anything about each other, do we?"

"Nah, not really. But that'll change, right?" Rion knocks his shoulder into mine with a small smile. I fight back a grin and nudge his shoulder right back. But I want to get to know Case better, too. What she did was shitty, but I'm not ready to write her off, like Rion seems to be. I can't help it. I like her. She's so smart, and good at things, so completely her own person.

And beautiful, too.

The crowds pick up again, and we continue down the streets in silence to avoid notice, dodging potholes and abandoned crates, climbing over low fences, holding our breath when we have to weave through alleys full of trash cans. The silence suits me better right now anyway. Rion's right. Going through weird messed-up stuff with people gets you close really fast. Like summer soccer camp: throw a bunch of us together for twelve hours per day, seven days per week of intense practice, and it's impossible to not come out the other side with new best friends, some awkward stories, and a thorough knowledge of who's hooking up with who.

Normally, I'm down for that. I loved those brief summer friendships. But I can't shake the feeling that I'm going to burn this all down at some point. We're going to get hurt or killed and it'll be my fault, because I'll wreck another ship or make the wrong decision or let my ego talk me into something stupid. It's only a matter of time. Hopefully crashing the shuttle gave the universe its due, and they'll be safe from me for a while.

The glorious scent of sautéed onions, garlic, and ginger takes over the breeze for an entire block before the restaurant below the apartment comes into view. We creep up to the alley behind the apartment, and I look around the corner, then wave Rion forward. We scurry up the fire escape like frantic squirrels just as a pack of young kids charges past the mouth of the alley, and we squeeze in through the narrow window, tumbling onto the floor in a tangled heap.

Safe.

I reach out and knock Rion on the shoulder, a goofy grin on my face, my unease fading. He returns the gentle tap with something more like a thump, leaning on me while he catches his breath.

Then I catch the feel of the room.

Stony silence.

Case sits at one end of the couch with her face in her hands. Zee sits beside her with a bloodstained antiseptic wipe in one hand, glaring at the side of Case's head. Asra ignores them both with fierce determination, aggressively folding origami lanterns and adding them onto the garland strung over her desk.

I didn't know you could fold aggressively, but there you go.

Great.

Time to play peacemaker.

EIGHT

IT'S THE WOBBLY TRICKLE OF blood mean-
dering down Case's arm that finally breaks through the
wall of awkward and puts words in my mouth.

"Okay, everyone. Look. I know we're in a shit situation, but this silent angst thing isn't going to help." I cross
to the couch and kneel down next to Case.

"Hey." I rest my hand tentatively on her knee. She's
trembling, and there's a faint sheen of sweat on the parts
of her face that aren't covered. "Hey, can you let Zee clean
that cut on your arm? You don't wanna get any weird
space infections, right?"

A single faint huff—a laugh, maybe? She pries one
hand away from her face and props it on the couch next
to her. Zee takes it and carefully begins to clean and spray
the lacerations there, clucking worriedly over her as if she
hadn't been trying to set Case on fire with her eyes a
moment earlier. Asra, seeming to sense the temporary
truce, settles onto the floor next to the table with the tablet Case stole and taps at it with a frown.

Rion glances up, meets my eyes, then flops back against the wall and leans his head against it. "I think maybe we should talk about what happened at the embassy."

Case stays perfectly still under Zee's prodding fingers, but takes a deep shuddering breath and lets her other hand fall away from her face. "As long as you guys promise to hear me out completely before bringing out the ax for my execution."

Her voice is weak and ragged, but it's a relief to hear a bit of her usual backbone in it. I squeeze her knee and take a seat on the couch beside her so she knows I'm in her corner.

Rion's lips quirk up at one corner, and he cuts his eyes over to mine before speaking. "I promise, definitely no axes, knives, or other methods of bloody death. I just want to know what happened."

I send him a tiny smile of thanks. What Case did was shitty, but I'd like to think we're not the kinds of people who would gang up on someone who just had a panic attack.

"Same for me," Asra says from across the table. She throws the stolen tablet down on the rug in frustration, then picks up her own tablet and hardwires the two together. "I've been in there a hundred times to *visit* Jace's office, and their security is pretty tight. If we hadn't had access to the employee entrance, it would have been nearly impossible. How'd you manage?"

Case hisses as Zee dabs at a particularly nasty cut on her shoulder where the flesh is ragged, gaping wide and raw. Her jaw tightens, but she grabs my hand and grips it tight, takes a slow breath through her nose, and talks through the pain.

"I commed my mom's friend, Ana, before I got there and told her to expect me. She took me to her office, I showed her the flight recorder, and together we went to the head of her division." She takes a deep breath and keeps her eyes fixed on Asra's patterned carpet. "It got weird. Like, instantly weird. He recognized me, and when I told him about the flight recorder, he started interrogating Ana, wanting to know if she'd seen what was on it. She had, but I guess she picked up on the vibe, because she lied, said she brought me straight to him."

She swallowed hard, and her cheeks darkened. "They had zero intention of ever hearing me out. Their number-one priority was getting the flight recorder away from me, and number two was locking me up where no one could hear me talk. I'm honestly surprised they didn't just kill me, but I think they wanted the publicity just in case it would bring you all out of hiding. Which it did, you complete asses," she says, and swats Zee on the leg. Zee swats her right back, then uses the opportunity to snag her arm and get a better angle on the gash to glue it shut.

"Oi, you're welcome, you know," Rion protests, half-heartedly throwing his balled-up and sweaty outer shirt at her. She twitches away like it's on fire, even though it came nowhere near her. Zee tuts in disapproval, chasing her with the can of skin bond.

"Hold still," she scolds. "What did you do to yourself, squeeze through a window of rusty nails?"

"Something like that," Case mutters, subjecting herself to Zee's fussing. "Ana was able to work with me to disable the lock on the door, and I'd memorized the layout of the building before I left, but it was still a near thing. I wanted to bring more back with me, but security was right behind me, so all I was able to grab was that tablet from the chief's office," she says, and points to the tablet in Asra's hands. Asra works in silence, ignoring us all.

I pull away from Case and turn around to fully face her, propping my arms up on my knees. She's looking much better, and the tension in the room has ebbed from "ready to kill" to "wary and annoyed," which I'll settle for. "Wait, so you memorized the layout of that whole building? Just in the time since we went to sleep?"

She shrugs with her uninjured shoulder and studies her shoes. "I have a good memory for diagrams. Kind of had to, when I was doing my engineering degree."

I shake my head. Bit of an understatement; she must have a near-photographic memory. "Right. Genius Girl. Almost forgot."

I drop my head onto my shoulder to rest for a moment, then think better of it. Ugh, I *reek*. Rion catches the face

I make, I guess, because he snorts and shakes his head.

"The smell," he says, "because I know you're all dying to know, is entirely Nax's fault. We had to duck through a bunch of back alleys to get away, and then O captain my captain here saw the goat herd in a paddock across the street and decided it would be the perfect hiding place. Apparently he had pet goats as a child, and it broke his brain."

He breaks off with a shudder. "The only herds we have in London are rats, bats, and corgis. The rats and bats mostly keep to themselves, and at least the corgis are potty-trained. Snappy dressers, too."

Zee, who's been drawing closer to eruption by the second, finally explodes with a loud, infectious laugh, her eyes bright with mirth. The rest of us follow in a heartbeat, even Case, because come on; in hindsight, the whole thing really is hilarious. I'm wiping tears from my eyes, something about sartorial corgis on the tip of my tongue, when Asra yelps, her furrowed brow relaxing all at once.

"I got it!"

She taps at the stolen tablet in her lap, then frowns again. "There's only one thing on here. It's totally wiped clean except for the most recently received message."

Asra pulls out her cables and sets the tablet in a short stand, then syncs it with the large screen on the wall. The message appears, with a logo preceding the brief words: two bright overlapping circles, one turquoise blue and one bright green, with a bold number one painted through the center.

All devices have been shipped to their final locations. Earth First personnel and any loved ones they want spared should make final preparations and arrange transport back to Ellis Station, if you have not already. Zero hour is 00:01 on 14|8|2194 UTC. Please click the attachment to securely delete this message.

Loved ones they want *spared*.

Spared from what?

Case sucks in a breath as she finishes reading, reaching out to clamp a hand around Zee's arm. Zee pats her hand, but her lips are pursed tight. Asra's eyes have gone dark and furious. Rion, though, lets out a disbelieving laugh.

"This is wild," he says. "It's ancient history. I can't believe I even . . ." He takes a deep breath and blows it out slowly. "I know what this is."

Everyone falls still and fixates on Rion. He stares at the ceiling for a moment, his lips moving, whispering to himself, then nods.

"Okay. So. The Global Colonization Commission was formed right after al-Rihla was discovered during the second space race, right? It was created in the first place because this really old treaty said that all space resources belonged to all of humankind, not just to the organizations

118

or countries that found it. No one wanted to stick to the treaty, so they needed someone to enforce it."

"Yep, that's Earth politics," Case says, her voice dry.

Rion huffs a derisive laugh. "Yeah, definitely not for me. So, at the same time as all that, there was a group that called themselves Earth First. They were against the creation of the GCC, because they were against colonization altogether. They wanted to make terraforming illegal and outlaw settlements outside of Earth and her moon."

I shake my head. Colonization has been a fact of life for the past hundred years, since long before I was born. It's strange to think of people actually debating it.

Rion continues. "Earth First was a small group, and they never did enough lobbying to get media attention, but they were weirdly powerful because they came from everywhere and believed in the cause for all kinds of reasons. Some were religious people who believed their god put humans on Earth for a reason, or that Earth was sacred. Some were scientists who believed it was wrong to change another planet's ecosystem, ecologists who thought our responsibility was to Earth first, that we should clean up our act there before messing up other planets. Businesspeople, economists, teachers, military officers, every kind of person you can imagine."

"Okay," Asra says, drawing the word out. "So that was over a hundred years ago."

"I've never even heard of these Earth First people,

and I minored in colonial history in college," Case says. She actually sounds affronted that there's something she doesn't know. I nudge her foot with mine and fight back a teasing smile. She nudges back and leaves her leg pressed against mine.

"There's no reason for you to know about them," Rion says, cutting everyone off before the discussion can derail too far. "The whole thing was swept under the rug before the movement could gain serious support. There was this guy, a member of Parliament, who shot himself in his office right after a major colonization debate. During that session, he said if Earth went through with the colonization of space, those loyal to Earth would correct their mistake. They voted in favor anyway, and the note he left was pretty threatening. Everything got covered up good. They were afraid of it getting into the media and gaining public sympathy, I think. Everyone loves a martyr."

"How do you know about all of this, then, if it was hidden so well?" Zee asks. Good point.

Rion shakes his head and huffs an ironic laugh.

"That's the wild part. I only know because my dad forced me into an internship with a local member of Parliament's office. I went through a lot of old paper records as part of an archiving project. Those records were never digitized, and they made me sign a nondisclosure agreement before they even let me into the file room. There can't be more than a handful of people alive who even know about that incident."

Asra slams the stolen tablet down on the tabletop, and the memo on the screen winks out. "Jace does, apparently. I saw this logo all over the back room of his office last time I broke in. I'd bet you *anything* that the money laundering I couldn't trace leads back to Earth First. He probably built up his whole scheme to help fund them. And here I thought I couldn't hate him any more than I already did."

Zee gathers up the bloodstained wipes in one gloved hand and takes off her exam glove inside out to wrap them up, then packs the med kit as she speaks. "It looks like these Earth First people never went away. It's ridiculous. Who could still be against settling in space after a hundred years of proving it works? But I guess logic doesn't matter much if you're obsessed enough. They must have been clinging to this and planning for decades, to get people into the positions they're in. Politicians? Military officers?"

Case's knuckles go pale as she twists and bunches the hem of her shirt. "And using the Academy as a launching point for their 'correction' of the 'mistake' has a certain symbolism to it, you know? It's like using the colonization system against itself."

There's a beat of horrified silence.

Then, *BANG!*

Behind me, a voice—"Go around the front, cut them off!"

I whirl around to see a head poking through the narrow window. The head of a uniformed enforcement officer, one of the ones who chased me and Rion from the embassy. Shit, did we lead him here? Rion plants his palm on the guy's face and shoves, hard. The face disappears, and the horrific *clang-CLANG* of the fire-escape ladder rings out, followed by a sickening crunch.

Ouch. That sounded like tears.

I slam the window shut, check the readout to make sure it's locked, then spin back around. Asra, Case, and Zee are all on their feet, breathing hard, their eyes wide. Below the floorboards, a door bangs open, and Nani's furious voice follows. I can't understand what she's saying, but it sounds like she's bitching them a new one. Her voice spurs Asra into action.

"She might be able to hold them up long enough that we can get down the stairs and into the basement. There's an exit there we can use. Grab your stuff," she says, already putting action to her words. She stashes the tablets and runs into her room, the sound of slamming drawers drifting after her. Case grabs the bag from the shuttle, and the rest of us stow our tablets, facechangers, and guns. Asra flies out of her room and motions for us all to follow. Case and Rion go first, and I hurry after them.

"Zee, cover our six, and be ready to kick," I say, grabbing the strap of her first-aid kit and slinging it over my shoulder. Another bang at the window sends a jolt of energy straight to my legs.

Time to go.

In the stairwell, our nervous breaths rasp and echo off the walls, but our feet are light. As we descend, the furious yelling gets louder, joined by a horrible battery of jangling clashes, like Nani is deliberately banging things in the kitchen to cover our noise. More voices join the chaotic jumble: some strangers, some the faintly familiar ones of Nani's staff, recent acquaintances from our brief stay.

Rion's and Asra's bright clothes practically glow in the dim hallway. They should have stayed in their sneaking-around clothes from earlier. If the enforcers get eyes down here, they'll see us for sure. Asra leads us with quick, sure steps, pausing only once to hold up a hand and peer around a corner. As we emerge onto the ground-floor landing on the other side of the wall from the commotion, the warm, pungent smells from the spice kitchen overwhelm my senses. If we're going to get caught, this is the place. My breath burns in my lungs.

Painfully loud crashes and clamoring reverberate through the narrow corridor, so I worry less about my footsteps and more about speed. Asra's bright orange hijab disappears around the corner into the narrow basement stairwell, then Case right behind her.

There's a sudden surge and clatter in the kitchen, and a new group of authoritative roaring voices—reinforcements. I press forward, my chest pushing against Rion's back in my haste to disappear into the darkness of the staircase. I make it down five steps when, right behind me, a deep voice calls, "The stairs!"

Zee whirls around, and through the gap between her legs I see a single enforcer who managed to find the dusty old door at the back of the kitchen. No, not an enforcer—one of the guards from the embassy. Zee wastes no time. Her leg arcs in a vicious drive, catching the man solidly in his right knee, then again in his jaw as he drops. Hard. Judging from his groans, he's still at least partially conscious, but not for long—I aim around Zee and send a pulse of sleep chem into the exposed skin of his arm. He won't be following us.

I stow the gun and back up farther to give Zee room to crowd into the stairwell, but she ignores me and grabs the man by the arms, then drags him over so his arms point toward the other staircase, the one we came from. She skips over the man's body, graceful as a blue-and-blond cat, then steps into the stairwell and closes the door behind her with an ever-so-gentle click.

I want to tell her "Good thinking" or "You're a genius," but any sound might screw over the brilliant advantage she's given us, so I do the most helpful thing I can: I get my ass down the stairs as quickly and quietly as possible.

When Zee and I emerge into the basement, Asra already has a crate of potatoes pulled aside, revealing a low crawl-space access hatch in the interior wall of the building. The bottom half of Case sticks out of the hatch, and Asra gives her a none-too-gentle kick in the ass to get her moving faster. Rion glances back, sees us coming, then drops to his hands and knees and disappears through. I put a hand between Zee's shoulder blades, guiding her forward, ahead of me. She doesn't argue, just follows the others. I look to Asra.

"You following after us?"

"Yes," she hisses, "but I'm gonna move this crate back as close as I can get it first. It might buy us some time."

"I'll help—" I start to say, but she cuts me off.

"You're a lot bigger than me, Nax. I can fit through with the door practically closed. You're wasting time—go!"

I put my hands up in surrender and scramble into the crawl space as fast as I can. Barely a second later, the hatch closes most of the way, and the crate scuffs closer. As my eyes adjust, I can barely make out the outlines of Zee, Case, and Rion crouched among the exposed pipes and wires, trying not to bump their heads and give us away. With a quiet scraping of fabric on metal, Asra squeezes through the hatch opening, less than a foot wide, and pulls it closed behind her. The last bit of light goes with it.

"How the hell are we supposed to see where we're going?" Case whispers in the dark, but Asra makes a sharp sound through her teeth to shut her up. There's rustling from her direction, then the glow of her tablet fills the narrow space with a pale white light, washing out our faces into ghostly masks. She crawls over to us, then motions for us to gather around.

"Listen," she whispers, barely audible over the distant footfalls above us. "This crawl space extends under the entire building, all the way to the end of the block. I have a place where we can hide once we're out of here, but we need to decide whether to make a break for it now or lay low for a while. Think about it while you follow me."

She drops to her forearms and knees, shuffling along with the tablet held in front of her, illuminating the mess of beams and plumbing that reaches down from the underside of the building like metal claws. We crawl behind her in a line, like a caravan of pack animals, and while a part of me is still logically terrified of being caught, a small part of my brain is furiously willing Rion not to fart in my face. I slow my pace a little, just in case.

By the time Asra comes to a halt against a mold-slicked wall, I'm feeling like an old man, all joint pain and cranky grumbling. I'm also no closer to figuring out what we should do next. Everyone's still pissed at Case, we're going to get *executed* if we're caught, and these Earth First assholes are . . . what, planning to blow up the whole damn galaxy?

One thing at a time, Hall. Don't get overwhelmed.

I elbow Rion out of the way and whisper to Asra.

"Is there a window somewhere? Can we get a look?"

She motions for me to follow, and the two of us shuffle our way around a complicated-looking system of digital readouts to a tiny grubby window. The bright noonday sun is barely visible through the grime, so I use the edge of my sleeve to wipe off what I can from the inside. As soon as I do, I jerk back; there's a pair of polished boots right next to the window. Military boots? Enforcers?

I lie down in the dirt, trying to get a steeper angle, maybe see some uniforms. I'm probably getting years' worth of mold and maggot crap in my hair, but I need to know whether it's safe for us to leave before risking the others. I angle my head toward the window, and there— the sand buildup and grime on the outside makes it hard to see specifics, but there's no mistaking the crisp outline of the navy-blue uniforms of the enforcers. I roll away and scramble back toward the others. If one of those enforcers had looked down at just the wrong time . . .

Asra rejoins us and puts her tablet in the middle of our little group, sliding the brightness up so I can make out facial expressions. It's serious frowns all around, for the most part, though Asra seems a little sick, too. Worried about Nani, I'd bet. Rion slumps back against the wall and rubs at his calf and thigh muscles. I get that; after the morning he and I had, the last thing I really wanted was more crawling, more running, more adrenaline and fear. My legs are screaming. I've never wanted a couch, a video game, and my dad's nonstop running baseball commentary so bad in my life.

"I know this isn't what you want to hear," I say to the group, "but I think we need to get comfortable for a few hours, at least until dark. I saw at least six enforcers out there, maybe more. If we make a run for it now, we'll get followed at best, and captured at worst. Asra, do you think there's any real chance of them crawling under here to check for us?"

She purses her lips, thinking for a moment, then shakes her head. "No, probably not. The building directly above us is abandoned and condemned." At this, Rion and Case immediately look up, as if the ceiling is suddenly going to collapse by mere suggestion. I'm about to make a snarky comment about it, but the ceiling gives a sketchy-sounding groan, and I barely manage to not flinch.

Asra grins at us, despite the circumstances. "Relax. It's been condemned for years. I doubt today will be the day it decides to fall. They won't chance searching it, though; too much risk to their officers. They could crawl through the way we did if they find the hatch, but I'm hoping they assume we escaped through the upper windows instead and are searching the streets." She shoots me a reassuring smile. "We'll be fine. I know a place we can go once we get out of here. We just need to sit tight."

Zee, who has been remarkably matter-of-fact throughout this whole thing, nods and sits down, kicking her long legs out in front of her.

"I agree in theory," she says, "but what about what we saw on the tablet?"

Rion swears. "Yeah, we don't really have half a day to waste. Earth First wants to attack the colonies? We're *on* a colony world. If we're going to steal this ship, we need to do it now."

"Does that mean you're all on board for my plan, then?" Asra says, her eyes locked on her tablet, reflecting its pale light as tiny white squares. Her voice is overly casual, deliberately calm, but the corners of her mouth are tense.

Case and I lock eyes. We were the only dissenters. I only see one possible path out of this, one way to help stop this. But Rion was right earlier—we all see different possibilities. I glance at Rion, catch his eye, then look back to Case.

"I'm in. Sorry, Case, but I just don't see another option right now."

"Hey, I tried to do the right thing and got screwed." Case's eyes are crushingly sad, but she forces a faint smile. "Let's steal ourselves a ship."

Zee studies her with careful consideration. "You're sure? No more running off, no more putting us all at risk because of your conscience? Can we trust you?"

"My conscience is as clear as it's going to get," Case says with a shrug. "You can trust me. Now we just need to figure out the when and how."

Asra nods. "The *when* is somewhat decided for us. The *Manizeh* is off-world right now, but it's scheduled to return just before midnight. We can give the enforcers a few hours to clear out, head to my safe house, make our plan, and go. Agreed?"

Zee reaches out to squeeze Case's shoulder. "Agreed."

"Agreed," Rion says, though he still watches Case with pursed lips and wary eyes.

I gesture with a grand flourish to Case, and she rolls her eyes at me, but it pulls a real smile from her anyway. "Yes. Tonight. Agreed."

"That's it, then." I toss her a wink as I borrow her earlier words. "Let's steal ourselves a ship."

NINE

I WOULD FEEL A HUNDRED times better right now if I could go for a run without getting arrested. I'm in that weird place between exhausted and amped, and staring at walls is the opposite of helpful. Back on Earth, August always meant soccer camp, endless distance running, drills, and scrimmages. Being cooped up with the curtains drawn is making me restless. Sitting around doing nothing while Asra, Rion, and Case work on our heist planning is making it worse. Zee and I tried to help, but we were only in the way; turns out a doctor and a pilot aren't all that useful for breaking and entering.

Asra has a few words with Tahseefa, the friend whose house we've temporarily invaded, and she says it's safe to run the staircase between the first and second floors to burn off some nervous energy without having to go outside. Just in time, too, because I'm about to climb out of my skin.

I cast a look over at Zee as I begin my calf and shin stretches. She's perched on the edge of the raggedy couch, staring unseeingly at the muted wall screen as her restless legs twitch and bounce. Asra catches my look, nudges Zee, and gestures my way. With an expression of blessed relief, she leaps off the couch, and I shift to give her some room. Zee nods her thanks, dropping into a stretch beside me.

I shuffle my feet out wider and lean over, feeling the stretch in the backs of my legs and sneaking a peek between my knees at Case and Rion, who sit in dining chairs pulled up next to the couch. I smirk, then glance over at Zee. "You gonna run with me?"

"If you don't mind," she says.

"Course not. Seems like we're having the same problem. Soccer, for me."

She ties her blue-and-blond hair back in a sleek ponytail and raises a disdainful eyebrow.

"Football," she corrects. "And same for me. I was in the running for the Kazakhstan national team earlier this year, and now my body doesn't know what to do with itself. If I don't run or kick something soon, an innocent piece of furniture will suffer, and that would be terribly rude. In my country, being a poor guest is almost as bad as being a poor host."

I bark out a laugh at that. I recognize it now, the way she moves, her build, her speed and strength.

"Let me guess. Midfielder." She strikes me as the brains of the team.

The corner of her mouth quirks up, that same cool and

confident expression she has when faced with blood and injuries. "Number ten. And you're a striker, obviously."

"Obviously? What's that supposed to mean?"

She snorts and lowers her voice. "Please. A hotshot pilot, great reflexes, always making jokes, and good-looking enough to have both Case and Rion trailing after you? Classic striker. You would have been endlessly irritating back on Earth."

Heat rushes to my cheeks, and I glance back to make sure no one else heard that. "Oh, but not you?"

She rolls her eyes. "I'm immune to strikers. Besides, this isn't really a good time, don't you think?"

"No, you're right, you're right." Still, though. I stretch out my arm for an excuse to look over my shoulder at Case and Rion. It's definitely mutual. Case is brilliant on a whole new level, doesn't let anyone tell her what to think, and I'd love to wrap my arms around her curves. And Rion . . . we just click, somehow. We don't always agree, but his sense of humor and smile are totally disarming, and he's unwavering in his beliefs. There's that *something* there, the thing I would definitely pursue were the time and place different. . . .

I shake the thoughts out of my head. New subject. Focus on Zee. "So, Kazakhstan? For some reason I thought you were Russian."

Her hackles go up at that, and she freezes in her stretch, but she quickly releases the tension. "My country has a complicated history. I'm mostly Russian by blood, but part Kazakh on my father's side. It's . . . yes, complicated is the best word."

And I've apparently stumbled into a minefield. Time to backtrack. I prop my toes on the baseboard to stretch my calves, and fumble for a new topic.

"If you were playing national-level football, how'd you end up doing the medical thing at the Academy?"

She holds her stretch for a few extra seconds as she studies me, then leans over to touch her toes. "I love my country, but they're very behind the rest of the world in some ways. They refuse to provide government identifications with anything other than sex assigned at birth until age twenty-one," she says, her voice quiet and even.

I look up sharply. "Are you serious? Places can still do that?"

"Yes." She stands straight again and smooths her ponytail before moving on to arm stretches. "When I got selected for the women's national team, it became a problem. So I decided to go into sports medicine, physical therapy, that sort of thing. Finished my secondary, worked as an EMT in Petropavl for most of the summer. Then went to the Academy and had the same problem."

"No." I keep my voice low to match hers, but it's a near thing. "That's illegal, Zee, they can't—"

"They can," she replies, completely calm. "The ID and the paperwork have to match. They can't reject me for being trans, but they can for that."

"Wow. Yeah, Zee, I don't know what to say. I'm sorry you had to grow up somewhere like that."

Zee shrugged. "I'm not. Yes, it was hard, and it still is, and I hope the push for change goes through soon. But I love my country, and my parents and grandparents and sisters. I traveled a lot for football and saw a lot of places. Mostly stadiums, to be fair, but I still think Kazakhstan is the most beautiful. I went hiking with my teammates a lot and got to see some of the best my country has to offer. I'm glad I grew up there. Burabai, Bayanaul, Kaindy Lake. But after what they've put me through, with football and with the Academy, I'm not sad to leave it behind."

She pauses, takes in a slow breath. Maybe not as unaffected as she seems, then. "What about you? Why'd they kick you out?"

A fresh wave of nerves sets me on edge. I'm not ready for this conversation. Not yet. What can I say?

"I, uh . . ." Stall. Stretch more. Think. "I have a history of . . . not making the best decisions. One of them caught up with me. My own fault."

Yeah, that's enough of that. I jump up and down a few times to test my muscles and find them limber and dying to move. And I'm dying to end this conversation. "So, are we doing this or what?"

Zee smiles and claps me on the shoulder. "After you, hotshot," she says in that pointed accent of hers.

I give her a mock half bow. "Whatever you say, Dr. Eyeliner."

My legs are coiled and ready to spring, but I turn back to check on the others first.

"How's the planning coming? Any updates?"

Case waves her hand at me without looking away from the tablet screen she and Rion are studying. "Go be jocks. We'll be done soon."

Asra leans over to point out something on her own tab, and Case's attention is reabsorbed by the task at hand. I look at Zee and shrug, then throw open the door and race down the stairs as fast as I can without slamming into the wall on the landing.

We chat on and off through panting breaths, mostly about football, but she also manages to get me talking about my family and tells me about hers back in Kazakhstan. It's easy enough to regale her with tales of North Carolina farm living, so different from her time in Kazakhstan's ultramodern major cities, and stories of Dad and Pa's Fourth of July fireworks accidents get her laughing so hard she can hardly run.

"What about siblings?" she asks when she gets her breath back. "Anyone to suffer through with you?"

The grin drops straight off my face. "Just the one brother. We don't get along." Not anymore, at least. Those days are long past.

Zee flicks her hand in a little wave, like a silent

apology. "Well, that's one bonus of being exiled from Earth. At least you don't have to deal with him anymore."

I put on an extra burst of speed and pound out my frustration on the stairs. If only that were true.

"Actually, he's out here. He works for spaceport security on Valen."

Zee's labored, even breaths break into chuckles. "I suppose you can just avoid that entire planet. Plenty of other options."

I'm about to make a snarky comment about him taking one of the best planets when the door to Tahseefa's flat opens and Case pokes her head out.

"We need you both for this next part," she says, wrinkling her nose at our sweat-soaked faces, "and you're driving me up the wall anyway. Think you can give it a rest and join us?"

I stumble back inside the flat, my T-shirt damp and clinging, and shoot her a winning smile. "As you command."

Her cheeks darken a bit as I drop into a low stretch, working my warm muscles into relaxation. I sense eyes on me as I move, so I make it a bit of a show, twisting back and forth, leaning over farther, pulling the bottom of my shirt up to wipe at the sweat on my forehead. Why not? When I turn back around, Case and Rion avoid my eyes, looking everywhere but at me. Theory confirmed. Zee looks to the ceiling and shakes her head, but I catch her smirking as she turns away.

In the kitchen corner of the wide-open living area, I flick on the tiny dim light over the sink and scrounge for something to drink out of. It takes me three tries to find a cabinet with glasses. The water smells a little metallic, but tastes mostly fine. It clears my head some, eases some of the tightness behind my eyes. Food would help, too. Crime on an empty stomach seems like a bad idea.

A bit of searching turns up a heavy cast iron pan and some eggs. Nothing wrong with eggs for dinner at ten o'clock at night when you're about to commit a crime. It takes a moment of fiddling, but I get the stovetop fired up and throw a chunk of ghee in the pan to melt.

"Okay, let's talk," I say, cracking a few eggs into a cleanish-looking bowl. "Asra, what's the next phase of the plan we need to figure out?"

She takes a deep breath through her nose, then fixes me with a solid gaze. "First off, I haven't said thank you yet. Seriously. I've been looking for people like you for months, waiting for the chance to try again, and I was starting to worry that . . . but I really think this is going to work. Thank you for trusting me." She glances down at her lap and fiddles with the edge of her hijab. "I actually quite like you all, you know."

I huff a small laugh. "Yeah, well, we like you too, especially the saving us from ourselves bit."

Asra ducks her head and pulls out her tablet, fixing

her eyes on its glowing surface, but the tiny curl at the corner of her mouth is there all the same. She bites her lip, then looks back up, straight at me.

"I *do* know that this is wrong, no matter how good the intention," she says, her eyes pained. "I don't want you to think I don't know that. I've made my peace with it as best I can, and I promise I won't back out on you."

I shake my head and wave it off. Honestly, I'm the last person to judge her. I don't really know how Asra is dealing with the fact that stealing is haraam, but I *do* know she's a far better person than her stepdad, and things will be better in Saleem if we pull this off.

I shoot Asra a small smile and whip up the eggs until they're nice and frothy, then slosh them into the pan.

"With everything that's happened over the past day, I think you've proved we can trust you."

The others murmur their agreement, even Case. The embassy incident really seems to have humbled her. Asra looks to the ceiling for a moment, then clears her throat and raises her voice to talk over the sizzling eggs.

"We'll run through the whole plan start to finish in a bit," she says, shifting back to business mode, "but we haven't talked about where we're going once we have the ship, and that's the part I wanted you both in on. Can we figure that out now?"

Huh. Whoops. Guess we've been so focused on actually getting the ship that we never bothered to think about *where* to take it. This is all going to go so well. I absent-mindedly scrape the bottom of the pan as the eggs start to scramble, letting the rhythmic sound lull the anxiety threatening to pierce claws through my heart.

"I guess if we make it off Jace's rooftop landing pad, we'll aim for high orbit and hope we don't get shot down, to start with. I promise I'll fly my heart out, better than I did getting us away from the station, but we do need a jump destination at least, so we don't have to figure it out while we're getting shot at. Any suggestions?"

Rion gets to his feet and wanders into the kitchen. "We probably all have some family or friends out here that would be willing to take us in while we work on the Academy problem," he says, reaching around me to rummage for five plates and forks. "I'm sure my uncle and his husband would have us. They're on Europa."

Case winces. "That's a bit too close to home for me. I'm not sure I want to be in the same solar system as Earth right now. Ana was my only contact out here, and you saw how that turned out, so I've got nothing."

"I have a friend on Xīnjiā," Zee offers, "but she only just graduated from the Academy and settled there six months ago. She's got two roommates and lives in the middle of a big city. I don't see how she'd be able to help us. I'd appreciate the chance to warn her about what's coming, though."

"Ditto for my uncles," Rion says. "What about you, Nax?"

I pause in my egg scraping for a fraction of a section, then catch myself and keep going. "Uh, nope. No contacts out here. Sorry."

Yeah, that sounds fake, but okay. I'm a terrible liar. I look back out to the group, trying to channel casual nonchalance, but Zee has me pinned with a puzzled stare. Crap.

"Really? No one?" she asks.

Damn it, I never should have told her about Malik. She's just so easy to talk to, and with my mind on the running, it was way too easy to overshare. There is literally no way I'm going to ask my brother for help, though, especially now that I'm a wanted criminal. Probably wins the honor of my biggest screwup ever. Zee has to let me have this one.

"Nope, no one able or willing to help. What about you, Asra? Know anyone on Umoja? I've always wanted to go there."

Asra taps at her tablet for a moment, and a long-view map of colonized space fades into view in the air over the low coffee table, with colonies marked in blue. "Everywhere you all have suggested so far has been too far away to be feasible in one quick jump with potentially low fuel levels, and Earth First probably has a large presence on all the official colonies," she says. She works for a few more seconds, highlighting five rocks in red, then taps three of the red worlds and numbers them.

"The red worlds are illegal settlements that the GCC and Worlds United have either decided to ignore or haven't found out about yet. Option number one is a changer named Serenity, but its terraforming operation was completely under the table," she says, tapping the world to zoom in on it. "The planet took to it well, and a decent-sized population has been living there for about twenty years. That one might be the easiest to disappear on if something bad happens, since the population is bigger and more established than the other two, and it'll definitely be easier to get clearance to land. The others are much newer."

She taps the second planet to zoom in and bring up its information. "Number two, Tau'ri, is a natural. It's smaller and has a good-sized main city, but they're kind of . . . insular. We can land there if we need to, but their traffic control might take some convincing. It's also where my ammu and sister went into hiding after they escaped, so I'd rather not draw attention to them if possible. I don't want to lead Jace there."

A quick gesture, and Tau'ri is replaced by planet number three. "Babylon is a bubble planet, which are personally my least favorite, and I also think they're the most inconvenient for our purposes. We can't guarantee that the ship will be stocked with vacuum suits, so if they refuse us entry to the dome and we run out of fuel, we'd be space junk."

Case shudders. "I never liked the idea of bubbles. They creep me out. I always thought I'd get claustrophobic, and I know it's completely illogical, but I keep imagining the dome cracking open and all the air rushing out. I'd prefer a natural, if possible," she says, looking around the room as if imagining unbreathable vacuum beyond it.

"Same," Rion says, "though I could deal with a changer, too. What about the other two worlds?" he says, indicating the two remaining red-marked bodies on the map.

"Those are a little far for a jump from here," Asra says, "but they're also controlled by some really nasty types. Not people I'd want to deal with, not even for honest trade. The GCC colony Valen is also in jump range, but like I said earlier, that should be a last resort."

"Definitely," I agree, gesturing with the hot pan of eggs as I carry it to the table. Zee studies me closely but holds her tongue.

"So, sounds like Serenity, right?" Asra asks, waving the map away. "They'll be best able to help us if we have to come limping in. They also have a reputation for hiding people who don't want to be found."

I set the pan down on a folded-up towel and dish out the eggs to everyone, serving myself last. "Sounds like the perfect place to park while we work on the Earth First problem."

Asra is shaking her head before I'm even finished, impatient for the first time. "No, I don't think so. At most, I think we can hope to refuel and resupply, if we aren't able to steal the fuel we need with the ship. There's no way they're going to let us stay once this ship gets reported stolen."

She bites her lip. "Jace may be an awful human being, but he has power and influence in a lot of places far beyond al-Rihla. They'll love that we did something to hurt him, but there's no way they'll bring his anger down on themselves by harboring us. We'll have to either ditch the ship and buy passage back to Serenity, or pay some major money to get the ship stripped down and rebranded, from her paint job to her motherboard. In the meantime, I think our best bet is to put down only as long as we have to, then keep flying while we hunt down the Earth First devices."

After a moment, Rion breaks the awkward, tense silence.

"These eggs suck."

My grip tightens on the eggy spatula. I will not smack Rion in the face with it. I won't. I . . .

I turn to him, and his face is lit with the biggest shit-eating grin, his plate clean and his mouth full of eggs. Bastard. His eyes are bright and mirthful and I can't help it—the corner of my mouth tugs into a grin.

"You're welcome to cook any time, *mate*," I say, stressing the Britishism. We were spoiled for our first day here, having Nani's restaurant right under our feet, but someone had to cook, and at least I bothered to learn to feed myself before leaving the Rock.

Case leans over and flicks Rion's ear, and he yelps, clutching at it like he expects blood. I add a second scoop of eggs to my plate, shake a generous coating of pepper over them just in case they are terrible, then knock Rion with the side of my foot for good measure.

Honestly, they aren't bad. I shovel the eggs into my mouth and swallow as fast as I can—then choke when the front door deadbolt slides open with a loud click.

My spine stiffens, and my breath stills in my chest. I fish under the table for our stash of chem guns, my heart slamming into my ribs because it's time, it's just *time* for something to go wrong.

The door cracks open—and I crumple in relief. Tahseefa, Asra's friend, whispers into the room and offers us a kind smile. She lays a hand on Asra's arm and a quiet conversation passes between them in Bengali. Tahseefa draws Asra up by the hand, and they scoot around the table toward the doorway.

"One second," Asra says, and disappears into the outside hallway with her. When they return, they each carry a small shoulder bag, and they're followed by none other than the fearsome and resilient Nani. Rion leaps up from the couch to make room for her and slides around to sit on my other side. Asra sits on the floor at Nani's side and pulls her bag into her lap.

"Okay, everyone," she says, throwing back the flap and digging through the bag's contents. "Tahseefa and Nani have made our lives a whole lot easier. They've put together some supplies to help us out, plus the last few things we needed for our plan."

Tahseefa brushes her thick, wavy hair out of her eyes and cuts in. "Just some medical supplies that I hope you won't need, a bit of food, clothes, extra ammo for your chem guns. I'm happy to help however I can."

Nani leans back on the couch and pulls her shawl around her shoulders. With her eyes firmly fixed on me, she delivers a quick and precise speech, which Asra paraphrases as, "She said if you get me killed, she'll kill you."

Yikes. No pressure. I swallow hard and lower my eyes. "I'll keep everyone safe. I promise."

Nani studies me hard, then nods. I feel like she can see right through me.

Zee pours a cup of tea for Nani from the pot on the table (it really is a compulsion for her, it seems) and hands it over with a frown. "Tahseefa, are you and Nani not coming with us?"

She and Asra look at each other for a moment, a pained expression passing between them, but she shakes her head and clutches Asra's hand tighter. "No. Asra has plenty of reasons to need to leave, and I completely understand them, but they're her reasons, not mine. I'd probably leave too, if I had her family issues, but I think I

146

can do more good here, for now."

"And you couldn't pry Nani from this planet while Jace still draws breath if you tried. She'd use every weapon in that arsenal on you," Asra adds with a wicked grin. "We'll have to stay in touch, though. If we haven't figured out Earth First's plan before the deadline, we'll come back for them."

"Sounds fair to me." I stretch, yanking the hem of my shirt down when it rides over my stomach, but not before I catch a few wandering glances out of the corner of my eye.

Then Case's wandering glance lands on the wall screen, and she launches herself from the couch and scrabbles for the control.

"Unmute it!" she commands herself, searching for the right button, then jabs her finger down so the news anchor's voice fills the room.

"—victim, Ana Velez, was found dead just after seven a.m. in the security wing of the Earth Embassy, just after the escape of recently captured suspect Casandra Hwang-Torres, who is believed to be behind the murder. Hwang-Torres was assisted in her escape by the other suspects wanted in connection with the Ellis Station attacks, Nasir Alexander Hall of the United States, Rion William Kwesi Turner, son of British member of Parliament—"

I snatch the control from Case's hand and mute the screen. Case's breaths are coming in short, rapid gasps, and she's half doubled over, her arms clutched around her torso like she's holding herself together. I wrap my arms around her, and her knees give way completely; we drop to the ground, kneeling together as a ragged scream tears itself from her throat.

"I didn't do it!" she cries, her chest heaving against mine. "They killed her, they *fucking killed her,* they—"

I tighten my hold around her shoulders and deliberately slow my breaths, coaxing her to follow my lead.

"I've got you, I've got you, I'm so sorry, I'm sorry . . ."

Zee gets down on the floor and throws her arms around both of us, rubbing soothing circles on my back.

"Loosen your grip some, Nax. Breathe deep for me now, Case, that's it. In through your nose, slowly, good, now out through your mouth, as slow as you can. Great, that's great, now again."

We huddle there on the floor for some unknown length of time as Zee counts Case through her breathing, with me unconsciously following along, until Case's death grip on my shirt loosens and the panic subsides. I keep my hold around her loose and easy, run a hand up and down her arm, press my nose into her hair, and just breathe. It's for her, of course, but for me, too; everything has been so *much* and having her in my arms quiets the roiling pain in my chest a bit. This is all too familiar, too close to home; it used to be Malik who got panic attacks over school stuff, but I eventually inherited my own brand of anxiety, too. Still, at least it means I know what to do for this, or what worked for me and Malik—close, quiet contact and slow, controlled breathing.

Eventually Case lets go altogether and wipes her puffy, bloodshot eyes, tears still clinging to long lashes. Her lips are swollen like she's had a minor allergic reaction to something, and her complexion is blotchy and pale. She covers her eyes and takes one more long, shuddering breath.

"Thank you," she says, as if surfacing from a nightmare in deep sleep. "And sorry. That hasn't happened for a really long time."

"Nothing to apologize for," Zee says matter-of-factly, two fingers on the pulse point at Case's wrist. She motions for Rion to get her a glass of water and takes an offered box of tissues from Asra. "Do you have anything you can take for it?"

Case shakes her head. "It was in my bag on the station. But I'm fine now. It's over. Just . . . give me a few minutes and I'll be ready to go."

"Are you sure?" Asra asks, an eyebrow raised. "We can put it off for a few hours if you—"

"No." Case braces herself on my shoulder and hauls herself to her feet, wavering only slightly. "Sorry, but no. We need to do this. Now more than ever, we need to do this. Besides, the longer we wait, the more time I have to psych myself out. Give me a cup of tea and something sugary and I'll be ready to go."

"On it," Rion says, making a beeline for the electric kettle. "If there's one thing I'm good for in a crisis, it's making tea. It's in my DNA."

Him and Zee both. That gets a small smile from Case, and something unwinds a bit in my chest at the sight. She really will be okay.

Once she has her tea and a pile of what Rion insists on calling biscuits, and Tahseefa has left to escort Nani home, Case does actually seem to bounce back. She conjures up a faint, watery smile for Asra and says, "Hey, you know what we all need right now? Show us our pretty ship again. The one that'll be ours in . . ." She checks her tab. "One hour and twenty-eight minutes?"

Hah, I *knew* she was a fellow aerosexual. Hot. Who can resist a ship like that?

Asra winks at her. "You got it. One Breakbolt Mark III, coming right up."

She grabs her tablet and brings up the same image she showed us earlier this morning, what feels like a lifetime ago. The ship rotates slowly in the air above the coffee table, all lovely curving lines and sleek aerodynamics. She's beautiful.

Still, everyone looks about ready to throw up their eggs from nerves, me included. This whole thing is actually happening. We're stealing yet another ship on the other side of the galaxy on the word of a girl we barely know. Completely ridiculous.

And yet . . . also kind of awesome. A foolish grin spills onto my face, despite everything, and when I look around at the others, each person meets my smile with one of their own. Case's is small but determined; Rion's is wide and sincere; Zee's is reserved, with something like pride as she looks around the circle.

And Asra? Her face glows with the kind of wondrous joy born of hope.

We're ready. As ready as we're going to be.

"Okay. We should move to our staging ground, get dressed, and go through this whole plan as many times as we can. Let's grab our stuff and get out of here."

"Aye, Captain," Rion says, and the circle dissolves into bustling preparation and last-minute showers and bathroom runs.

This whole thing is cracked. Way dangerous; god, I know it is. We have to trust one another. We each have to execute our roles perfectly. Grenades flying, weapons firing, beefy security guys . . .

I hope everyone's trust in my piloting isn't misplaced. I hope I don't screw this up like I did the landing. I hope we all live. I hope I'm up to this.

I take a deep breath.

"Okay," I say, my hand on the door controls. "Let's do this."

TEN

"IS THIS THING STILL WORKING okay?" Rion asks, turning to face me in the darkness. I squint; the facechanger is projecting well, but there's a tiny glitch, a gap in the textures right over his left cheekbone.

"Something's blocking it a little bit, right here," I say, brushing a finger over the spot. "Let me—"

I reach out and tug at his collar, tucking it away from the tiny projector on his jaw and pinning it with a black safety pin. The texture over his cheek evens out, and he's fully someone else. Still tall, still black, still handsome (focus, Hall), but his eyes are a different shape, a new shade of brown. His nose is crooked now, and his mouth slips into an unfamiliar smirk.

"Better now," I say, and finally remember to step back out of his space. Way to be awkward. "How about me?" I ask, to cover up my blunder, presenting each side of my face for inspection. A last-minute check can't hurt.

"I like the other one better," Rion says, his grin

widening, reaching out to cover the primary projector on my chin.

We've only known each other for a short time, but seeing someone else's grin on his face is weirdly disconcerting. I avert my eyes and bite back a smile. "Thanks, I think?"

"You're welcome. But seriously," he says, covering each projector in turn. "I didn't notice before we left, but I think your facechanger might be broken. It's like this one here on your cheek is projecting a different face than the rest."

Asra appears from nowhere and snatches my tablet from my pocket without warning. "You probably damaged one of the projectors when we were running away from Nani's. That one's not communicating properly with the app anymore. We'll just have to find a face setting where it's not as noticeable."

She and Rion stand back as she cycles through the options. Then they both wince.

"That's the one," Asra says.

"There's definitely . . . plenty to distract from the inconsistency," Rion adds, his disguised nose wrinkling in distaste.

I scowl. "What, am I hideous now?"

"Let's call it *distinctive*," Rion said.

Ouch. If I'm getting the diplomat-level tact, it *must* be bad.

I cast a quick glance around to check on Case and find her fiddling with her facechanger's settings. She seems to be doing much better, and though I wish we could take more time to let her come down from it all, we don't have the luxury of time. I watch her for a moment longer, then grab the bag Asra gave me for part one of our plan.

It has the few items I deemed worthy of making the trip out into the black: a share of the food and clothing Tahseefa supplied us, a portable charger. The tab synced to my facechanger goes in my right front pocket, tucked carefully away in case I need to mess with the settings again. Rion grabs his pack, too, and we head for the front room, the others following behind.

We're hidden away in an abandoned second-floor apartment one block from Jace's compound. It's just after midnight thirty, which means we have about five minutes before go time. Case shifts from foot to foot, her eyes closed, her lips moving. Probably reviewing maps of the compound in her head. Zee puts a hand on her shoulder, and some of the tension bleeds out of Case's posture. Good; she seems to be recovering well, all business and laser-tight focus. Something about compartmentalizing techniques, she said.

Asra is absorbed in her tablet, hopefully monitoring the cameras she hacked in and around Jace's warehouse. We're all dressed in dark colors like thieves from some ridiculous cop vid, but hey, it's practical for a night heist.

I walk up and peer over Asra's shoulder at the tablet screen. "How are things looking over there?"

"As we expected, so far," she says, her voice far calmer than mine sounded. "Two guards outside the door, and no one in the warehouse. Two guards on the roof. Jace is staying at his other house in New Dhaka tonight. The ship's crew left together as soon as their cargo was unloaded, and I haven't seen them return yet, which is perfect for us. Hopefully they won't come back until we're long gone."

"We can only hope," I say. Asra glances at me, then her gaze slides away. The others are doing the same. No one will meet my eye. Something ugly rises in my chest.

"Okay, what?" I snap, sharper than I meant it. "Is it just the facechanger, or nerves, or are you all having second thoughts? This is our last chance to talk about it, so make with the touchy-feely share time, people."

That earns a few snickers, and Case's eyes flick up to mine for a brief second. "I'm just nervous," she says, "but also that face is weirding me out. The other face is better. Your face, I mean."

I snort. Two in a row, score. Unless I'm so hideous now that anything would be better. Why am I thinking about this? Time and place, like Zee said. I shake my head a little, like I can physically clear out the distracting thoughts, and take a breath to ease the tension from my chest. "Okay, everyone. If this goes down according to plan, we'll be in the air in about ten minutes. Are you ready?"

Zee is calm and put-together as always; she even managed to borrow some eyeliner to get back her trademark look. Asra practically vibrates with the nearness of her goal. Rion and Case avoid each other's eyes, though, and I sigh internally. I wish we could go into this with complete trust between us all, but we can't put it off until folks get over their issues. Even I can't shake the tiny seed of doubt—is Case really as okay with this as she claims? Is she ready to commit a premeditated crime?

But ready or not, the time is now.

Asra stashes her tablet and looks around the circle, lingering on each of us. "Thank you for trusting me. I know it probably doesn't seem like it, but you all are saving me right now. I appreciate it."

My stomach lurches, but I manage a nod and a half smile. "I hope you'll forgive us if we wait to say you're welcome until we actually manage to pull this off."

After all, I have to successfully pilot us out of here before we can pat ourselves on the back. I breathe through the stab of fear to my heart and force some pep into my voice.

"Okay, people, let's get this party started. Rion, you're with me. Everyone else, Asra will lead you in once we've distracted the guards." I pause, my lips pursed. Saying good luck seems dangerous. What was it the theater kids used to say?

"Break a leg, everyone. We'll see you on the other side."

Thirty seconds ago, I felt brave and leaderly and profound. Now I feel profoundly stupid. Every step toward the compound is like walking into a pit of quicksand, merrily letting it draw me down and crush the air from my lungs and—

Rion and I pass through the open gate in the outer wall around Jace's compound, and there are the guards: tall, muscular, and angry looking. Rion's gait doesn't falter; it's relaxed and casual, and his breathing stays completely steady. He has some nerve. His diplomat act is unbreakable, but I guess it would have to be, interning with politicians all the time. He strides smoothly forward, as confident in his surroundings as the people we're impersonating would be.

We've been over this plan a hundred times by now. I should really be more chill than this, like him. I try to force my shoulders to uncoil, let my arms dangle and swing naturally at my sides. Am I swinging too much? How do I normally walk? What do I do with my hands when I walk?

My chem gun presses against the small of my back, cold and hard on my spine. I hope it doesn't somehow fire. It's only sleep chem, but I can't help the irrational fear of blowing my own ass off with one wrong step. I've only fired a gun a handful of times on Earth, under very controlled conditions and with lots of safety equipment. Then, once in the stairwell at Nani's, at an already unconscious enforcer. This is so, so different. And this walk is taking *forever*. It's only fifty feet from the main gate to the two guards, but I feel like I'm aging a year for every step we take, past stacked crates, empty load lifters, and broken-down pallets.

The guards snap to tense alertness once we cross the property line, their hands resting on the sidearms at their belts. I'll take it as a positive sign that they haven't drawn them yet; they must be buying our act for now. Shitshitshit, we're there, we're stopping, and my mouth has gone dry, and—

"Delivery from Ms. Begum, right on schedule," Rion says, his voice bored and sarcastically cheerful. Confident. Perfectly on script. How does he do that? He unshoulders his bag slowly, but the guys don't make a move.

"What happened to the other two guys? What are their names, Ravi and Sudeepta? Something like that?" the guard on the left asks. He scratches one terrifically bushy eyebrow, his body language relaxing with practiced ease. His eyes are anything but casual. This is a test.

"Rabi and Nirjar. Not even close on that last one, mate," Rion says, still cool. How can he do this without a single tremor in his voice? I always heard that politicians could smell fear, so maybe his diplomatic training just happens to lend itself incredibly well to crime. "They're out on another job tonight. Boss decided we could handle making the delivery this week, and if we manage not to screw up, we might even be your new regulars."

Or Asra bribed them to clear off for the night, but you know, close enough.

Rion lets a little grin twist his unfamiliar lips, like he's letting the guards in on a joke. I try to mimic him, raising an eyebrow for effect.

The guard on the right looks straight at me, then over to Rion. "Your friend here ever speak?" he asks.

"Nah," I say with a small chuff of a laugh. May as well play off what everyone's been telling me. "No one wants to hear what my ugly face has to say."

The second guard lets out a surprised laugh, his professional cool relaxing somewhat. "You got that right, friend. That is one unfortunate mug you're sporting there."

"Hey, that's my momma's face you're insulting!" Gotta draw this joke out as long as I can. In my head, I'm calculating: Where are the others now? Are they across the lot yet? Have they disabled the camera yet? My eyes flick unconsciously up to the camera over guard number two's head; the light is still burning steady green. Shit.

The guard follows the direction of my gaze, and his eyes harden again. "All right, gents, I think that's enough

159

of that. Hand over the payment, we'll count it, and if it's all there, then you can go back to your boss and tell her that you were good little delivery boys."

Rion's expression twists into confusion, and for a second I start to panic. Does he not know what to say next? Is it time to start shooting?

But it's all part of the act, of course. He has this under control. Can't help it—I'm *damn* impressed.

"We don't deliver to someone inside?" Rion says, letting his brows furrow. "I thought Nirjar said we were supposed to deliver to Mr. Patel, the warehouse guy? Or is he the accountant?" He looks to me, as if to verify his memory of the delivery instructions. I play along, biting my lip in uncertainty.

"I . . . think he said the warehouse guy. Is that not right?" I say, turning to the guard on the left. No good, no good, I'm the worst liar *ever*—his hand is back on his sidearm, and he's popped the safety off.

"No, that's not right," he says, voice low. "You have ten seconds to hand over the money." The second guard follows suit, drawing his gun out of its holster.

"Whoa, whoa, lads, no need for all that!" Rion protests, sliding the last brown strap off his shoulder. "Just a little bit of misinformation, some lines of communication crossed, no big deal. We're giving you the money right now, okay? How do you want to do this? Should I hand you the bag? Put it on the ground? Should I take the money out and hand only that to you?"

Rion has a skill for babbling, it seems, because he's drawing this out longer and longer and we still aren't dead, but it can't stay that way for long. Maybe I should shoot first. My heart is hammering so hard it sounds like a kick drum of pulsing blood inside my ears, playing some ridiculously fast, angry electronica beat. I discreetly wipe my palms on my pant legs. No way I'll be able to grab a gun with the Amazon River gushing down my hands.

I see the moment they make the decision. The guards' eyes meet for the smallest fraction of a second, and god, this is going to all go sideways before we even get inside, before we even get close. Forget about the rooftop problems, because there's the *fffwissh* sound of metal on leather and guns in my face and a gun in my hand, and I'm diving to the side—

No, the guard is falling to the side, Zee's boot firmly lodged in his right kidney. They're here. And with that realization, time moves again, and my head clears. I whip my gun around to find the guard on the left, just in time to see Rion fire. The guard crumples to the ground.

I swing back, aiming at the guard on the right again and, by sheer luck, land a chem splatter on his cheek. It seeps in through his skin barely a second later, and its soporific effects are instantaneous. His hands, clutching at his side where Zee kicked him, relax and fall to the ground. The camera—yes, the little light is burning red now. Asra and Case jog up, and Asra wastes no time waving her tablet at the lock pad beside the door. It hums, and the door emits a soft click. She yanks the door open and waves us in, the impatience of the gesture betraying the cracks in her calm.

Case steps through the door first, her chem gun held awkwardly in front of her. She hadn't wanted to carry a gun at all, but I insisted. Even without any training, even without ever having fired one, it's better to have it just in case. It's nonlethal, so what's the worst that could happen?

Zee darts through the door next, running flat out toward her designated target: the weapons storage area. And *damn* is she fast. I would have loved to see her on the soccer pitch—I bet she was a star. She'll be much slower on the way back with a box of grenades in her hands, though. And I thought running with scissors was bad.

I go in next, then Rion, and Asra pulls the door shut behind us. Case leads us with sure movements, muttering turn-by-turn directions to herself as she rounds corners without hesitation. A right, then a left down a row of foodstuffs, then another right, and there's the freight elevator. Next to it are fuel containers and ship ammunition crates, just as Asra said—except they aren't preloaded on carts like they're supposed to be, ready for tomorrow's shipment. Because the carts aren't there. At all.

Balls.

The fuel is stored in a huge metal cylinder that comes up to my stomach, with two thin silver handles sticking out on either side. I grab the handles and heave, but damn, this thing is heavy as a brick of lead. It doesn't even budge. I try an underhanded grip and heave again, but it's useless.

"I can try to find a cart," Case begins, but I cut her off with a gesture.

"No time," I say. "Call the elevator. We'll roll it on there and deal with it when we get to the top. Rion, can you lift at least one of the ammo crates?"

Rion replies by crouching down, wrapping his arms around the crate, and lifting from his knees. He nearly topples over, his groan telling me just how heavy is.

"It's awkward to get hold of, but I got it. Tell me you've already called the lift."

A pleasant-sounding chime punctuates his sentence, and the elevator doors slide smoothly open. Asra leaps forward to hold the doors open while Rion staggers inside, bracing himself against one wall to ease the strain. He's sweating and breathing hard through his nose, but his arms are steady. Still, better hurry.

"Help me with this," I say, waving Case over. "Tip it toward me and we'll roll it."

It takes a few seconds of rocking, but eventually the

cylinder tips onto its bottom edge. It's heavy even with the ground taking the brunt of the weight, and it's hard as hell to control. I roll it right past the door on the first try. I have to rock it back and forth in several small crescents to get it in, but eventually a *bumpbump* vibrates through the handle as the cylinder glides over the door track. I'm in. With the fuel tank still braced against my right side, I wave Asra away and mash the level-four button inside the elevator.

"Get up the stairs and blow the guard quarters the second Zee gets back!" I yell as the doors start to close. "I'm gonna be pissed if a bunch of reinforcements show up on the roof!"

Just before the doors seal shut, an echoing boom cracks the air: an explosion. Like a grenade going off.

"Zee!" I nearly drop the cylinder as I lunge for the doors, but it's too late. My hands scrabble at the seam, but the elevator is already moving, and oh god, if something went wrong, we're going to be on that rooftop alone. They were supposed to take out the reinforcements, blow the stairwell, but . . .

"Rion," I gasp, my breath coming hard and fast. My lungs burn, though whether from exertion or fear, I don't know. I rock once, twice, then let the fuel container fall back to a flat sitting position. My arms feel like they're floating without the weight. "Rion, put down the crate, forget the ammo. If the others got in trouble, we're going to have to take on the rooftop guards alone. Put down the crate and get out your gun, man. Do it."

He lowers the crate as gently as he can in the cramped space of the featureless steel elevator, though it still drops the last few inches with a thump that makes me cringe away from it. Munitions are not a great thing to drop. It doesn't explode, thankfully, so I draw my gun with my left hand and Rion draws his with his right, and we press our bodies together in front of the door, ready to charge.

"No hesitation. Run straight at them, shoot as soon as you have an angle, then find cover to finish it. We have to get back to help the others." I give Rion's shoulder a nudge as the elevator chimes its warning. "I bet your dad would flip if he saw you right now."

He glances over and flashes his killer grin. "You know just how to sweet-talk me."

Then the doors slide open, and we charge.

ELEVEN

DING!

Two guards turn their heads lazily toward the elevator, probably expecting the ship's crew back from the bar, legless and happy. What they get is two reckless guys charging at them with chem guns spitting. My first shots go wide, which gives my target plenty of time to draw her gun and take cover around the ship's curved underbelly.

At the first *pop*, muscle memory takes over and I drop to the ground, roll—this is twice now in a few days' time I've been shot at. Not just by a chem gun or a jolter, but a real gun with real bullets that will really kill me on the spot. I want to look over, want to check on Rion, but I need cover, need to hit my target so we can check on Zee and the other—

Pop pop pop!

"Aaugh!"

Oh god, Rion.

Cold horror seizes my chest, knocks the breath from my lungs. I throw myself behind a stack of supply crates, my head swimming with adrenaline and pure fear. I chance a look in Rion's direction. He's pressed against a small electric cargo hauler, one bloody hand clutching— his shoulder? His chest? Was he hit in the chest? Oh my god, please not Rion, please! He fires wildly, his injured side propped up on a crate for stability, but his shots do little more than distract the second guard.

A bullet pings off the metal of my hiding spot, and I sink lower, pressing the heel of my hand into my forehead. I can't breathe. This isn't going to work. I can't just hide here and let them walk over and shoot me. The erratic fire from Rion's hiding place has slowed—is he losing consciousness? I have to do something. I have to get to Rion. I have to get to Zee. I have to do this. No time to sit and think and plan.

I take a breath. Another. Move into a crouch. Check the chem levels in my gun—half gone already; god. I can do this. Count backward, three . . . two . . . one!

I explode from my crouch and sprint toward the ship, angling around to where my original target has taken cover. She's waiting for me, has me sighted down her barrel, but I throw myself to the left, then again, then to the right, moving forward all the while, building momentum. The guard's eyes go wide and her eyebrows climb. She's figured it out: I'm not planning to stop. Full-on bull rush, with all my athlete's speed behind it. She changes her stance to deal with the close range, sights down her gun barrel again, and *bang!*

God, I should be dead, should have hot blood pumping from a hole in my chest. Maybe I am. Maybe I just haven't felt it yet, but as soon as her finger moves I'm on the ground, my finger tight on the trigger, a steady stream of chem pods firing wildly, and—

A tiny splatter of green appears on the underside of her chin. She tumbles to the ground.

I want to stay right where I am, just lie down and be still. My body is already protesting, telling me I've done enough, but all I can see in my mind is Rion, the blood pouring over his hand, his face crumpled in pain. His shots stopped at some point. What if he's dead? I charge back around the ship, angling for Rion's cover, and then WHAM! The ground slams into my face, or I slam into it, and before I can process the fact that I'm horizontal again, a gun barrel presses hard against the back of my head.

"Who sent you?" a voice asks, oddly delicate and lightly accented. "Tell me," she says, "and I'll kill you right now instead of giving you to Mr. Pearson. Trust me when I say you should prefer my bargain."

I open my mouth to start BSing, my cheek dragging across the harsh concrete, but what comes out instead is: "Is my friend alive?"

She snorts, like she's amused at my ineptitude. "Dead, dying, same difference. You were stupid to come up here with just two of you."

A door bangs open somewhere—the stairwell?—and I strain my eyes as far as I can. Three figures, thank god or the universe or whatever. Zee can help us, she—

But it's not them. Three more guards stroll onto the rooftop, their hands resting casually on their weapons.

"Took you long enough," my captor says, practically spitting at them. "I radioed for backup last year, assholes. We're fine now; you can go back to picking your ass or whatever it is you do in your downtime."

One of the guards holds his hands up in surrender, his sidearm hanging limp in his grip. "Hey, chill, okay? Looks like you have everything under control, so we'll just—"

The man stops. Just . . . stops. Then his eyes fall shut and he topples over.

The gun pressing into my skull eases up, then slides away. A second later, a full-grown woman in light body armor comes crashing down on top of me.

"Oof! Goddamn—"

Two more thuds, right in front of me. I force myself up on my forearms with a groan, the woman's body sliding sideways off my back. All three reinforcement guards lie on the deck, out cold. Case, Asra, and Zee stand just outside the stairwell doorway, shoving guns back in their respective holsters. Asra spares me a quick glance, but no more—she makes straight for the ship, pulling out her tablet on the way to work on the locks. Case starts toward me, but I get one arm free and wave her off.

"Preflight checks!" I yell at her. None of this will matter if we don't get the ship in the air. She hesitates for a moment, but runs to Asra's side. Good. Thank you.

With a heave, I pull myself the rest of the way out from under the weight of the passed-out guard, get my legs under me, and scramble over to Rion's last hiding place, waving Zee over as well. As soon as I round the corner, the hot burn of bile rushes into the back of my throat.

Rion is slumped against the cart, his clothing and hands stained with fresh blood. I drop to my knees and push two shaking fingers against his throat and this is all so horribly, *horribly* familiar, and for a second I can't remember if it's Rion or Malik under my fingers. Where the hell is the pulse point supposed to be? Am I too low? Was that a beat, or was that my hand shaking? I push harder, and no no no, maybe there's no pulse to find, maybe it's not there, maybe—but there.

There it is.

I'm not sure if it's the right tempo, but it's steady and it's there. That's all I know. All I care about.

"He's alive!" I yell as Zee skids to a halt, crouching down beside me. "Help me get him up. We have to get him on board, take him with us!"

"Of course we do," she says, her voice even and sure. "But not yet."

She rips the bag off her back and pulls out a roll of

thick, stretchy bandages. While I support Rion from his uninjured side, Zee winds the bandage tight around his entire shoulder and upper arm, tying it off tightly right over the bullet's entrance wound. The blood begins to seep through within seconds, but Zee only adds a pad of gauze over top and nods to me, pressing her palm hard against the wound. She's incredible, completely incredible, so in control, so everything I'm not, and thank the stars for that.

With careful coordination, I maneuver Rion's uninjured arm over my shoulders while Zee wraps her arm around his waist from the other side, trying not to jostle his wound too badly. We lift, and he is *so* much heavier than he looks, the bastard. His head slumps onto his undamaged shoulder, his short curls brushing against my cheek. A whisper of a groan escapes his lips—was that my name?

"Hold on, Rion," I whisper, pressing my cheek against the top of his head. I don't know if he can hear me, but I think I'm talking just as much to myself as I am to him. "This is almost over. We'll be in the black and home free before you know it." I readjust my grip on his side and grimace. "We'd get there faster if you'd wake up and help us, asshole."

His legs dangle uselessly between Zee and me, and it takes a lot of effort to not kick his ankles with every step or catch his sneakers on some discarded tool or scrap. Just a few more steps. The beautiful lines of the ship gleam faintly with the light of the risen moons, the white beams of light disappearing inside the open hatch. Asra appears in the doorway as our boots hit the ramp, and she hauls Rion off my shoulder without a word. I start to protest, my hands gripping his shirt, his bicep, but she shoves me away with her hip.

"Go," she says. "I've got him. Close the ramp and get us in the air. Case is done with preflight. We're right behind you."

That gets me going. Rion's wounds won't matter a lick if we get shot out of the sky because I take too long getting us up. The sooner I get us to safety, the sooner Zee can give Rion some real help. I hit the door controls and tear off through the impressively large cargo bay, trusting the hatch to do its job and seal properly behind me. A left turn at the brightly marked central corridor, past the forward maintenance room; then the bridge door stands open right in front of me.

As soon as I'm in, with the winking lights of the pilot's console beneath my hands, a fresh jolt of adrenaline erupts behind my breastbone. *Ground rushing up, the screams behind me, awful screeching crunching shriek of metal on metal and the front of the vehicle rushing toward me, then the blackness . . .* My hands tremble.

It won't happen again. I won't let it. I'll just channel some of Zee's level confidence and do what needs doing.

Case glances over from the navigator's terminal as I drop into my chair. Her expression is calm, determined, no trace of her earlier panic, so I take a deep breath and shove the nerves away. The plush cushioning of the pilot's seat molds around me, and while I adjust the seat so my boots rest comfortably on the rudder pedals, the back of my mind luxuriates in the thought of owning a classy, comfortable ship like this. I want to take a moment, take it in, study all its tiny details, but there's no time. Gotta get away with it first.

"We ready?" I ask, my finger hovering over the ignition switch. Case finishes a last few keystrokes, then looks over and meets my eyes. Nods. Takes a breath.

I hit the ignition.

The ship roars under us, an unbelievably sexy sound that sends a gentle shudder through the metal skin of the vessel. It vibrates through my chair, even more through the pedals at my feet and the control stick in my hand. This ship's controls are more like a fighter jet than a shuttle, which I'm both more comfortable with and more afraid of. I bet this ship has some major mods under the hood. I give the engines a moment to warm up, but only a moment; Case hasn't said anything yet, but she's leaning closer and closer to her display screen, so I know there's bad news coming.

Asra and Zee burst onto the bridge, moving as fast as they can with the unconscious Rion between them. They manage to get him strapped into a chair; then Asra waves her tablet near the ship console's wireless interface. Delivering coordinates, probably. As soon as her tablet beeps, she throws herself into the seat behind Case and straps in. Zee plants her feet and bends her knees, hanging tight to the back of Rion's seat with one hand.

"Aren't you going to strap in?" I ask her.

"I'll be fine. He won't," she answers smoothly. "Once his bleeding slows, then I'll worry about sitting down."

There's no time to argue. I ramp the mag coils smoothly up to full power, lifting us off the deck without a bump, then engage the thrusters. Jace's mansion compound falls away beneath us, and I gently guide us out of the maze of Saleem's tallest buildings and into open sky. The city glitters below, its steel and glass towers shrinking as our altitude increases. It's gorgeous, both the sight and the feeling of open air around me again. If I weren't carrying lives I'd rather not lose, I'd be putting the ship through her paces, rolling and banking and getting myself in trouble again, no doubt. As it is, though, I stay tight and focused, overly conscious of my responsibility.

Once we hit minimum safe distance, I dial the throttle higher, the ship's humming pitch rising along with it. "Do you have a heading for me, Case, or should I just take the most direct route to orbit?"

Asra answers instead. "Head for orbit straight over the center of the city, if possible. The city has ground-to-orbit munitions, but they won't want to rain shrapnel down over their own citizens. They'll probably send—"

"Fighters incoming!" Case cuts in. "They're still seven klicks out, flying in from the next town over, but they'll be here in about ten seconds."

"Just so," Asra finishes. "Same thing, though; if you stay over the city, they won't shoot us down. They'll try to crowd you in, force you to land or fly over the desert. Don't let them."

"Oh, don't let them! Great idea, Asra, I'm so thankful for your brilliant advice," I snap, wrenching the stick back and opening the throttle. Zee stumbles and swears behind me as we rocket into the night sky, the viewport completely filled with pinpoint stars and glowing moons.

Wait. *Moons.*

"Case, the largest moon is directly over the city right now. It'll take extra time to get out of its gravity shadow, won't it?" My fingers tap wildly on the throttle control like it'll somehow make the ship go faster.

"Yes," Case says, her voice laser sharp as her intense stare burns a hole through the navigator's display. "Once we're in low orbit, we can angle away if you think it's safe, but it kind of depends on what happens with these fighters."

As if on cue, the roar of powerful engines shredding atmo bleeds through the background rumble of our own ship. I glance up at the rear cam display and see a pair of fighters closing in, painted the same rust red as the beach sand. The comm light blinks on, and a voice fills the bridge.

"Pilot, this is Lieutenant Haque of the al-Rihla enforcement First Fighter Wing. You are in possession of stolen property. You are ordered to land and surrender your ship at once."

My HUD squawks the second the fighters come into firing range, and I set the ship to dancing, pulling every maneuver I can at this speed. Zee swears again, and I can hear her rummaging around for something in her bag, but it's looking worse for her by the second.

"You really need to strap in now, Zee," I say, breaking hard to starboard as the fighters move in around us. "You can't possibly do anything for Rion right now."

"Just let me . . . give him this . . . injection . . . ," she grinds out, then makes a little noise of triumph. "Got it! The bleeding should—"

"Sit *down*, Zee!" Case orders. She is *not* fucking around. "And put on your damn harness."

"It would really help," I add. The second I hear Zee's restraints click, I jam the stick back and to the left, darting around a fighter trying to cut us off. My head bounces off the headrest with the force of the maneuver—I hope I'm not jostling Rion's wound too badly, but I think he won't mind terribly, considering the alternative.

God, Rion.

Now's not the time.

With my eyes locked on my display and my hand glued to the stick, I ask, "So should we say anything back to the good lieutenant, or just let them wonder?"

Case raises her voice to be heard over her furious tapping. "I don't think there's anything to say, real—"

The comm clicks on, and Asra's voice rings out from behind me. "Lieutenant Haque of the al-Rihla enforcement First Fighter Wing, I think there are greater wrongs you could be righting than the theft of a drug-running ship from a horrible man who poisons our community. How long have you been looking the other way while our stepfather ruins Saleem? What is it, Aasim—money? Fear? Or are you really that oblivious? Either way, of the two of us, you are the greater criminal here."

The comm clicks off, and the bridge is filled with a severely awkward silence. I have no idea what to say, and no spare brainpower to make my mouth work anyway. More fighters join the first two and slip into formation around the ship: one off each wing, one in front, and one behind. We're boxed in.

The fighter in front fills our massive viewport, its engines growing larger as we race toward it, so close now I can read the service designation painted on the sleek black wing: TIGER SQUADRON, CPT. ISAAC THOMAS, with a row of kill marks underneath. Oh hell, *Tiger Squadron.* I completely forgot they were here assisting local enforcement. They failed at shooting us down over Earth, but I doubt they'll let us get away this time. This just got even better. I thumb a switch on the control stick, shifting our avionics over to close-range dogfight mode, surprised it even exists in a ship this size. This must be a custom job through and through.

The comm clicks again. "Asra? Is that you? What are you doing?"

"What you never had the courage to do," she snaps back over the comm. I risk a glance away from the viewport and over at Case, but she's making no move to cut off or scramble the transmission. Actually, I think she has a tiny smile on her face, but I have to look away before I can be sure. The formation is tightening now, and I can't juke the ship without nicking one of their fighters. It would probably hurt them more than us. *Probably*. But worst case scenario, we end up too damaged to make the jump, or one of the fighters crashes and kills civilians in Saleem. Neither option is acceptable. Gotta think, gotta think . . .

"Do you really think this is what Ammu would want you to do?" the lieutenant's voice says through the comm. Some of the command is leaking out of it, replaced with something else—sadness, or weariness.

"I think she would prefer this to seeing what you've become this last year. I hope one day you'll wake up and be the man I know you can be, insha'Allah," Asra replies, her voice quieter now. "Until then, I'm happy to do this one small thing to help our city. And since I know these transmissions are recorded for public record, let me say this: to anyone who is still unaware, whether through optimistic oversight or deliberate ignorance, know that nearly every person in our community who has disappeared over the past fifteen years can be tied back to my stepfather, Jace Pearson, Saleem city councilman. Some were forced to work making drugs for him, and some were killed for debts or disputes. The proof is readily available for anyone willing to dig. To my people out there—you know who you are. Spread this recording far and wide. Bring him down. Astaghfirullah."

Asra plays all this off so relaxed, but that small moment of seeking forgiveness is telling; this whole thing with her stepdad is killing her inside. There's barely a second of silence before an angry voice bursts from the speaker. "This is Captain Isaac Thomas of Tiger Squadron. We have you surrounded and we will—"

The comm clicks off, then plays a little double beep.

"I shut the comm down so we won't have to listen to their whining anymore," Asra says coolly. I want to reply, want to ask about her brother and the things she said, but unless I do something in the next few seconds—

A fifth fighter appears on my HUD, joining the other four boxing us in, but this one directly above us, forcing us down. We're going to collide unless they match our speed. What in the hell am I supposed to do now? We're so dead. I've got nothing. I knew I'd probably kill us this time out, but—

Unless.

"Case," I ask, my voice coming out surprisingly even. "Can you give me any more power to the engines? I'm gonna try something that might be . . . not good."

"Oh, lovely," Case says, "We aren't using the weapons systems right now, so I can cut them off and reroute that power. Other than that, all I can do is override some safety protocols and hope the ship doesn't explode. Are we in favor of that?"

"Of not exploding?" I ask, incredulous.

"Of the override, Nax," she snaps, her fingers flying over her screen.

"Do it," Asra says.

My hand shakes over the throttle control. This is exactly the kind of thing that always backfires on me. I try to get too fancy, try to show off, try to push myself . . . but right now, if we have any chance of getting out of here, I have to do this.

I have to.

I blow out a slow breath. "Okay. Tell me when you're ready."

"It'll only take a . . . okay, now!" Case shouts, and I cut the engines off completely and shove the control stick forward, throwing us into a freefall. The ship screams in protest, with some help from Asra, but the fighters leap past us at full speed and we're free of the aerial blockade. I jerk the stick back up, and for a sick second, we're sailing forward on our leftover momentum alone—then I wrench the stick over, kick in the afterburner, open the throttle wide out, and shit, Case was *not* kidding. Without the safety engaged, this ship can move.

It is *unbelievably* hot.

We blow past the fighters, and I don't even bother with evasive maneuvers that might slow us down, just rely on out-and-out speed to get us up and away. The fighter formation wavers behind us for a moment, and I can imagine them chattering over the comm, trying to hail us, trying to figure out what the hell just happened, but fortunately we don't have to listen to any of that crap. A thrill builds in my chest, like the swell of a shout bubbling under my ribs, and a grin tugs at the corners of my mouth. I actually pulled that one off. The atmosphere turns wispy, and its drag on the ship falls away bit by bit.

Our momentum pushes my head into the back of the chair, crushes all my organs back against my spine in a way that will never stop being exhilarating. My grin turns cocky, and I roll my head over to share the moment with Case. If we can keep up this pace, we can make the A-jump in just over a minute. We're home free.

Worst. Thought. Ever.

What is wrong with me?

As if summoned by my arrogance, a screeching

warning erupts from the HUD, and I slam my foot down on the right rudder pedal, yanking the stick back and over. A rush of energy surges past us in the wake of an enormously fast projectile, the bullet winking away into the distance. The ground-to-orbit railguns. Not good.

The largest moon looms huge and craggy off our right wing, its pockmarked face staring down at us as we rush toward it. And I have another idea. Instead of angling away from the moon, into clear space, I maneuver us toward it.

"Case, I need your help here," I say, keeping my hand light and easy on the stick. "I'm using the moon to block their shot, but if we're not out of here soon, those fighters will be back to shoot us down anyway. I need to use the gravity of this moon to slingshot us away. It should get us into A-drive range, right? You know the physics stuff better than me. Can we—"

"Yeah, yeah, shut up so I can math. Level out for now, I'll send you the trajectory. Get ready . . . okay, there, go!"

My HUD lights up with a path showing the exact speed and angle to follow. I pull the stick gently back until the nose lifts into alignment with the path, then level out the wings with the pedals and match our speed to Case's calculations. I'm so tempted to push it faster; after what we pulled earlier, I know this ship's got more juice, but the angle, the speed, the acceleration, it all has to be perfect for this to work, and the breakaway point is coming up soon.

A flash, a shrill warning, then bullets ping at our shields. Not again. Please, don't let this happen again. Pleasepleaseplease, I couldn't take it if—

"Stay the course!" Case shouts over the hail of bullets. "Our shields are holding, just a few more seconds!"

The comm clicks, and Asra's voice fills the bridge once more. "Aasim, if that's you back there, I hope you know I can never forgive you for this."

"Asra—" the voice from the fighter starts, but Asra cuts communications again. I feel her cold fury like a physical presence at my back.

Then my instruments flash green, the stick leaps out of my hand as the autopilot times the slingshot maneuver, and we're launched off into the black with an exhilarating force I've never experienced. It's a rush, nearly painful, but more fun than any thrill ride on Earth.

Until I hear Rion groan in pain behind me. Shit.

My head swims with the suddenness of the maneuver, but we're not out of danger yet. "Case, are the jump calcs ready?"

"We're going, Nax, just give me a few seconds . . ."

The ship's humming changes, ramping higher and higher. The vibration studders, and space-time starts to scrunch before the drive even fully engages, the stars sucked away until only a blank empty center remains—

Then we're nowhere. Gone.

I hope when we come out the other side, things go

better than they did last time.

No crashing this time.

I promise.

I hope.

(Rion, please be okay.)

TWELVE

THE REAPPEARANCE OF THE STARS is just as disconcertingly sudden as their disappearance, but their pale winking light is a relief nonetheless. Several glowing lights on my console blink for my attention; we're running hot, but as we seem to not be crashing, leaking atmosphere, or dying, I take a few indulgent seconds to sink into my cushy pilot's chair and let the adrenaline drain from my system.

I'm sure I'll start shaking any moment now, for but the time being, everything is clear. Calm. Quiet. Nothing but us and the stars, drifting along in shared silence. I nudge us gently out of the jump arrival zone—no use getting killed by a jumping ship right after our daring escape— then collapse against the headrest.

A shuddering breath breaks the silence beside me, and a wet sniffle comes from behind. A sudden pressure burns behind my eyes and in my throat at the sounds, live and pained. Case leans with her elbows braced on the console in front of her, head in her hands. Her chest and back rise and fall with deep, fast breaths, just this side of hyperventilating. I want to reach over to her, run a hand through her hair or rub her back as it heaves with sobs, but there's an entire center console of controls separating us. At least these aren't panic-attack sobs—just regular, completely understandable thank-god-we're-alive tears.

The brief stillness doesn't last.

The click of Zee's safety restraints pulls me back into our current situation. Now that we're relatively safe, drifting alone through the black, all I can think of is the drying blood that stiffens the shoulder of my shirt. I flip a few switches, venting some of our excess heat into space and engaging the autopilot, then pull myself out of the pilot's seat, moving to help Zee with Rion's unconscious form. Between the two of us, we manage to get him unbelted and back over our shoulders like before, his head lolling to one side. It takes a lot of awkward sideways shuffling down the cramped central corridor, barely wide enough for two people, and several wrong turns, but we eventually find what could generously be called a medbay.

It's more like a storage closet for medical supplies that happens to be large enough for a single bed. I prop Rion's limp form against the wall and support him as Zee rolls the bed into the hallway; there's no way we'd be able to maneuver him in such cramped quarters. She lowers the bed so we can ease him down, then rolls it back into the tiny room and drops into a crouch beside him.

Seeing Rion lying there, his eyes closed, complexion ashen and dull, hits me far harder than expected.

The medbay barely has standing room for two, so I back myself into the doorway, available but unobtrusive while Zee works, deliberate and careful. My body must recognize that I finally have a moment to myself, because a wave of dizziness slams into me, and I have to close my eyes and lean my forehead against the doorjamb to regain my balance.

Spots dance on the insides of my eyelids, and my skin goes hot, then cold, then weirdly tingly. Part of me distantly wonders if I'm finally losing it, but the majority of my brain is dedicated to replaying the moment when a tiny piece of metal buried itself in Rion's shoulder, when he screamed and fell and bled all over my hands just like Malik did. What are we doing? One of us actually got *shot*. Shooting *kills* people. *Oh my god.*

"Deep breaths, Nax," Zee says from inside the tiny room, her voice even and calm. I open my eyes just as she finishes untying her hasty bandage job from the rooftop. She tuts when she sees the state of the wound, a dark, sticky, twisted mess.

"I wish I'd taken the time to cut away his shirt before I wrapped it earlier. This is going to be much less pleasant for him. I hope he stays unconscious," she says, eyeing the shelves around her. She digs through drawer after drawer, slamming each one progressively louder.

"Seriously?" she finally says, throwing her hands in the air. "What kind of medbay doesn't have bandage scissors?"

I snort half-heartedly. "This ship is so pumped with illegal modifications, I wouldn't be surprised if they cut the medbay in half to use the extra room for more engines or coolant or something."

"I have to cut this before I can do anything else," she says. "Bits of it have dried into the wound. I have some scissors in my pack on the bridge. I'll be right back. While I'm gone, wet a cloth and hold it over the wound. A spray bottle with water would be great too, if you can find one. Soak the shirt."

I leap to follow her orders, glad to have something to do to help. I rummage through cabinets that barely have room to open in this confined space and find a pile of squishy white hand towels. I run the warm water in the room's tiny sink and wet the cloth, then lay it over the wound. Most of the spray bottles in the narrow supply closet hold cleaners or chemicals I don't recognize, but I finally find an empty one and fill it with more warm water. The fine mist evenly soaks the shirt around the bullet hole, and I use the cloth to dab gently at the edges of the wound, where blood has congealed on the fabric.

I hope this isn't hurting him. I've hurt him enough already. Probably he wants to get the hell away from me and this ship the second we put down on solid ground, and with his smooth words, he could probably do it, too. This whole thing, it's the same kind of shit I always pull, some wild scheme that ends up hurting people, and—

"Hey, mate, stop thinking so loud," Rion croaks, and I jump, nearly dropping the cloth. Cool relief washes through my chest as his deep russet-brown eyes blink open and meet mine.

All I can do is stare for a long moment. Rion's eyes have a dark ring around the outside, and a tiny freckle next to his right pupil. I never noticed. I have to swallow down a thick surge of emotion before I can speak, can diffuse this intensity.

"God, man, you scared the hell out of me. I thought you were unconscious!" I manage. "How are you feeling, you bastard?"

He manages a weak smile and tips his head toward me. "Oh, you know. Fine. Just catching up on some sleep. I think I have a chunk of metal stuck in my shoulder, which may or may not be on fire right now, but I'm sure I'll be up in no time." He pauses, taking a slow breath. Pain shows in the lines around his eyes, but he pushes on with good humor. "Where are we at? Are we dead in the water? Venting atmo again? Planning another crash landing?"

"Okay, you're obviously fine. Think I'll just leave you here to bleed," I say, masking the flare of panic his words provoke with a small chuckle. I actually managed to not

189

almost kill us this time, thanks, but the fact that he can joke around like a dickhead means he'll be okay, I think. "We're floating in the black right now, just outside Serenity's controlled space. I honestly haven't thought much past that. Haven't looked at fuel levels, diagnostics, anything. I'm assuming the ship would have screamed at us if something major was going wrong."

I rub my thumb gently along the edge of the rough cloth, watching the individual fibers of the weave bend and snap back. The cloth goes cold after a moment—am I supposed to resoak it to keep it warm? I look up and catch Rion staring at me, and I freeze, my heart rate skyrocketing. His lips part, and I fixate on the tiny motion, a rush of heat darkening my cheeks, but my eyes won't obey my command to look away, damn it. I try to say something, some kind of apology for getting him shot, or a "glad you're not dead" speech, but my mouth goes dry.

And then Zee comes bustling through the door. The moment shatters.

"Back up, please," she says with cool efficiency, and I do as she says, transferring the damp cloth to her hands. She crouches by Rion's side and gives him a small smile before lifting the corner of the cloth.

"Sorry for the wet," she says, "but this will hurt less than me ripping dry cloth from the wound. I'm going to cut off this part of your shirt, okay?"

He grunts his assent. Probably couldn't say more if he

wanted to, with her tugging at the fabric like that.

She goes slow, carefully snipping the fabric around the wound, then counts backward before pulling each scrap away from the ragged hole in Rion's shoulder. Rion sucks in a sharp breath through his teeth, but all he says is "Yeah," tight and pained. I'm assuming that means "Yeah, hurts like a mother."

A double beep jolts me out of my fixation on Rion, then Case's voice comes over the all-ship intercom.

"We need you on the bridge," she says without preamble. "We're having an . . . issue."

My stomach sinks. What now? Is the ship dying? Are we getting shot at again? I would love it if someone else could deal with this. I take one last steadying breath to clear my head, glance back at Rion, then nod. Back to the bridge for the next crisis. Zee's and Rion's quiet murmurs fade, and when I get near the hatch, a different set of voices takes over—two of them, though Asra is the only one I recognize. The problem quickly becomes apparent.

"—but is there really no way we can work something out? Or at least refuel? We can put down far outside of town, on the dark side of the station, fly without transmitters, whatever you want, we just—"

"I'm sorry, ma'am, but the decision is final. Come back once you've had the ship scrubbed and we'll welcome you and your credits with open arms and wallets, but until then, we can't risk word getting out that we harbored the people who stole Jace Pearson's precious toy. Now, we don't mean to be unfriendly, but we're gonna have to ask you to move along out of our airspace. Right now."

Asra sighs, shakes her head. "Understood."

"Fair winds and friendly skies, sister," he says, sounding almost regretful, and the line goes dead.

We're silent for a moment. I drop into the pilot's seat, tip back against the headrest, and close my eyes. Probably not a good idea; I could drop off to sleep any second. The hours are melting away in a flood of adrenaline, and each day the weight of what happened at the Academy feels more ominous. Four days. Evacuating loved ones they want "spared" from the colonies . . .

I open my eyes and blink a few times, then shake off the exhaustion, fixing my gaze on the bright blue arc of Serenity on the horizon. It slides away under our portside wing as I turn us around and re-engage the autopilot, then let my hands fall away from the controls. I'm too tired to guide the ship, and my eyes keep losing focus. Better to let the computer have a turn.

"So," I say, unable to keep the weariness out of my voice. "I guess we need to have a meeting. Figure out where we want to go and what we want to do about Earth First now that we're free."

Case pulls out her tab. "I'll download the ship status, fuel levels and all that. Meet in the mess hall?"

I rub a hand over my face. My brain feels like it's full

of molasses. "Uh, yeah. If we have a mess hall."

Asra stands and stretches, then leans her shoulder against the side of her high-backed chair. "I'll go round everyone up. See you in a few."

"Yeah," I say, sagging back into my seat. "Two minutes."

Her footsteps echo down the hallway, followed seconds later by Case's quicker steps.

And I'm alone.

The quiet of the bridge wraps around me, a blessing after the past two days of constant company. I start to drift off almost immediately, the adrenaline crash catching up with me.

We made it. We're here, in our own ship, off the Rock, in the black. Free. It's my dream made real.

But all I feel is exhausted.

I can't breathe. We're crashing, again—I can't get anything right, can I? The atmo is venting, hissing out through bullet holes in the hull, and everyone's screaming, screaming. Rion is bleeding everywhere, and Zee glares at me, stern and disapproving, blaming. Case's breath rasps in her chest, coming way too fast, a panic attack for sure, where's her medicine? Asra will get it for her, Asra . . . just shakes her head. Slowly. Sadly. She shakes it and shakes it, side to side, over and over, but now her neck is twisting too far, and it's not natural—how is it doing that? Then the

*ground is rushing up and none of it matters because there's
a flash of light and I brace for impact, and the door to the
bridge bangs open—*

"Nax!"

I wake with a gasp, lurching forward in the pilot's
chair. It's dark and calm. No alarms. No screams. A gentle hand rests on my shoulder.

Case.

"Sounded like you were having a nightmare," she says
quietly. I scrub my hands over my face and blink hard.

"How long was I out?"

"Only a few minutes. The others are in the mess hall,
ready to meet." She pauses. "What was your nightmare
about?"

I close my eyes again and breathe.

"Crashing again. Rion bleeding out. Zee trying to
save him, telling me it's my fault. Making you have a panic
attack."

When I open my eyes, her mouth is drawn tight.

"Well," she says with a little self-deprecating laugh,
"now you know why I washed out."

"The panic attacks?"

Her hand slides off my shoulder, leaving a trail of
warmth behind. "I had medication and a signed medical
waiver. My doctor said I was fit to serve. It wasn't supposed to matter." A hard exhale. "They decided it did."

I shake my head in disbelief. "I can't believe they'd

wash out someone like you, an actual no-shit genius."

She scoffs, waves the comment away. "I'm just good at school. There's always a next thing to work on, a grade to shoot for, an assignment to complete, and I just always pushed myself for more. I ran out of high-school work right before I turned fifteen and panicked because I had no direction anymore. Hence college. It gave me something to focus on while I waited to be old enough for the Academy."

"So you always knew you wanted the Academy?"

A shadow passes over her face. "Not always, but early enough. I figured if I was stuck on Earth until I aged into the Academy, I might as well get a degree that would help me be a systems specialist when I got there."

"Which was?"

Case bites her lip in a thoroughly distracting way, then looks up at me. "There was a lot of overlap, so I ended up double majoring in electrical and mechanical engineering with a focus on ship systems."

She looks up at the ceiling and blinks rapidly. "Guess the effort didn't matter much. All that hard work for nothing, you know?"

I get to my feet and turn to her, but she doesn't step back to give me room. Her shoulders are slumped, her eyes closed, lips pressed hard together. She sways into my chest and bunches my shirt in her hands.

"I'm sorry. Just give me a minute," she says. Her grip

on my shirt tightens suddenly, then relaxes. She lifts her head up and looks me straight in the eye, her face inches from mine, radiating determination and fury. "I'm still so angry about it. I'm about two seconds from screaming at any given time because it's so unfair. But you know what?"

Her ire cools into something harder, more dangerous, the quirk of a smile playing at the corner of her mouth. "When we save the galaxy from these Earth First douchebags, they'll regret passing us over."

Damn right. I can't help but grin back at her, feeling a little dangerous myself after everything we've done. This beautiful, brilliant girl deserved so much more than to be cast aside for something like this.

Then her gaze flicks down to my lips, back up to my eyes.

My brain comes to a screeching halt.

Is she—?

Her mouth is on mine before I can process her movement.

My hands lift automatically to thread through the hair I've been dying to touch, like strands of silk through my fingers. Her lips are soft and tentative at first, a gentle brush to test the waters, then she breaks away, takes in my stunned reaction, and returns with more confidence. This time, her kiss is firmer, longer, moving toward more, and it's like a shot of heat straight to my stomach, to my chest—

A shot.

Rion.

I pull away with a regretful groan and lean my forehead against hers.

"We can't do this," I gasp, even as a portion of my brain screams, "No, what are you *doing*?"

She pulls back to study my face for a moment, then her eyes widen.

"Shit, I'm so sorry, I know you and Rion—I shouldn't have—"

"No, that's not . . ." I cover my eyes with one hand and wince. "You're definitely . . . I mean . . ."

I should just not talk ever. How can I say this? "I'm bi, so that's definitely not the problem, and you're both awesome, but there's a whole life-or-death thing going on?" Then I remember Zee's words from this afternoon.

"This isn't really the best time, you know?"

"You're right, you're absolutely right," she says, shaking her head ruefully. "I came here in the first place to tell you everyone's ready in the mess hall. If Serenity won't let us land, others may not, either. We'll be drifting. We need a plan."

Case smooths out the wrinkles she caused in my shirt and looks up at me one more time.

"And if it *is* Rion, then it's fine, really." She sucks in a deep breath and forces a small smile. "But if not, maybe another time."

She steps back, gives me a shy smile, and turns down the central corridor with her head held high, hips swaying.

I watch her go in a daze.

Holy *shit*.

I might be *completely* cracked.

THIRTEEN

MY HEAD IS STILL BUZZY and light from the kiss when I step into the combined galley and mess hall for our crew meeting. I need to get my brain together before I have to look Case in the eye again, but my lips are still tender and tingling, my fingers hypersensitive where I touched her hair, her waist—

Okay, not helping. Focus.

The mess hall is much grander than the medbay. I guess Jace had his priorities when he ordered this ship from the manufacturer. The kitchen half of the space is separated from the dining table by a half wall topped with a long metal countertop. Stools are tucked up under the counter, like a bar, and everything that sits atop a flat surface is lightly magnetized to prevent sliding during maneuvers, right down to the salt and pepper shakers on the metal dining table. The kitchen equipment is nicer than anything I've seen, even back on the Rock. Clean and powerful appliances, sleek cabinets, and top-of-the-line pots and pans. Amazing.

The dining half of the room is occupied by one long rectangular table with four chairs on either side, plus one at each end. Case, Zee, and Asra have taken three of the chairs at one end of the table, nursing metal cups of water and munching on a box of cereal scrounged from somewhere. There's enough room to host dinner parties here; there's even a little magnetized flowerpot with a silk flower arrangement stuck in the middle of the table. For some reason, that one little detail makes this whole space feel unreal.

Rion's hospital bed sitting at the head of the table doesn't help with that feeling.

My chest gives a sharp pang, and I head straight for Rion. He starts to sit up when he sees me, but I push gently back on his good shoulder. His clean sleeveless undershirt is soft under my fingers and wholly at odds with the rest of the crew's battered and ragged appearance. I study his face for a moment, then look to Zee.

"Should he really be here?"

"You try arguing with him," she replies without missing a beat. "I'm still not entirely sure how I agreed to this."

"I have my methods," Rion says slyly.

I pull up a chair next to his bed and sit, inspecting the neatly bandaged and immobilized shoulder. There's no more visible blood; it's like he's perfectly healed and the bandages are just a fashion choice. His face tells another story, though; his complexion is ashy, and his eyes are half lidded with exhaustion. Time to get this moving so he can rest.

I grab the pepper shaker and tap the side of it against the tabletop three times like a gavel before setting it back down on its magnetized bottom.

"I hereby call this crew meeting of the RSS *Manizeh* to order." I feel like I should say something leaderly, like "Status report!" or "Where are we at, people?" What actually comes out is a weak-ass smile and a vague hand-wavy gesture. "So?"

"Rion is doing surprisingly well," Zee says, getting straight to the most important point. "There are a lot of really bad places to be shot in the shoulder, but the bullet missed the artery and the bone. A pretty minor wound that could have been a lot worse, to be honest. Probably just a ricochet. I got the bullet out, and he'll be weak from the blood loss and sore for a while, but pretty lucky overall."

I close my eyes and breathe. He's going to be okay. I didn't get him killed. This is all too real. Case and Asra surround Zee with a hug from both sides, and I reach across the table to squeeze her hand. What would we do without Zee? She's completely amazing.

"Hear that?" Rion says. "I'm fine, so let's move on to the real stuff. How are we going to deal with this Earth First thing? We've burned through a lot of time just getting our shit together. We have, what, a day and a half left? It's time to take the fight to them."

Case leans back in her chair with her arms folded and props one foot on the edge of the table. "Here's what we know so far. Earth First has shipped some kind of device to all the colonies. They're evacuating all their people back to Ellis Station so they'll be 'spared.' Whatever the devices do, whatever they want to be spared from—they're going to do it just after midnight on August fourteenth, UTC. That's a little over a day away."

"And that's not much to go on," Zee says as she pours me a glass of water from the pitcher on the table. "There are really only two options that I see. We don't have our evidence anymore, so we can't prove anything." Case winces, but Zee continues on smoothly. "Either we figure out a way to warn everyone, or we hunt down one of these devices and try to figure out what the plan is and how to disrupt it."

Asra is quick to correct, as always. "There's no way to warn everyone. We'd have to plant a message on a dozen different courier ships, hope they all get through without Earth First intercepting it, and hope the people on the ground believe us instantly despite our wanted notices and have enough time to find the devices and do something about them. Even if everything went perfectly, we don't have the fuel to make more than one jump. If we had some supertransmitter, we could warn all the colonies right now, but they don't exist."

"So our next jump has to count," Case says. She

balances her chair on two legs and stares at the ceiling while she thinks. "The devices would have to go through the major spaceport on each planet, I would think, just like all other shipments."

Asra picks up her thread right away. "If we could get access to the spaceport records, we might be able to find where the device on that planet was taken, and steal it."

"One problem," Rion says. "Spaceport security is no joke, from what I've heard. Just as bad as on Earth."

"True," Zee says. "But I think we might have an in."

My stomach sinks. I know what's coming. God, why did I open my damn mouth? We were running, and I always babble when I run, and I never thought telling some random stranger about my family would matter but—

"Nax. You know where we need to go," Zee says, her eyes intent on mine.

I shake my head once, then more firmly. "No. Not gonna happen."

Her gray-green eyes are soft, pleading. "We have to. It's our best chance. It's *everyone's* best chance. There's too much at stake."

I thread my fingers into my hair and clutch hard, yanking at the roots. No, no, no, *please*. "There has to be another planet close by. Asra can fake us documents, we can—"

"Faking documents takes too long," Asra interrupts,

studying me warily. "What's the deal, Nax?"

My leg starts to twitch and bounce all on its own under the table. I take a long drink of water to stall, then stare into the empty cup. There has to be another way. Anything. *Anything.*

But this isn't something we can screw up. We need the best option, the fastest one. Lives are at stake. Millions. This is bigger than me and my family issues.

I flop back in my chair and rest an arm on Rion's hospital bed railing, drumming on the cool metal with restless fingers. "My brother," I begin, then pause to shove down the surge of mixed, unpleasant emotions the two words bring. Start again. Breathe.

"My older brother, Malik, works for the spaceport authority on Valen. He's a security specialist."

Case's chair falls back on all fours with a clang. "Nax, that's perfect! That's exactly what we need."

A faint brush of fingers against mine draws my attention.

"So what's the problem, then?" Rion asks, his voice slipping automatically into negotiation mode.

I force away my irritation, covering my eyes with a hand to give myself a moment. He doesn't know what he's asking.

"We don't get along. Not anymore, at least. We haven't spoken or written in two years. I don't even know for sure that he'd be willing to hear me out."

"What happened between you?" Asra asks. "Would he be on our side, do you think?"

I guess if anyone would understand brother issues, it would be her, but I just . . . I can't.

"It's complicated," I finally say. "He'd probably help us, though, if he listened. He's always wanted to live in the colonies, but he stuck around a few years after high school to help Ammi and Dad." Until I fucked up, that is. I swallow hard. "He'd want to protect his home out here, for sure. But I can't completely guarantee he'll believe me."

"Well, we'll have to come up with a plan B, but . . ." Case catches my gaze and holds it. "This is our best option. We have to take it."

"Sorry, Nax," Zee says, nudging my foot under the table. "But I agree. We have to."

The ugly thing in my chest twists and writhes, but I clench my fists, then release, letting the tension bleed out.

"Fine. We'll go, I'll contact him, we'll try it." I close my eyes for a second, then look to Zee. "Moving on. Next issue. Please. Supplies?"

"Zee found a whole box of condoms in the medbay," Rion says with an eyebrow waggle.

The others bust out laughing like twelve-year-olds, but the sour feeling in my stomach keeps me from joining in. Zee throws bits of cereal at Rion, and he catches one in his mouth.

"What? Apparently this ship's former crew liked to

205

have a good time, that's all," Rion says around a mouthful of crunch with his best "Who, me? I'm innocent" face.

"Medical supplies," Zee says, steering the conversation firmly back to the practical. "They won't matter if we don't stop Earth First, but I used the last of our waterproof bandages on Rion. If we happen to come across a source for supplies, we should stock up."

"Or—and I know this is ridiculous, but hear me out—we could just not get shot anymore," I add. It had to be said. And I'm still feeling salty, so what?

"That would be best, smart-ass," Case agrees with an indulgent eye roll. "This box of cereal here is all the food the former crew left on board for us, so we'll have to figure something out once we're down there."

"Fuel and ammo, we're screwed, obviously," Asra adds. "You know where we're at with that. So there's just one last order of business."

"Which is?" Zee prompts.

Asra scowls. "There is no way I'm calling this the RSS *Manizeh*. It's my ammu's name, and that's weird. The ship deserves a new name to go with her new life."

"We could just keep it simple," Rion says, rolling slowly onto his good shoulder to face us. "Call it the ESS *Jace Is a Wanker*."

"It's kind of a mouthful," Zee says, one finger tapping her bottom lip. "But it does have a ring to it."

"Except we can't call it the ESS anything, considering

the E would sooner see us in jail than in possession of a legally licensed spaceship," Case says. She makes it a joke, but the thought is sobering.

"I would love to go down to Earth Command and give those arseholes a swift kick in the head," Rion says. "They have no idea, none at all. No, better yet, I'd like to have Zee do the kicking. She could probably launch a person into orbit."

Zee smirks, but says nothing.

"It's true, though," I say, reaching across the table to poke Zee in the arm. "A swift kick to the head got us off Ellis Station alive, then got us out of Asra's place after that."

"And I think you've just named our ship," Asra chimes in. She traces some words in flowing script on her tablet, then projects them into the air. "The *Swift Kick*. The *Kick*, for short."

Silence reigns over the table for a long moment.

"Um," Rion says finally. "I love it."

Case grins and claps Zee on the back. "Me too."

Zee actually laughs, a lovely sound. "It'll do," she says.

And it's so perfect it actually breaks through the heavy cloud of my looming reunion with Malik. Their excitement is infections, and I let myself grin.

"That settles it, then." I grab the pepper shaker and bang it on the table again. "I declare this boat reborn as the *Swift Kick*. We'll worry about the prefix after we get her stripped down and registered one day, but for now—to the *Kick*!" I declare, lifting my drink.

"To the *Kick*!" the others echo, clinking their metal cups of water together.

It's nothing. We're still drifting in the middle of nowhere, drinking recycled water and eating the stale leftovers we found in the cupboards. But it's our nothing. And this feels like a *moment*. I stare into my cup for a few seconds, then look up at the crew. My friends?

"Okay, sailors," I say, standing and stretching. "I don't know about y'all, but I need at least a few hours of sleep before I have to face my brother and all this Earth First stuff. I know we're pressed for time, but we won't do anyone any good if we're delirious. It's late morning on Valen, so why don't we take a look at the crew quarters and stake our claims, get a few hours of sleep, and plan to arrive in early evening? Hopefully Malik will be off work then."

That name again. I haven't said it aloud in two years, and now it feels like it's every other word.

I receive a chorus of sleepy agreements, so we wheel Rion back across the hall to the medbay and say our good nights to him, then funnel into the hallway. The communal bathroom and showers are directly behind from the mess hall, and the individual quarters are behind the next three doors on both sides of the hallway, six rooms total. Five of the rooms are identical: small but functional boxes with a single small bed, a nightstand, a small desk, and a tiny refresher station with a sink and mirror. The final room is much larger, with one bed big enough for two people, a private bathroom with a sink and toilet, and a larger desk. I have a thought, the kind of thing that would have made Malik crack up laughing before he ditched me, and I can't resist.

"Okay, hear me out. I have an idea," I say. "The five of us each take one of the five smaller rooms. This single bathroom in here is the pooping bathroom."

"What the hell, Nax!" Asra shoves my shoulder, bumping my knees against the big bed, and I nearly let myself fall onto it, but I know I'll never get up if I do. The temptation to sleep through the next twelve hours and let the others deal with Malik is so strong. Case and Zee snicker behind their hands, though at my idea or at the sight of Asra pushing me around, I'm not sure.

"Hey, it makes sense, okay? Why stink up the communal bathroom when there's a separate one right here? Or we can use this as a rec room eventually. Get a projector mounted to the ceiling in here, upload some games, watch vids—it wouldn't be too expensive, really."

I'm babbling, I know I am, but I can't stop myself. Rec room plans are a much more pleasant thought than the alternative.

"That sounds great, Nax," Case says, her jaw cracking with a yawn. "Think I'll worry about redecorating in the morning. Or . . . you know, whatever five hours from now is. Tomorrow we'll have to calibrate the day cycle simulator how we want it. Space is confusing."

Asra snorts. "Try figuring out how to pray at the right times. Fortunately, there's an app for that."

She waggles her tablet at us as she shuffles out the door behind Case, with Zee right behind. They each disappear into one of the identical rooms and shut their doors with muttered good nights.

Just like that, I'm alone again. A weird chill crawls up my spine, and I look over my shoulder. Nothing there. I just haven't been alone while awake since leaving Earth, and the sudden silence is disconcerting. I eye the oversized bed, thinking again about letting myself fall onto it, about how nice it would be to share it with someone. Not fair, though. I should take one of the small rooms like everyone else.

I'll go check on Rion one more time, I think. Then sleep. Lots of sleep.

In my mind, I watch the ship crash over and over. Blood drips. Rion's, or Malik's?

Yeah. Sleep.

Maybe.

My next wake-up call doesn't involve Case's lips, and I'm not sure how to feel about that. My tablet chimes gently again, and again, and again. I groan and roll over, burying my face in the pillow and trying not to think about some stranger's dandruff getting all over my face. Or the reason I have to wake up. I'm being cuddled into blissful oblivion by this warm, cushy mattress, and I'd much rather focus on that.

Chime. Chime. Chime.

"Fucking UGH!" I yell into the pillow, then lift my head. What in the hell possessed me to set an alarm? Why would I do such a thing? I was obviously delirious at the time. Five hours of sleep isn't gonna last me. I swat at the tablet until it shuts up, then slump back onto the pillow. Whose sweat am I rolling around in right now? (Gross.) Who used to call this little box of a room their home? The thought brings a small pang of regret—whoever they were, they're probably out of a job now. And I have their stuff, now that I think about it.

Curiosity piqued, I pick my head back up and look around the room, the sleep fog lifting from my brain. I didn't bother studying my surroundings before bed, just face-planted on the pillow and passed out as soon as I got back from the medbay. Now, all around me I see tiny touches left behind by the room's previous inhabitant. The wall over the desk holds a magnetically mounted piece of abstract artwork, its neon colors the brightest point in the otherwise featureless room. I roll over and swing my legs off the bed, then pull open the top drawer of the nightstand.

Ick.

Boxers, all black with neon accents. Of all the things I imagined having to deal with while stealing a ship, some other person's underwear didn't even make the list. The bottom drawer contains three sets of identical all-black clothing, all of which smell of laundry soap. I unfold one of each; the pants are a size too big, but the shirt should be a decent fit. I'm not wild about wearing some rando's clothing, but I was only able to bring one set with me, so I can't complain.

The only other notable thing in the room is a small photo tucked into the corner of the mirror over the refresher station. Five people of varying gender presentations, all with their arms thrown around one another, a puppy pile of smiling faces and rude gestures. They wear identical all-black clothing, like what I found in the nightstand, and they all have matching tattoos around their biceps. They're young, none of them much older than the five of us. It has to be the crew. Or rather, the former crew.

I pull the photo loose and look closer, running my thumb along the edge of the glossy paper. They don't look like bad people. They look like a family. Why were they working for such an awful guy, hauling drugs around the galaxy? I guess everyone has their reasons, though I can't imagine what theirs could be. Then again, I'm sure others would look at our crew and think, such nice kids, wonder where they all went wrong.

Except Malik, maybe. Was he even surprised when

my wanted notice came through?

If I have to face my brother today, I'm at least going to be as clean and respectable as a wanted criminal can be. I tuck the photo back into the mirror frame and let myself into the hallway, making for the communal bathroom down the hall.

Steam billows from one of the stalls, and when I step closer the heat radiates from it. Someone's trying to burn their top layer of skin off, apparently. Maybe they also had the realization they were sleeping on someone else's dirty sheets. I wish I could burn away the gross feeling that comes with having to ask my brother for help, but there's nothing in the universe that can help me with that. The mere thought of seeing Malik's face again puts knots in my shoulders and makes my heart race.

I slip into the empty shower stall, then yank off my clothes, chucking them into a haphazard pile right outside the door. The shower has a digital readout where I can punch in my preferred shower settings, so much fancier than back home. It chimes happily, accepting my input and displaying a ten-second countdown to optimal shower temperature.

The water comes slowly at first, then ramps smoothly up until it rains down over me in a steady stream. I close my eyes as the beep signals the incoming scrubber chems, and the dehumidifier dries me off at the after the last of the water trickles away, leaving my skin prickling and fresh. I really don't want to put on yesterday's clothes, now that I feel so clean. I'll just walk back in boxers and put on the borrowed clothes when I get there. We're going to be risking our lives together, so they can deal with a bit of skin.

I crack the stall door open to grab my boxers, pull them on, and climb out of the shower—then find myself face to face with a freshly showered Rion, wearing a towel around his waist and a waterproof bandage wrapped tightly around his left shoulder. And nothing else. My eyes lock on a single drop of water slipping its way down Rion's neck, sliding over chest and stomach until it disappears into the edge of the towel. My tongue darts out to moisten my lips, wishing for that drop of water to be—*oh no, I'm staring.*

"You're up!" I say, wrenching my gaze back up to his face. My skin feels electric, charged by the proximity, every hair standing on edge. "Good to see you on your feet. Uh, how are you feeling?" Eyes up, Hall, keep it together.

Rion's smile is a slow, liquid thing that slides onto his mouth with ease. "A little put out that you all chose rooms without me, you arse, but fine otherwise. Still hurts like hell, of course, and it's stiff, but Zee does good work." His eyes flick down my body, then back up to my mouth. "And you?"

Case chooses that point to wander in, see us standing there talking in our boxers and towel, roll her eyes, and climb into the shower. "Don't mind me," she says as the shower beeps its acknowledgment of her input. Her shirt flies over the stall and lands on the floor outside, and the sound of raining water starts a second later.

I blush, a wash of heat flooding my body down to the tips of my fingers. Apparently we aren't going to be a particularly modest sort of crew. I may not survive this. My brain is bouncing between soft curves and hard lines and I *really* need to get out of here.

"I'm glad to see you up and around, Rion. Really. And hey, if the bedroom we left you is really that bad, you can have mine. I owe you."

Rion bumps his good shoulder against mine, the tiny brush of skin-on-skin contact sending a pulse of awareness through my body. Then he heads for the door. "You don't owe me shit, mate. But you better believe I'm taking your room if it's better!"

I chuckle and follow him out, my dirty clothes wadded up in my arms. And if my gaze wanders a bit as I walk? Hey, we might die soon, so why not? I couldn't ask for a better distraction from the thing I am absolutely not thinking about (Malik's judging stare, his hard scowl and folded arms). New topic, new topic . . .

I pop my door open and chuck the clothes into the corner, then poke my head back into the hallway and point Rion to the door next to mine. "That's the empty one. Think it'll meet your high standards, posh boy?"

The door to the bathroom bangs open again before he can reply, and a waterlogged Case bustles out, fully dressed and rubbing at her hair with a towel.

"That was fast," Rion says, eyebrow raised.

"My umuni is an air force officer and Mamá is always running late to everything. I was trained to shower fast from birth." She hits the door controls and chucks the wet towel in ahead of her. "Come on, boys, let's get moving. We've got a galaxy to save."

Her words have the desired effect. We have to go. No matter how much I stall, this is happening, and the sooner we get it over with, the sooner we can help people. I get changed in less than a minute, and take another minute to get my head together. My stomach roils, and it feels like I have a thousand-pound weight sitting on my chest, but it's been two years. Maybe it won't be so bad. We've both changed a lot.

Or maybe it'll be a disaster and this will be the last thing I ever do.

No point. Get moving. Out the door, into the hallway. I step up into the bridge and nod to Zee, the only other person there, then lower myself into the pilot's seat. There's a lot I could say right now, but none of it is good or helpful, so I start preflight checks and bite my tongue, pushing through the nervous jitters the pilot's seat brings.

"For what it's worth, Nax, I'm sorry," Zee says, her

voice soft. "Are you okay?"

Damn it. I close my eyes and breathe.

"I know we have to do this. It's our best option. I just hope this doesn't blow up in our faces."

She reaches forward and squeezes my shoulder. "I've got your back, no matter what. We'll get through. And I'm sorry I had to force the issue of your brother. I wouldn't have if I thought we had any other option."

The corner of my mouth tugs up in a grim smile. "Yeah. I know."

Doesn't stop me from being bitter about it.

Case arrives next, dropping into the navigator's seat and instantly switching into Focused Case Mode. "Preflights will be done in two minutes. The others are right behind me."

As if summoned, Rion and Asra barrel through the door and buckle themselves in, breathing heavy, like they raced here. We're all feeling the urgency, now that we've had a bit of sleep and a shot of adrenaline. I steady my shaking hands on the controls, then look over my shoulder.

"We ready?"

Four affirmatives. It's time. I take one last look at Serenity, luminous and vivid against the star-dotted blackness, and send them a mental middle finger.

God, we're really doing this.

I turn to Case and smile, though my mind is an endless replay of crashing, bleeding, alarms, and I can hardly *breathe*, but I have to hold it together.

I have to do this.

"All right. Let's go see my brother."

FOURTEEN

I MAKE THE RUN UP to the jump point and hit the target speed, and the A-drive engages at Case's command. The rumble of the engines drops in pitch, the sound stretching as we pierce the fabric of the universe— hover in the empty black void for a maddeningly long moment—then pop out the other side.

It's unsettling; we went from looking at one blank field of stars to a different one, but all the stars are in different places. New constellations, new reference points—and a new planet, blue-green and bright in the distance, watched over by an unfamiliar and distant sun. I throttle up to cruising speed, taking us out of the arrival zone and closer to the planet, its blotchy colors resolving into continents and oceans as we approach. As soon as we cross into Valen-controlled space, Asra takes control of the ship's comm system from her tab and punches in the comm code I gave her. The repeated tone of a tight beam call sounds in the bridge, over and over, each repetition adding to the crushing pressure in my chest. I'm not ready, I'm not ready, I don't want to do this, I—

A click, then the faint hiss of an open line.

"Hall here," a voice says with a note of wariness. Malik.

God.

I'm silent for a long moment. My grip on the controls tightens to a strangle. I bite the inside of my cheek.

"Is there anyone there?" Malik says with an edge of irritation.

"Yeah." The word bursts out, overly loud from being withheld. "Yeah. Hear me out before you hang up."

A clatter comes from the other end of the line, then a door slam. "Nax?" he whispers.

My throat closes up, and I have to force the words out. "Yeah. Listen . . ."

God, this is *mortifying.*

"I . . . need help."

A gust of breath on the other side of the line. "Are you *trying* to get caught?" he hisses. "They've been questioning me twice per day since the station went dark. They're watching me."

I grit my teeth. I really wish the others weren't here to listen to this.

"Well, you weren't exactly my first choice, Malik, but this was our only option. Everything they've told you about us has been a lie. Some bad shit is going down, and we need a place to refuel or we're really screwed right now. Can you *please* just give me a break and help us?"

A long silence. In my mind, I can see him covering his face with one hand and shaking his head like he always used to do, every time I screwed something up.

"I'm transmitting you coordinates to a mechanic shop a friend of mine runs," he finally says. "It's outside the city limits, and her radar-jamming net should keep you from being noticed. Fly dark, all nonessential systems off, and approach low and from the far side of the city."

"I know how to fly, I'm not a—"

"Enough," he cuts me off. "I hope you have money, because you're going to need to get that ship stripped down while you're there. There's no way she's going to let you sit that stolen ship on her lot as is."

"We'll take care of it," I say, my tone clipped and bitter.

"Good," he replies. "I'm still at work. I'll come meet you as soon as I can. Don't go anywhere or do anything until then."

With a quiet double beep, the transmission ends.

I slam my hand down on the console with a frustrated growl. The shock of pain radiates through my hand and up my arm, but I don't give a shit, because it feels like I've torn open a badly healed gash in my chest. My cheeks burn with shame and embarrassment and all the ugly things between Malik and me, somehow made worse by the fact that he's actually helping us. Yet another thing where I'm a mess and he has to clean up after me, hating me all the while. He ditched me after the last time. Who's to say whether he'll actually follow through this time?

"We have the coordinates," Case says, unusually subdued. She swipes two fingers over her display, and the course slides over to my HUD, layered over the other data splashed across the viewport. I grab the throttle control and edge us onto the highlighted route, my hands and feet doing the work automatically while my brain stews in a mess of boiling resentment and anxiety.

"It's good that your brother has this mechanic contact," Rion says from behind me. "I was worried we were going to have to figure out how to land and sneak out of the spaceport."

I press my lips together and shake my head. After the past few days, my skin still prickles with danger sense. We can't seem to go anywhere or do anything without something terrible happening. The fact that this is going without a hitch so far is making me more nervous instead of less. The last thing I need is to wreck this ship on my brother's doorstep. I'd never live it down.

"I don't even know what he's doing with a contact like that. He's always been the precious one who did everything right and never got in trouble. Now he's hanging with a mechanic who's willing to doctor a stolen ship? Doesn't make any sense."

Zee hums her agreement. "Can you look anything up about this mechanic, Asra?"

"We just crossed into Valen's net range. I'm looking now." Asra taps at her tab for a few moments, then hums in interest. "According to at least one source I trust, this woman is very good at what she does, and very good at being discreet. She's also selective about who she'll work with. If I'm reading between the lines right, she deals exclusively in illegal modifications, but only if she deigns to work with you. I'm hoping that means she's got some personal code of ethics, because I'd rather not share a dock with space murderers. But you never know."

"A fair concern, especially considering our pursuers," Zee says. I almost laugh—wouldn't it be ironic for us to roll up in our stolen ship, only to have Jace and his Tiger Squadron buddies hanging out in the next bay? I shake off the image, weaving us into the pattern of light space traffic in orbit around Valen.

"We're about to make our final approach. Knowing our luck, we can't guarantee there's not about to be some major bad turbulence here, so check your restraints," I say, wiping my palms on my pants. Our last landing nearly killed us. I really need to not screw this up. Especially with Malik watching.

"Quit being such a downer, Nax," Rion says. He claps a hand on my shoulder and squeezes. "Just chill out and let things go well for once. I could use a few moments without bowel-shaking doses of adrenaline and fear, okay? I'm trying to enjoy this one. Don't be a buzzkill."

I give a weak chuckle and lean back, letting my hand rest gently on the stick as I guide us down into the atmosphere and angle for the coordinates for the mechanic's shop. Deliberately landing instead of crashing means we actually get a view of the planet's surface on the way down, bathed in the golden light of its sun. Lush trees, abundant flowing water, and plant life in colors that are close to Earth, but not quite close enough to look completely natural. It's like someone ran the whole planet through a color filter and shifted everything toward the blue end of the spectrum. This planet is a changer, but it's good enough to almost pass for Earth in some places. The European Space Union really lucked out; the terraforming tech was new at the time and the whole thing could have failed horribly.

Instead, they got this: wide-open fields between low, rolling mountains, about as close to my part of North Carolina as you can get outside of Earth. The sight out the viewport tugs at my heart. Of *course* Malik would end up somewhere so much like home. Figures. The planet's land masses are only about 60 percent habitable, unlike al-Rihla, which is close to 90, but what they do have is definitely worth the trip.

Asra and Zee have their noses pressed against the starboard-side viewport, watching the terrain rush past. I grin, catching Case's eye and nodding in their direction. "Like what you see?" I ask them, taking us closer to the waving treetops for their benefit.

"Always wanted to take a vacation here," Asra mutters, going up on her tiptoes to see more below. It's kind of adorable.

Case hums her agreement and keeps one eye out the window as she monitors our progress. "Wish I had my camera equipment. Would love to take some photos here sometime. Al-Rihla, too, on those red sand beaches."

"You do photography?" Zee asks without looking away from the view.

"Sometimes. I'm not any good at it, but it's relaxing."

I never would have guessed that about her, but in a way it makes sense. Even she has to have some hobbies that don't include school. And I bet she's far better at it than she thinks.

After a moment, the forest gives way to a sweeping open plain of dry brown grasses, then to scattered buildings and a few small outlying settlements. I pull back on the throttle as we approach, not wanting to come in too hot and appear threatening, sticking tight to the vector Malik sent us. A hulking building comes into view, perched on the far outskirts of a sizable city; our destination. I shift power from the engines to the mag coils as soon as we're over their iron-inlaid runway, then set us gently down in a yellow-painted ground-landing zone, guided by a two-person ground crew. No raised landing pads anywhere in sight. Less conspicuous, I guess.

As soon as we're settled, I power the ship all the way down and revel in the silence for a moment. No vibrations, no gunfire, no venting atmo, just the even breaths of a crew not panicking. How nice.

A tinny knocking comes from far up the corridor. The comm crackles.

"Please allow my people on board for an inspection." The mechanic, I guess?

"Yes, ma'am. On our way," I say. Pays to be polite to people who might work with space murderers.

I unbuckle my restraints and motion for the others to do the same, then lead them all to the entryway. My heart pounds, still half expecting this to turn into shooting and adrenaline all over again, but so far this has been the most peaceful landing we've had as a crew. Without me saying anything, the others grab their chem guns from their quarters and line up on each side of the foyer before the ramp, like a welcoming party. We may not be military, but we're a damn good crew.

Giving everyone a last glance with a smile I really, honestly try to wipe from my face, I call out, "Ramp coming down!" and hit the controls. The doors crack open, the ramp descends, and the rich smells of Valen's vibrant flora mingle with the slightly stale recycled air of the *Kick*.

Four people stand at the foot of the ramp: three in stained coveralls and one in a more clean-cut, nondescript uniform. Their hands rest casually on their sidearms, still holstered at their belts, as do ours. The lead guard gives me a once-over, then nods and comes up the ramp, extending a hand to me. I take it and give what I hope is a firm, confident shake.

"Nax Hall. Welcome to the *Swift Kick*, sir. Thank you for having us." I think belatedly that it might have been smarter to give a fake name, but it's too late now. Malik probably told them to expect us anyway. And honestly, these people deal in unsavory types, and we're probably the most savory of their clientele. Unsavory lite. Diet savory? I don't know. Hopefully this won't be one of those split-second decisions that comes back to bite me.

Either way, the guy gives me a slight smile, like I'm an adorable child, but he returns my firm handshake and motions for the rest of his people to come aboard. They do, giving polite smiles to the rest of the crew. The head guy moves into the bridge area and pokes around while the rest of his group wanders through the back of the ship, presumably inspecting the guns, mess hall, and medbay.

"I hope they aren't planning to inspect our quarters, too," I murmur with a glance at Rion. "I'm pretty sure there's a pair of dirty boxers hanging from my desk chair."

Rion snorts a laugh, doing his best to smother a grin

227

in his shoulder. "And what were you doing that they ended up there?"

I blush and turn my eyes to the ceiling. Honestly, I just chucked them over my shoulder when I was getting changed, but now it sounds so much worse. Case watches our interaction closely, but she glances away as soon as I catch her looking.

It feels oddly like we're back in elementary school, all of us standing in neat rows waiting for teacher to let us go play at recess. The head guard returns to the entryway and waits for his crew with a pleasant, neutral expression. And he just . . . stands there. Silent. Unmoving.

I cut my eyes to my right; Rion has his hands folded calmly in front of him, his serene diplomat mask in place. Across from me, Zee shifts her weight back and forth, restless. Probably wanting to get back out into fresh air again. Case is tense and unfocused, like she's lost inside her own head. Asra taps away on her tablet, completely ignoring the situation, until her tab chimes a new message alert that feels horrifically loud in the awkward silence. I barely suppress a snort of laughter. Asra scowls down at the screen, though, then glances up at our guard.

"Do you mind?" she asks, gesturing with her tab down the hall to her quarters.

"Fine," the guard says, then falls silent once more.

Asra turns to me with the slightest roll of her eyes. "Be right back."

She slips away just as footsteps come echoing up the hallway. The rest of the guard's crew trickle in to the foyer and bend their heads toward their supervisor with quick gestures toward other parts of the ship. After a brief, hushed conversation, they head down the ramp without another glance at us. The lead guy stops in front of me.

"You'll meet with Ms. Brenn now," he says. "Follow me."

"Great!" I say, gesturing for the others to follow. "Just let us get Asra from—"

Our guide turns, though, and holds up a hand.

"Just you," he says. "The rest of you need to stay on the ship and get her ready for service."

I probably look like the greenest, wimpiest criminal in the world, because my eyes go wide like a frightened animal. "Uh, can I bring someone to advise the mechanic on the particular work we need done?"

He considers me quietly for a moment, then nods. "One." Then he retreats down the ramp to wait.

"It needs to be Asra," I say, trying to make it sound like a firm decision. Case would have been best for the mechanical details, but Asra's the only one of us with any real experience on the other side of the law; hopefully she'll know what to say and how to say it. Case struggles with the whole illegal thing on the best of days. And . . . okay, I still feel a little awkward around her. The kiss really threw me off, but she seems completely unaffected. She's a mystery—high-strung, angry, anxious, but also

229

totally confident in herself and her skills. Well, maybe that makes more sense than I thought.

"Okay, y'all. While Asra and I are gone, can you get some things packed up? Med kit, extra clothes, anything on the ship you think might be useful. I don't know if Malik is going to take us somewhere else, so we should be ready."

"Assuming he agrees to help us," Case says with a raised eyebrow. I wince and shake my head.

"Don't even think it. I'm gonna go get Asra and make this deal. Be safe while we're gone," I say, bumping knuckles with Rion and Zee before I head for Asra's quarters. Her door stands open, and a voice drifts out into the hallway from within—a deep male voice. I slow my pace and pause just beyond the doorway, listening.

"—doesn't have to be the end for you. If you call in a tip about the suspects, I'll turn your entire trust fund over to you. And as much as it hurts me . . . we never have to see each other again, if you don't wish it. I'll parade you as the hero who stopped the Ellis Academy fugitives, tell the city how happy I am to know you're safe, and it'll all be over. You can even keep the ship, if you want—I've already ordered another."

I hold my breath as Asra's tab dings with a downloaded attachment. The voice—Jace's voice, obviously—continues. "I don't know which world you'll be on when you receive this, as I sent ships to every colony world, so I've included a list of contacts for each. All you have to do is tell one of the contacts where to find the fugitives. You don't even have to be involved. Just send a message, and it will all be done. I hope you see the mutual benefit in this situation."

Jace's voice softens, cracks at the high end. "Everything I've ever done, I've done for you and your brother and sister. You want me out of your life? Fine. But if you don't do this simple thing for me? I'll be on the heels of you and your so-called friends every step of the way, along with Tiger Squadron, the GCC, and forces you haven't even begun to tangle with yet."

A pause, then the voice comes through low and clearer, like Jace leaned in closer. "Let's do this the easy way. Money and freedom, Mazneen. Just send a message, and it's all yours. I love you."

Asra snorts. "Yeah, whatever you say, you miserable excuse for a—" and she trails off into Bengali, muttering angrily as she slams every drawer in her room. I guess that means she's not planning to sell us out? But she could be angry because she feels conflicted, could still be considering—

"I know you're out there, Nax. You may as well come in."

Busted.

I poke my head around the doorframe first, then lean my shoulder against it and clear my throat.

"So. Planning to give us up?"

Asra's expression darkens, and she looks away. "You really think I would do a single thing to help that man? After everything you've seen? And he still thinks I don't know about the Earth First plan, what he and his buddies are doing to the colonies. Didn't even bother to warn me about it. Guess I don't count as a loved one to be 'spared.' Not that I particularly want to be dragged back to whatever Earth First commune they've got set up for when they make their grand return." She barks a harsh laugh.

I scrub a hand over my face, dragging my fingers over two days of generous stubble and hair that badly needs some kind of product. I'm too tired for this shit.

"I guess not, Asra, but you should tell the others about the message too, okay? You shouldn't have to deal with this on your own. But for now, we have a deal to make. They said I could bring one person with me. I chose you."

A little niggle of doubt teases at the back of my brain after hearing the message, but she's still probably the best choice. We've trusted her this far, for better or worse. It's too late to back out now. "Will you come?"

Asra's eyes soften, and her mouth uncurls from its twisted frown. She nods. Smiles, just a little.

"I'm with you, Captain," she says. "Give me a minute to calm down. I'll be right there."

I let the door close on my way out and hope, yet again, that I've made the right call.

Time to go make a deal with a criminal.

I'm feeling less sure of this mechanic, and my brother, by the second.

Our guide leads Asra and me out into the chilly Valen air and across the tarmac, past a collection of bizarre frankenships that completely suit my mental image of what a space murderer might call home. The ships look like they were once stock models of reasonably affordable commercial-line cargo haulers, but they were put under the knife young and never learned how to be civilized. Every possible part has been modified: engines definitely, shield lenses usually, whacked-out paint jobs required. Is this what the *Kick* will look like when this woman is done with her?

"Murder chic," Asra mutters under her breath, waggling her eyebrows. I cough hard to cover the laugh that bursts out of me, then wipe my eyes.

"We need her to look different, but I'm not sure this is the aesthetic we're going for."

"So we ask for what we want," she replies with a quick, cautious glance at our guide. "We're paying, so if you want a flashy, shiny pinup of a ship, then that's what they'll give us."

Paying. *Shit.* "We don't have any money. How exactly

are we supposed to pay?" I mutter, keeping an eye on our guide's back. I will throw myself off the nearest tall building before I'll ask Malik for money.

My stomach sinks, twisting in on itself. We're out of immediate danger now, but there are still so many ways that this whole thing could implode around us. I've never paid a bill in my life—now I'm supposed to negotiate getting our ship illegally stripped?

"Actually . . ." Asra trails off.

I look up sharply. There's a weird note in her voice, a hesitation I've never heard before. Normally she's so self-assured. I tip my head and study her, and she seems . . . defiant? Embarrassed? At the same time?

"We should be fine on money for a while," she says, like it's a challenge. "I took the liberty of lifting some from Jace's accounts right before we took off."

My mind screeches to a halt, and I stare at her. I don't know what to think.

"How much?" I ask, my tone as neutral as I can make it.

Asra purses her lips, and her eyes narrow. She lifts her chin and says, "One hundred thousand credits."

I'm speechless. That's a lot of money. A *lot* of damn money.

I take a breath, then nod. Asra's shoulders relax minutely.

"Okay, on the one hand, yay for money, but on the

other hand . . . maybe tell us next time, since we're your accomplices and all. We share the blame. And it kind of brings Jace down on our backs even harder, doesn't it?"

Asra shrugs. "He's going to be after us no matter what. We've publicly embarrassed him by stealing this ship and—sorry for this part—that bit I said over the comms on our way off al-Rihla probably had him spitting mad. He'll do literally anything to save face. I guarantee his priority is making sure he's still powerful and respected and comfortable once the colonies go down. Hell, he probably has people back on Earth airing out the giant house he left behind when he emigrated."

Asra's mouth twists into something between a snarl and a sob for half a second, then the expression is gone. "You heard him on the recording. He has a trust fund for me somewhere that he won't let me touch. I would have taken the money from there, but I've never been able to find the account."

She snorts. "I chose the amount deliberately. It should be enough to get the ship stripped and rebranded, with enough left over for a few loads of fuel and basic supplies, but that's it. From there we'll have to find work. Yes, I still stole it, and I know it's wrong, but it's money he earned by doing awful things, and it's not like I cleaned out his accounts. I'm not him."

"Fair enough," I say. "That makes everything easier on us, at any rate."

Beyond the last of the ships looms a four-story building with a cavernous mouth gaping toward us. It's big enough that I bet they bring the ships inside on mag coils to do the actual work. I figured we'd be walking in through the giant ship-sized double doors, but the guard veers off, leading us to a smaller door flanked by barred and tinted windows. A faded, rusty sign on the door reads MAIN OFFICE. Asra raises her eyebrows and mouths "murder chic" again, and this time I can't hold back a snort of laughter. Our escort glances over his shoulder but doesn't comment.

"Thanks for coming with me, Asra," I murmur, nudging her elbow with mine. I can't imagine myself walking into Brenn's office, a seventeen-year-old kid who knows more about fixing cows than fixing ships, trying to talk on her level. She'd probably laugh me right out of her garage.

The door creaks horrifically as one of the door guards pulls it open for us. It's surprisingly nice inside, though. Compared to the outside, this place is almost homey. Warm colors, worn but comfortable-looking furniture, and a reception desk. I smile at the receptionist, a young russet-skinned guy who can't be much older than me, and try to channel some of Rion's charm.

"Good afternoon!" I say. "Or morning. Or whatever it is on this planet right now." Off to a strong start, right?

"Almost dinnertime," he says with a grin. "You can go

right in—Brenn was able to clear some time to meet with you."

He stands and motions for Asra and me to follow him down a narrow hallway.

"A word of advice," he mutters over his shoulder. "Wipe that grin off your face before you see her. You give her that pretty smile, and she'll take you for every credit you got no matter who your brother is. Serious face, yeah?"

I wince at the mention of my brother but wrestle my features into something more neutral.

"Thanks. Appreciate it." Serious face. I can do that. I discreetly wipe my palms on the sides of my pants and wiggle my fingers to get my nerves out. Please, *please* don't let me screw this up.

At the end of the hall, the man knocks twice on a door marked THE CHOPPER and pokes his head in. After a brief word, he winks and heads back into the main reception area, whistling an off-key tune.

"You gonna come in or what?" a stern, twangy voice calls from the office.

I glance at Asra, take a breath, and stroll in as casually as I can.

The office is exactly what I expected. Junk parts everywhere, fluid stains on everything, a diagram of a Ford S528 projected on the wall, and a recessed terminal built into the desk. Then, there's Brenn herself.

She is tiny, but tiny in the way that vicious little dogs

are tiny, and looks about as likely to chew my hand off. She can't be more than five feet tall, and I'd guess even less than that. Her slight figure makes it hard to judge her age. Maybe mid-twenties? Her skin is incredibly light, with freckles peeking out from under the rolled-up sleeves of her coveralls. She sits in her high-backed chair with her arms folded, one ankle resting on the opposite knee.

"Sit," she says, and I do. Immediately. I'll admit it—I'm intimidated as hell. This whole act she has going on? It's working. Asra sits in the chair next to mine, much more composed. I'll bet she's not intimidated.

Brenn looks me over with raised eyebrow. "So, you're Malik's troublemaker little brother. You two are practically identical."

"Only in looks," I snap, then bite my tongue. It's really not going to help our case if I piss her off.

She clucks her tongue once with a little shake of her head. "He's missed you, you know."

I barely suppress a derisive snort. If he wanted to see me so bad, maybe he shouldn't have stormed off into space in a hissy fit and abandoned me. I shift in my seat, feeling like I'm fifteen years old and in the back of my ammi's cop car all over again. Brenn gestures toward me as if to say, "Well, get on with it," so I swallow and fall back on drilled politeness.

"Thank you for seeing us," I say, picking at the lint

on my pants. "Our ship, the *Swift Kick*, needs some rebranding work, and Malik said you were the person to see."

"Model?" she asks. She doesn't move when she speaks. It's kind of unsettling.

"She's a Honda Breakbolt Mark III," Asra says, smoothly jumping into the conversation. "She's been lifted, so she'll need a full rebrand from the inside out. Transmitters, DR codes, paint job, and external scarring at the least, plus anything else you find in your inspection that could allow the ship to be connected back."

My pulse jumps; it seems completely counterintuitive to come out and say we stole the damn ship, but I guess that's the kind of place we're at. Malik would have told her, anyway, and it's obvious from the kind of work we need done. I keep my mouth shut as Asra taps her tab screen a few times and projects an image of the ship.

"We'll give you thirty thousand for the whole job," she says, totally cool, setting the tablet down on Brenn's desk.

"Forty," Brenn replies without missing a beat, her expression impassive.

"Thirty-two," I shoot back. Now this I know. This is a game I can play, and I learned from my aunt, the master haggler, on my trips to Pakistan. Try me.

Brenn frowns. "Forty. I don't negotiate."

"Thirty-two," I say. "I don't overpay. We're only here

239

because my brother recommended you. I'm sure we could go elsewhere."

We stare at each other. Her eyes are so hard that after a moment, I actually worry she'll refuse to work on the *Kick*. Did I push too hard? Maybe I should I have backed down. It takes all my effort not to glance over at Asra. Brenn taps one stubby nail against her lower lip.

"Thirty-five. Take it and consider yourself lucky I don't shoot you."

I grin, but only a little bit, the receptionist's warning in the back of my mind. "You got a deal."

She stands and puts out her hand, and I grab it in a firm shake. Her eyes never leave mine, probing and curious, and she holds my handshake a moment too long. I feel like I'm being analyzed, but there's something in the way she looks at me, almost sad, or worried. The moment passes, though, and she sits back down and kicks her feet up on the desk.

"Your lady's new name will be the *Swift Kick*, you said, correct? We can do VSS or ESS registry codes here. Which do you want?"

"VSS." Part of me feels like I should be running this decision by the rest of the crew, but logically I don't think we can get away with passing ourselves off as an Ellis-sourced ship. Too many possible legal hang-ups, ways to get caught and deported, get the *Kick* taken away. Can't risk it. And for better or worse, our home is out here now, and Asra's always has been. Assuming everything doesn't get destroyed tomorrow night. It's the right choice. The safe choice. Clinging to Ellis Station and to Earth is pointless now.

It's all I can do not to close my eyes against the emptiness that thought brings.

"Right then. Ellis-based registry woulda cost you extra anyway. Damn pain, that is," Brenn says.

She pulls a small tab out of her back pocket and taps it a few times, then holds it out toward me. I pull out my own tab and wave it near hers. It receives the data packet and chimes happily.

"That's instructions for transferring payment once we run our full inspection of the ship's systems. Once we have your credits, we'll move her in and get to work."

"And how long should the work take?" Asra asks without looking up from her tab. Playing it casual.

Brenn smirks and folds her arms over her chest. "Should take about two or three days, assuming no one more important than you shows up."

Assuming we're not all dead before then, too. Asra and I lock eyes for a moment, and she nods slightly, just a dip of her chin.

"Well," I begin, drawing it out. "I don't know what Malik told you, but we might need to leave in a hurry. Two days isn't going to work for us. Can we do the most critical stuff now, have her ready to fly by the end of the day, then move on to the less important stuff?"

Brenn's mouth curls into a tiny wicked smile. "It's gonna cost you something extra. Ten thousand additional for the rush job, and the whole amount in advance."

I wince and open my mouth to haggle further, but Asra cuts in. "Fine. But you'll have the ship space-worthy by nightfall, and we can come back any time to get the remainder of the work finished?"

"Yes, so long as you leave your credits here, you can do as you like," she says with a vague hand wave.

I barely suppress an eye roll. "Great. Thanks. Pleasure doing business with you."

She stares at us. I take the hint.

I step over the spare parts littering the ground and head for the door with Asra right behind me, somehow managing to weave around the mess without getting her jeans dirty. I swear she has a classiness field around her that keeps her looking clean and composed at all times. You'd never peg her for an underworld hacker queen.

"I'm so glad you were there," I tell Asra as soon as Brenn's door closes behind us. "She would have scared the piss out of me if I'd been there alone."

"I don't know, Nax, I think you were plenty terrified even with me there," Asra says, biting her bottom lip to hold in her grin.

"The woman is like a tiny Texan velociraptor!" I say in self-defense. "Vicious, and calculating, and can you

242

imagine a pack of Brenns surrounding their unsuspecting prey, ready to tear their throats out?" I shudder.

"I thought she was pretty nice. And her accent was fun." Asra's full-on smiling now, but I think she's being serious. She actually liked that woman. I shake my head.

"Whatever you say."

I smile at the receptionist guy on the way out and push open the outer door—

—and run straight into Malik.

I'm not ready.

I wasn't ready for this.

My world tilts on its axis, a feeling of unreality settling like a fog over my brain.

Malik.

His narrow eyes fix on me, the same flinty near-black as mine, looking down at me over the same nose. His expression is completely unreadable. Am I supposed to be able to read him? He left home two years ago, and I haven't seen him on a video message for almost as long. Whenever Ammi and Dad watched them, I always found somewhere else to be.

The scar is still there, though. The one unchanging thing about him, cut right into his jawline as a constant reminder.

I close my eyes against the intense pulse of sense memory (momentum, stomach lurching, sharp pain, *so loud*) and take a deep breath, letting the cold, clear air carry the rich scents of soil, greenery, and ship fluids into my lungs.

I'm *not* ready.

But it doesn't matter.

"Come on," Malik says, the first words he's spoken to my face since the day he left. "We can talk on the way."

He puts a hand on my shoulder to guide me out the door, and I flinch so bad that he snatches his hand away as if burned. Without another word, he turns and leads the way out.

That's it? That's all I get? Two years since he completely abandoned me, and that's all he has to say? The words pile up in my chest, boiling into a hot stream of anger and a million other things I can't even begin to untangle. I shove a hand into my hair and yank once, blow a hard breath out my nose, and count to five. Slowly.

Then I follow. So does Asra.

The hulking forms of vicious, torn-up ships loom over us as we cross the tarmac to meet up with the others. And there, on the edge of the landing zone, the *Swift Kick* sits peacefully in the golden-yellow light of Valen's sun, awaiting the start of her new life. I hope she gets it. I hope I'll be around to see it. Between Malik and Earth First, it's not looking good. And Jace's people. And Tiger Squadron. Is there anyone else who wants us dead?

They'll have to get in line.

FIFTEEN

ONE SET OF AWKWARD INTRODUCTIONS and an uncomfortable car ride full of explanations later, we pull up to a small cottage in the middle of nowhere. One of the bonuses of colonial living: huge plots of cheap land with no neighbors for tens of miles. I'm surprised Malik would choose to live in a place like this; back home, he was always driving into the city with his friends to "escape hickville." Enormous shade trees tower over the house, throwing dappled evening light through the windows of the aircar as it comes to a rest in the landing space.

We spill out of the car in silence, and the others immediately gather behind me and a bit away, leaving me alone in facing Malik. They left me to do all the talking on the way, too, left me fumbling to explain the massacre at the station, the situation on al-Rihla, stealing the *Kick*, the plan for the spaceport . . . all of it.

Yeah. Thanks, y'all.

Through the whole thing, Malik was totally blank. He still hasn't reacted, in fact. Nothing to say, really? Framed for a massive attack, colonies in danger, *you* included, and . . . nothing?

Malik gestures for us to follow him as he walks toward the house, fiddling with his tab. He leads us to a side entrance under a covered work area where a half-rebuilt speeder bike rests in greasy pieces. His tab pings when he waves it at the lock, and the door clicks open. Inside, the house is bland and functional, done up in simple patterns and solid navy blues. Malik has always been a flashy person, though—this doesn't strike me as his style at all.

"Whose house is this?" I ask.

"My girlfriend's," Malik says, waving the lights on as he goes. "I haven't been home since you—since the attack. Too many eyes on my place in Center City."

He leads us through to a small combined kitchen and dining space with a table crammed against one wall and a small pile of dirty dishes in the sink. Malik rolls his eyes and sets the hot water to run, filling the basin with soapy water for soaking. Some things never change. So offended by a few dirty dishes.

"You may as well sit down," he says, pulling several containers of prechopped vegetables from the refrigerator. "I didn't get my lunch break at work today, and I've gotta eat before I can think about any of this."

Sure, remind me again what an inconvenience I am, why don't you? I haven't heard it enough in my life.

I lean against the wall just inside the door, leaving the

four chairs at the table free for the others. Malik throws a pile of veggies into a hot oiled pan with a dramatic rush of sizzling and leans back against the counter, poking at the food as he studies me.

The rich, spicy smells and the scrape of the spatula in the pan remind me so much of home. He learned all of Ammi's recipes during his summers home from college, and if I close my eyes I can almost pretend it's her cooking instead, with my dad whipping up batter for cupcakes right beside her and luring me into an argument about the fate of our favorite TV characters. I get my sweet tooth and my taste in bad television from our dad. Malik, of course, hated both of those things. The reminder of home should comfort me, but my senses are on hyper-alert. Waiting for the inevitable attack.

"You know, there's one thing you still haven't told me," he says.

My stomach twists. Here it comes. Please don't ask, Malik, just—

"Why did you wash out? I mean, you'd be dead if you hadn't, so I'm glad you did, in a way, but satisfy my curiosity."

I stumble over my words, stutter like a guilty child.

"Wh-what does it matter? We should—"

"Did they find out about your record?"

"No. Can we not do this please?"

"Which was it, the wreck, or all the break-ins?"

Damn it, Malik.

The silence is heavy and awkward, punctuated by the occasional pop of oil in the pan, but I can barely hear anything over the blood rushing in my ears anyway. Five sets of eyes pin me against the wall, but I can't look at any of them. We've only been together a few days; they're probably thinking they don't actually know me at all. We're all criminals now, but I bet I'm the only one here who had an actual record back on Earth, who was a criminal by choice rather than necessity. I take a shuddering breath.

"How did you even know about the break-ins? You'd already left by then."

Malik scoffs. "I actually *talk* to our parents, Nax. Was it that, then?"

I chew on my thumbnail for a moment, then close my eyes. He's not going to agree to any plan to help us unless I tell him. I give a helpless, bitter laugh.

"I failed my piloting test."

"What?"

I risk a look up at the others. Case's mouth is still hanging open from her exclamation. Asra is wide-eyed, her lips pulled into a small frown. Zee and Rion have their blank wait-and-see expressions on. Expectant. I guess I owe them an explanation. A lot of explanations. Malik huffs a laugh, though, and turns back to his cooking.

"Ah, I should have guessed. Pushed it too hard?"

My blood boils. "I wanted to make wing leader. I was on target to make top score on the practical piloting exam, but I needed the cushion room in my points total in case the girl with the next-highest score did better than me on the written exam we had to take afterward. I pushed it too hard."

I swallow, my throat sore and my face hot with remembered embarrassment and fury.

"You're right. I did what I always do. I just had to go that little bit too far, had to show off and be all extra about it. And I crashed the sim. Automatic failure." A bitter laugh. "Honestly, it's a miracle I haven't killed us all before now. I never should have gotten behind the controls with you all on board. I only ever did because we didn't have another option."

"And . . . the rest of it?" Case asks. God, I hate that she looks so suspicious.

"It's not what you think," I begin. Malik snorts, and I shoot him a glare. "Really, it's probably less bad than you're all thinking."

"You almost killed us both with your piloting," Malik snaps, visibly angry for the first time since our reunion. "You were in the hospital for two days, Nax, and me for weeks, and it cost Ammi and Dad a ton of money. We couldn't go anywhere in town without people bringing it up. You made Ammi look bad, embarrassed the hell out of her at work—do you have any idea how much stress you

249

put on us all? And then after it all, you wouldn't let any of us help, you just cut me out completely like I was—"

"Stop it!" I snap, covering my eyes and dropping into a crouch. I take a shuddering breath and look back up at Malik, though in my mind I see him as he was then, bloody and unconscious, a jagged piece of metal lodged in his jaw right where his scar sits now.

"I know, okay?" My voice comes out ragged. "It was my fault. The biggest of all my many screwups. I'm perfectly aware."

I shift my eyes to the others and brace for the impact of their mistrust, their disgust.

"I was fifteen and had just gotten my learner's permit. Malik was in the car with me, supervising a practice fly. I'd been simming since I could reach the pedals and had flown with my ammi, and I was already a confident pilot, so I thought I could handle it. Like he said, I was too much of a hotshot. I wrecked. We got hurt."

I take in a slow breath through my nose and fix my gaze on Zee's face. She's always been understanding. Stay calm. Get through it.

"My ammi's a cop. I think I told you that. She responded to the scene, tried to keep it as low-key as she could. But we come from a small town, so everyone knew what happened. But I swear, after that wreck, I was always so careful. I never let anyone ride in the car with me, never flew hot outside a closed course, never put a toe out of line after that."

"Except for the breaking and entering?" Case asks, her eyebrow arched. Skeptical. My judge and jury. I actually snort at that—not with much humor, but compared to the wreck, this part is downright hilarious.

"The breaking and entering really *is* just . . . you're going to laugh, but after the wreck I was restricted from flying, and I was so beyond grounded. I had to come home straight after soccer practice every day, which meant no extra sim time at school. Our parents couldn't afford to pay for extra sim time at the training center after my accident cost them so much money, so . . ."

"Oh my god, you *didn't*." Rion's lips twitch as if he finds the whole thing immensely funny. "You complete nerd!"

I chuckle a bit. At least he can find the humor in this. "I did. I started sneaking into the school on weekends, and sometimes in the middle of the night, so I could get more sim time. I know it was utterly cracked, but you don't understand. Being a pilot is all I've ever really cared about, and after the wreck I couldn't keep my skills at Academy level with the hour or two a week they gave me at school. But I started getting cocky again, and I was gone more and more until Ammi finally busted me. Again. That one we dealt with privately, no record."

I'm too afraid to look up at the others, to see their reactions. The silence has gone from awkward to oppressive.

"I know you have no reason to trust me after hearing all that," I continue. "Obviously I don't have a great track record for decision making or—" I close my eyes against a flash of memory, the crash on al-Rihla *(screeching metal, shattering glass, hard ground rushing up)*. I clear my throat. "Or safe piloting, I guess. But I would never do anything to deliberately put you all in more danger. And, if you'll have me, I still want to be part of this."

A hand appears in front of my face—Zee, offering to help me up. She pulls me to my feet and taps me on the cheek twice, like something my ammi would do.

"You've led us this far," she says. "You've proven yourself to us. To me, at least."

"And me," Asra and Case say in unison, then lock eyes and bust out laughing.

"And me," Rion says from the closest chair, just loud enough for me to hear. Our eyes meet for a long moment. I press my lips into a hard line and look back down at the floor, feeling my face flicker between shame, gratitude, embarrassment, disgust. I really can't screw up this time. Everything is riding on this. My eyes skitter away from the scar on Malik's jaw, and I squeeze my eyes shut again.

"He has good reason to be angry at me. And I know you hate me, Malik," I say, forcing myself to look him in the eye and maintain the contact. "But this is bigger than me and my issues. This is . . . everyone. Millions of lives."

I swallow hard. This is the big question.

"Do you believe me? Will you help us?"

Malik purses his lips, his eyes darting over my face, flaying me open to expose all the ugly innards. He sighs, though, and turns back to the stove, adding broth to the pan and turning the heat down to a simmer.

"Nax, I don't know where you got it that I hate you, when you're the one who completely cut me off. You wouldn't even see me before I left for Ellis. I've *never* hated you."

The urge to lash out rises hard and fast in my chest, but I clamp down on it at the last second. My cheeks and eyes burn.

Malik continues. "But you know what? We don't really have time to play family meeting right now. You may not have the best track record, Nax, but that doesn't mean I don't trust you. You've never been a liar. If you say this planet is in danger, that *everyone* is in danger, then we need to do something about it. I'll help you."

The tension pressing down on my chest releases so suddenly that I get lightheaded, and I steady myself on Rion's shoulder for a moment. I still feel the thrum of shame hot under my skin and beating in my chest—airing all my failures in front of everyone like that, what an *asshole*—and I don't think I'm ever going to be able to look Malik in the eye again. Not that I'd ever planned to. And the others . . .

how am I supposed to fly the *Kick* with them on board, knowing that they *know* my piloting history?

But Malik's going to help. We're going to stop Earth First. That's more important than my issues. I'll just have to deal.

Malik puts a lid on the pan, then gestures for all of us to follow him through the living room into the single bedroom. We pile in, crammed awkwardly around the giant bed that takes up most of the room. From the corner, Zee catches my gaze and smiles encouragingly, tapping her hand twice over her heart. Asra fiddles with her tablet and projects the list of GCC contacts her stepdad sent her while Malik throws open the closet and digs into the hanging clothes.

"Getting you into the port will be easy, but moving around once we're there will be much more difficult." He tosses me a crisp black spaceport security uniform jacket identical to the one he's currently wearing, then throws two more jackets and three pairs of pressed black slacks onto the bed.

"That's all I've got," he says. "We can't take everyone, and honestly, the fewer the better. Less conspicuous, and—"

His eyes zero in on Asra's list, lighting up the bare wall above the bed.

"What's this?"

Asra bites her lip and turns to the group. "I guess now's as good a time as any to tell you all that I received a message from Jace. He wanted me to rat you out. Offered me lots of money, but conveniently neglected to mention that I'd never get to spend it because I wasn't on the list of 'loved ones to be spared.' He sent this list of people I could sell you out to."

Malik narrows his eyes.

"I recognize some of these names." He steps closer and scans the full list, then traces a circle around a group of four. "These people all worked in IT at the spaceport. They were fired last week. We all assumed they'd been involved in some shady net-hosting issue. Lots of new policies, no more offsite access, and we got a memo that the new server they installed wouldn't be accessible until next week. These two," he said, indicating two more, "just left on vacation two days ago. The first guy on the list is my boss. Daniel Akiyama is head of spaceport security."

"Let me guess," Asra interrupts. "Also on vacation?"

"Just left yesterday." Malik presses his lips into a grim smile. "I think it's safe to say they're all heading for Ellis Station to avoid the upcoming . . . whatever. Damn, I can't believe this has all been happening right under my nose. Though it does explain a few things."

Case waves a hand for him to elaborate. "Like?"

"I think at one point they were trying to recruit me.

Feeling me out, seeing what my views were. If I were given the option to permanently return to Earth, would I take it, that sort of thing."

My heart thuds painfully. I've been carefully avoiding asking myself that same question. "And what did you say?"

"That I missed my family and would love to see them again, but that I loved my life and my work out here and wouldn't trade it. That I had made my decision when I left and I was happy with it." He pauses, looks up at the ceiling. "Besides, I knew you would be out here as soon as you could, so I'd have you to think about, too. I was hoping we'd be in touch."

His words are like a knife to my chest, far more painful than I expected. I've been hating him with everything I had for two years, but he thought of me. He wanted me out here.

Have I got this all wrong?

I shake out the uniform and hold it up against my body. Looks like a perfect fit. We really are almost twins, now that I've grown a few inches and caught up. Except for the scar, of course. I quickly force my mind off that train of thought.

"This is a good thing, though," Rion says, grabbing one of the spare uniforms to pass to Case. "These people were definitely involved, so their offices and the projects they were involved in are a good start for the investigation.

I'm assuming Case needs to go so that if the weapon is there, she can use her fancy genius degrees to figure out what it is and how it works. Anyone else?"

I look the others over one by one, considering. We probably won't need Zee's medical expertise, and if we do, then we're probably boned anyway. And as useful as Rion's ability to talk his way in or out of anything can be, I think Malik will be better at talking his way around trouble, since he works for the spaceport and knows the people. Asra, on the other hand . . .

"Asra, what do you think about the whole server install thing, the IT people who got fired?" I ask.

She's already snagged a jacket and a pair of trousers, though, two steps ahead of me as usual. "I guarantee that's a private server for Earth First stuff. If they have records of their shipments, that's where they'll be. They'll have it locked down and quarantined on the network, but I can work with that."

The others agree. Case slips the uniform jacket on and holds the slacks up to the curve of her waist, checking the length. She's not as tall as me, but she's definitely not short, so we should be able to make it work. Asra, though . . .

"I've got some slacks that should work better for you. You'll drown in those," a new voice says from the bedroom doorway.

A familiar voice.

"Brenn?" I gape. "What are you doing here?"

"This is my house," she says. She squeezes past us to open a dresser drawer and tosses a much shorter pair of dress trousers to Asra, then pulls my brother down for a peck on the lips. "When you didn't come say hi while you were at the shop earlier, I got worried you'd decided to kill your little brother. Thought I'd take off early and see if you needed help burying a body."

Are you *serious*? Malik and Brenn? I really don't know my brother at all anymore.

Malik smiles, but there's no amusement in it. "No, there really is some major stuff going on. I need to take these three to the spaceport with me to try to figure this out. We might need to be ready to go in a hurry, though, so can you pack some stuff and swing by my neighbor's house to pick up the dog?"

He has a dog? *Malik*, despiser of farm chores, has a dog?

"Sure," she says. "Stay in touch. We'll keep an eye on things here. The folks back at the shop have the repairs well in hand, should be no trouble having the *Kick* ready for whatever comes next."

Asra, Case, and I take turns getting changed into the security uniforms, then pile into the small kitchen to make last-minute adjustments and apply facechanger projectors while Malik and Brenn work together to finish off the meal Malik had started. Rion stands close at my side to work on my facechanger, sticking the tiny projectors along my jawline with a feather-light touch. Brenn and Malik pass hot pans and Tupperware back and forth like a well-oiled machine until four servings are packed and ready to go.

"We'll eat on the way. You spill anything in my car, I turn you in to the cops," Malik says.

Aaand *there's* the old Malik. At least all that's familiar isn't gone.

Rion squeezes my forearm. "Be careful."

"We will."

And I take a little risk. Not much of one. I let his hand slide down my arm so I can catch it in mine and squeeze back. His fingers twine around mine for a moment, then let go.

This is so not the time. Really.

Case's eyes are on me the whole way out the door.

SIXTEEN

A CHEERILY GLOWING SIGN WELCOMES us to Valen Central Air and Space Port, a bright beacon for travelers and semicriminals alike. People of every kind flood in and out of the enormous glass-fronted building, cutting one another off with wheelie bags and slamming into their neighbors with overstuffed duffels. We weave into the crowd and allow ourselves to be herded inside, chins up and expressions blank and professional, trying our best to look like this is just another night of work for us.

The majority of the crowd shuffles into orderly queues for ticketing and security, or presses into anxious clumps in front of the arrivals zone, chattering in a blurry cacophony of languages. Malik breaks off to the left, cutting around the entire crowd. He spares us only the briefest look over his shoulder to ensure all three of us are still with him, then leads us off to a staff entrance door at the end of the long ticketing counters.

The port looks completely different behind the scenes. Outside, everything is shiny, brightly painted and lit, warm and inviting, so maybe you won't give the employees hell when your flight gets delayed and you're stuck there all night. The hallway behind the security door is all hollow metal bones and wired veins, loud orange safety paint and caustic lighting. Malik leads us around a corner, past a violently yellow fire-suppressant system console, and down several long hallways with shouting red signage:

CAUTION! MUNITIONS DELIVERY ZONE
GCC PERSONNEL GATE
VALEN IMPORT AUTHORITY

We turn a corner and find ourselves face-to-face with a pack of chattering flight attendants pulling overnight bags. I scoot closer to the wall and keep my eyes fixed on the back of Malik's head, internally begging them not to look too closely at us. My steps falter a bit, but the group passes us by and turns the corner without the slightest break in their conversation. *Close.*

The next hallway is marked with a solid black stripe down both walls, with SECURITY WING painted in bold block letters within. Malik scans his work tab once at the entrance to the hallway, which has no visible effect, then again at a door marked DANIEL AKIYAMA, HEAD OF SECURITY. A freshly printed sign hangs on the outside of the door, crooked and hastily stuck up with tape.

**THE HEAD OF SECURITY IS CURRENTLY
OUT OF THE OFFICE ON VACATION AND
WILL RETURN ON 30|08|2194.
PLEASE DIRECT ALL QUESTIONS AND REQUESTS
FOR SERVER ROOM ACCESS TO SARAH DZUBENKO,
DEPUTY CHIEF OF SECURITY, IN ROOM 207.**

Malik sniffs and clenches his jaw, then motions for Asra to step up to the door. Case and I hang back, hands on our holstered chem guns, keeping eyes on both ends of the hallway while Asra runs her custom lock-popper app. It feels weird to not have Zee and Rion here watching our backs, but part of me is glad to know that at least two of our group are safe, will have a chance to get away if this goes badly.

A faint click signals Asra's success, and we pile into the office and lock the door behind us. Asra immediately sets to work on the door at the back of the office labeled SERVER ROOM, while Malik hits a control on the wall, illuminating an enormous collection of screens covering one entire side of the room. Security camera monitoring. Some of the cameras seem to be motion triggered, following travelers and employees as they walk, while others cycle through several different angles on the same room. Another click, and by the time I turn around Asra has already disappeared into the server room. I catch the door before it closes behind her and watch her hardwire into a terminal for a faster connection.

"The new servers are probably masked, but still on the network. It'll take me a bit to locate them and get to digging, but unless you have a better idea, I'm going to focus my search on anything that looks like shipping records," she says, tapping away at her tablet, then turning to the main console display. "I figure if they shipped some kind of device here, it probably happened within a few days of the attack on the station. This could take a while."

"Do what you need to do. We'll watch your back," I say, then leave her to focus. Out in the main office, I catch the tail end of a conversation between Malik and someone on his tab. He swipes the screen off and turns to me.

"Brenn said her people have finished their final inspection. They're doing a last bit of tuning on the engines, but she's basically good to go."

"Perfect," Case says. "Text her thanks for us."

"Yeah," I agree, then shake my head. "What are you doing with a girl who deals in illegal tech and strips stolen ships, anyway? You judge me for my issues, but she's somehow fine?"

This isn't the best time to start another fight, but this issue is like a loose tooth—an ever-present irritation, and painful yet weirdly satisfying when you poke at it.

Malik shoots me a glare, obviously unimpressed with both the question and the timing. He turns back to the bank of camera feeds and darts his eyes from screen to screen, following the motion.

"A big portion of her business comes from refugees fleeing failed terraforms and unofficial colonies. The Valen government doesn't want to admit them, so we have an arrangement. I do deals with air traffic control so they skip over her part of the sky, and she does affordable or at-cost work on the arriving ships so they can disappear."

Should have known there'd be some noble reason behind it. Ugh.

"Hey, Nax?" Asra calls. "Think I found something."

We all shuffle into the sweltering little room, stepping over coiled cables and squeezing in between stacks of warm, humming computers. Asra flicks a message from the main console to her tab, then projects it for us all to see. It's a shipping manifest, and a vague one at that. The logo of the GCC takes over the top center of the page. Under Items Shipped, there's only one thing listed: "receiver, qty 2, weight 27.2 kg, ID Num 428." The head of Valen spaceport security is listed as the recipient, and the sender was . . .

The package came from Ellis Station. Shipped on 11|8|2194, the day after the attack, *after* all travel and shipping in and out of Ellis Station had been banned.

"This has to be it," Case whispers. "The weapon, or whatever it is they're planning to use against the colonies. Are there any others like it, or is this the only one?"

"I did a search for other shipments coming from the station and got nothing on either the new private servers or the main ones. I think this is it."

"Do they list a storage location, or has it already been taken off-site?" Malik asks, bracing a hand on the back of Asra's chair to peer at the screen.

"There's a shelf location, but no warehouse designation. Why bother giving us the specifics if it could be in literally any storage closet in this whole port?"

"Not *any*," Malik says, tipping his head back to stare at the ceiling. "There's an SPZ warehouse near the GCC personnel gate. I'd bet anything that's where it's at."

At my blank look, he elaborates. "Special patrol zones are blocked from regular employee access. Only certain security personnel are allowed in, and only to patrol for five minutes at a time. I was just in there doing rounds earlier today. It's the only active SPZ we have right now. If there's something they don't want messed with, that's where it'll be."

"That's our target, then," Case says. "Time to get a look at this mystery device."

Asra cuts the projector and returns to her furious tapping. "I need to stay here and dig deeper. They might have more hidden partitions or something with more information about their plans. If the device doesn't give us any ideas on how to stop all this, we'll need a plan B."

"One of us will have to stay here with you, then," Malik says, but Asra shakes her head without looking up.

"I'll be fine here. I'll lock the door, jam the code, and

keep my gun out. You'll need all of you to locate the device as fast as possible. Honestly, I'll probably be safer here than you'll be out there. I might even be able to loop some cameras for you."

I shift my weight from foot to foot, a hand over my mouth. I don't like this. If she gets into trouble, she'll be totally alone.

"This is my choice, Nax," Asra says, pausing in her efforts to look me in the eye. "I'm choosing this. You do what you need to do, and I'll do what I need to do. You won't be gone long. Don't worry about me."

I take a deep breath and nod. "Yeah. You're right. Okay." Then: "Be careful." Because it had to be said. I wave a hand at the door and meet Malik's curious gaze.

"Lead the way."

He purses his lips for a moment, but does as I ask all the same. I bring my hand to rest between Case's shoulder blades, just a brief touch. "I'm here," it says. "We've got this." She glances at me out of the corner of her eye, quirks a tiny smile, then refocuses forward.

Time for business.

Malik has always been one of those people who could easily look like he belonged anywhere, but here, in this place, he looks like the master of his domain. He leads Case and me confidently through the hallways, shoulders back, spine straight, a steady stream of work-related training speeches flowing whenever someone happens to pass near us. It's how I feel when I'm in the pilot's seat . . . so long as no one is in the ship with me.

My tablet vibrates in my hand, and I glance down at the lit screen.

managed to loop the cameras in the warehouse. can't guarantee re: other security

I pass my tab to Malik and Case without comment, then accept it back after they're done reading. That's one point in our favor. Hopefully Malik can account for the others.

We turn a final corner and come to a door, unlabeled except for a temporary decal above the lock mechanism declaring SPZ5 in bold letters. Malik turns to us and murmurs, near silent.

"Once we unlock this door, it starts a timer. If we're not out in five minutes, it trips a silent alarm."

I bite my lip, thoughts racing. "Okay, Malik, as soon as we're in there, do a loop through the warehouse to make sure we're alone. Disable any secondary security you can. Case and I will look for the device. What was the shelf code?"

"Seven zero two WH," Case replies, the numbers rolling off her tongue without hesitation.

"Let's do this, then. Ready?" I ask, turning back to Malik. He studies me for a long moment, then turns back to the door and holds up his fingers in a silent count.

Three . . . two . . . one . . .

Click!

As soon as we're inside, I take a quick scan of the layout: one long hall down the center, solid wall to my right, rows of shelves to my left. Case ducks down the first row to begin examining shelf labels, so I sprint to the other end of the stacks to start there. Malik takes off for the far end of the room, peeking down each aisle as he goes, totally focused on his task. He's always been incredible at everything he does, my complete opposite. I'm glad to have him on our side.

At first, the shelves seem to have no logical order to them whatsoever. Four hundreds are mixed in with fifteen-fifties are mixed in with boxes that don't have a number at all. How the hell are we supposed to find anything in here? It's been at least a minute since we walked through the door. Four minutes left.

I try the next aisle, but find the same nonsensical grouping of numbers, no goddamn order to it at all, what the *shit*, people? I turn to try the next aisle when something in my brain finally rearranges, recognizes a pattern: the letters. The letters are grouped vertically and ticking downward, but aren't in any particular horizontal order at all.

"Case!" I say as loud as I dare. "The letters—"

"I found it!" she snaps, tense and excited. "Help me with this!"

I dart around the next two rows of shelves to find Case dragging a pair of footstools together in front of a row of crates.

"There!" She points to a box just above my head. "Let's lower it slowly, together. We don't know if there's anything explosive or toxic in there."

I climb onto my stool and grasp my side of the box, and with a "Ready, go," we slide it inch by careful inch forward until we have all its weight supported on our forearms.

"Careful now," I say, my legs burning with the effort as we crouch lower and lower, bringing the box to settle on one of the stools. We set it down without a single bump, and the breath I'd been holding bursts out of my lungs just as Malik rounds the corner.

"Two minutes," he hisses, but Case waves him away impatiently.

"There are no warning labels on this crate like there are for some of the others," she says, pulling out her multi-tool. "We'll have to risk it. Agreed?"

"Agreed," I say, and help her pry the lid off the crate before I can let the sheer danger of the decision really sink in.

And the weapon . . . looks like nothing. A bland metal box rests inside the crate, no displays, no wires. Just a brightly painted logo on the top: the concentric blue-and-green circles and bold number one of Earth First.

"Well, this is definitely it, but—what are you doing?" My eyes go wide as Case begins unscrewing the top panel of the device.

"There's no way to tell what this thing does from the outside, Nax, what did you think I'd have to do?"

Oh, stars, this is so cracked. Nothing for it, though. I take the top panel from her once she gets it free and turn on my tab's LED to give her more light to work with.

Case swaps the multitool for her tab and runs a scan on the device, then peers closer at a few of the components. Behind her, Malik starts bouncing on the balls of his feet.

"Nax, we're out of time, we have to—"

A voice from Malik's tab interrupts him. "Lieutenant Hall, we're picking up a silent alarm from the SPZ. Your tab is synced to the lock. Report."

"Damn it," he spits, then lifts his tab to reply.

"Dispatch, just finishing up my SPZ rounds, stopped to inspect a loose vent cover. Sorry for the alarm."

Case switches back to her multitool and deftly removes six tiny screws holding a bright blue board into the device. She swaps the screwdriver for a pair of clippers and, with a tiny *snick*, severs the wires holding the board in. She shoves it at me, then snatches the top panel back and replaces it on top, shaking her head, her mouth hard. What exactly am I holding here? Is it going to kill me? I start to ask, but the dispatcher speaks up before I have the chance.

270

"Lieutenant, we're not seeing you on the cameras."

Malik's eyes burn into mine, desperate and angry. "Really? That's strange," he says, his voice high and strained. "I'll swing by IT on my way out, see if they can have a look at it. Maybe those guys who got fired screwed something up, eh?"

Wow, he sounds fake as hell. He can lie about as well as I can. Family trait, I guess—we're painfully honest. The responding silence isn't encouraging, so I nudge Case's boot with my toe and shove the board she gave me into my back pocket.

"Leave it," I say. "They already know what we're here for. No point in concealing it. Where's the other one?"

Case shakes her head. "There was only one on the shelf. The other one's missing. Probably already deployed, ready for . . . whatever."

Of course. Of *course* it is. Nothing we can do about it now.

"We're out of time," I say. "We need to go."

Then *my* tab is the one to chime, a new voice call from Asra demanding attention. *Shit.* I accept the call as we run for the door.

"Asra?"

"Guys, you have incoming, and I have bad news." Her eyes shine with unshed tears, and my heart seizes.

"There was a scheduled message on the server that just went out. Another reminder message, like the one

Case found at the embassy on al-Rihla, but this time . . ." She swallows hard. "Nax, they're testing the weapon to make sure it works in less than an hour. On Tau'ri. My ammu and sister are there, we have to—uh-oh."

Her head whips to her right. A loud clang, shouting, muffled voices—and the line goes dead.

I pull out my chem gun and look to Case, running at my side.

"Is this thing in my pocket going to kill me?"

"It's just a receiver, was hooked up to a powerful signal repeater. No time to analyze it right now. That's how it's activated, though—by receiving some kind of trigger signal. I have the scans to look at later."

We come to a stop on either side of the door, our guns at the ready. Malik trots up behind us and pulls out his own weapon.

"There's a quick way back to the parking lot from here. Follow me and—"

I cut him off with a sharp wave. "We're going back for Asra first."

Malik shakes his head, impatient. "There's no time, she'll have to meet us outside if she can. They'll be all over this sector, and—"

"We're going back for her, Malik. You don't like it, you're on your own," I snap.

Case meets my gaze, we exchange a nod, and I hit the door controls.

SEVENTEEN

THE SECOND THE DOOR ROLLS back, before I can even see what's beyond, I squeeze the trigger.

One body down, then another by Case's gun. Two more left. I drop to a crouch just inside the door and press my back against the wall, cold metal biting through my shirt. Breathe, breathe, turn—three more shots, one of which splatters across a security officer's jacket but fails to touch bare skin. Malik, towering above me with his own chem gun, nails the last two on his own with frightening accuracy.

Clear. For now.

I motion for Malik to take the lead.

"Are you going to help us get her back?"

He searches my face for a moment, a longer moment than we really have time for. Please, Malik, I think at him. Trust me.

Something in his face shifts, and he nods, takes off down the corridor, back to the security wing.

We stop to check around every corner, encountering

pairs of security officers more often than not. Malik is a wicked good shot, and with Case and me as passable backup, we manage to get back to where we started with a trail of unconscious people in our wake. We had the element of surprise up until now. The moment that changes is the moment this gets really dangerous.

We round the final corner and . . .

Yeah, *now* we're screwed.

In the middle of the hallway, one security guard has Asra's arms locked behind her back. One pulls the door to the head of security's office closed. And two have their guns aimed straight at us.

Think fast.

"Okay, okay, you got us," I say, holding up my hands, gun clenched tight.

"Drop your weapons!" one of the guards barks.

"Hey, it's cool, we'll do that, okay? We're gonna *drop*," I say, meeting Asra's eyes on the last word. She winks at me. I tap my index finger against my gun, then point to the left. I have no idea if the others saw, but here goes nothing. I hold my free hand in front of me in a placating gesture.

"On the count of three, we'll drop, okay? It's fine. Here we go. One . . . two . . ."

On three, we dive for the cover of the hallway opening and Asra goes dead weight, pulling her arms free from her captor's grip. He scrambles for her, but she dives between his legs, kicking at his ankles with her hands

274

cuffed behind her back, and he's distracted enough that I manage to lean around the wall and land a hit on the top of his bald head. A chem pod whizzes straight past my ear, and I slam myself back against the wall, my lungs burning with a heady mix of panic and breathlessness. There's a heavy *thud* as Malik drops another guard with a crack shot, followed by running footsteps, getting closer, what are they—

Case slams the heel of her hand under one guard's chin as he rounds the corner, and his teeth make a sickening *clack* before he drops to the ground, a smear of chem from Case's gun dripping down his neck.

The last guard is smarter. He comes in low and fast, and takes Malik out at the knees, toppling them both to the floor and landing in a flurry of kicks and punches. It's impossible to aim, no way to shoot without possibly hitting Malik too, and I am *not* carrying his ass out of here.

Screw it.

I holster my gun and dive into the fray, wrestling one of the guy's arms away from Malik's throat and pressing a knee hard into the small of his back with all my weight. Malik breaks the guard's grip and slides out from under him, a pair of handcuffs at the ready. He snags the other arm and pins it, and the *snick* of the cuffs signals the end of the fight. The guard thrashes anyway, kicking at Malik's shins, then flops over on his back.

"Over here!" he shouts at the top of his lungs. "They're

in the security wing!"

Malik pumps a shot of sleep chem straight in his face. The guy slumps a moment later, silent.

No time to recover. I race back around the corner and find Asra struggling to get to her feet without the use of her hands. Malik follows close behind, rifling in his pocket. He withdraws a small ring of physical keys, the kind used for mechanical locks, and inserts one into a tiny hole in Asra's handcuffs. Digital locks just aren't a great idea for some things.

Asra shakes the feeling back into her hands, then yanks her tablet from the pocket of her former captor.

"Nearest exit?" she asks.

Malik looks over his shoulder, then back down the hallway.

"Follow me."

We meet little resistance after that. Malik leads us through service corridors, into maintenance access hatches, and down ladders that lead to basement passages. A few small patrol groups give us a bit of trouble, but before long Malik bangs through an unmarked door and out into the frigid night air. We sprint side by side, him slightly ahead, guiding us back toward the car. Then he slows suddenly, pulls his tab from his pocket. It vibrates in a repeating pattern: long, short short short. Long, short short short.

"It's Brenn," he gasps, then takes the video call. "This is a very bad time, is everything okay?"

Loose bits of hair stick to Brenn's sweaty face, and the image wavers as if held in a hand that can't keep still. Not her hand, because she's got hers busy with flight controls.

"Don't come home," she says, her eyes on her flying rather than the tablet. "Place is surrounded. We're en route to the garage. I've instructed the crew to have the *Kick* refueled and ready to fly by the time we get there."

"Are Rion and Zee okay?" I shout, hoping the tab will pick up my voice.

"They're fine, they're with me. Zee's holding the tab. Rion is wrangling the dog in the backseat." A deep, throaty bark distorts the speaker, followed by a string of colorful swears. A blur of dark-skinned arm and honey-colored fur streaks past in the background, and Brenn breaks off to shove a hand behind her. "We'll be there and ready for you in ten. Be careful."

"You too," Malik says, and ends the call just as an aircar slides down the row of parked vehicles and straight into our path. Six police officers spill out, taking cover behind their doors. We dive behind the nearest car before the shooting can start.

"I was hoping not to have to use this," Case says, digging in the front pocket of her borrowed security vest. She pulls out something small and shiny.

One of the grenades from Jace's warehouse.

"Slide your weapons out from behind the vehicle and come out with your hands up!" one of the officers calls.

Case's grip on the grenade tightens. "I'm going to aim for the cars on the other side. I don't want to kill anyone. As soon as I throw, run for it. Ready?"

Asra, Malik, and I all nod. Case closes her eyes, blows out a long breath, and heaves the grenade into the next row of parked cars. We're up and running for a full two seconds before the explosion grenade detonates, and a wave of heat and sound hits us from behind. Angry shouts, secondary explosions, a scream—no time to look back. The car is in sight. We're almost there.

"Nax," Malik calls. "Catch!"

My hands raise automatically to catch the thing flying at my face. A digital key fob, the Mazda logo raised in gleaming silver—the key to the car. I double-click the button to unlock the doors and fling myself into the driver's seat, hitting the ignition as the others pile in.

Sirens wail in the distance, drawing closer by the second. I glance behind me to make sure Asra and Case are strapped in, check Malik in the passenger seat, and floor it. Forget about proper flight lanes and speed limits—our only chance is to lose them. I take us up and over the entire parking deck, weave around a ship coming in for a landing, and turn into the maze of streets at the heart of Center City. Malik barks directions at me, taking us down shortcuts and backroads, through pop-up neighborhoods and modular construction sites until the sirens fade farther and farther into the background din of the city.

It isn't until we're flying full-out over the highway back to Brenn's that it hits me.

Malik is in this car.

Malik, with his scar, who I nearly killed last time he flew with me.

My breath chokes me from the inside, my airway seizing up as my knuckles go pale on the steering wheel. I try to remember my breathing exercises, try to count, but all I can hear in my own head is white noise turned up to max, blocking everything, turning my vision darker, darker. . . .

"Nax!"

I suck in a ragged gasp at Malik's shout, feel his fingers bite into my shoulder. He gives me another good shake and leaves his hand there, a comforting presence, just like when he used to help me with my homework, or teach me something on the computer. It works, a bit. Once my breathing begins to slow, he speaks.

"Nax, you're an incredible pilot. That flying you did back there, in the city? Mind. Blown."

I huff a little self-deprecating laugh, but he cuts me off before I can say anything.

"I mean it. You've got this, Captain." He squeezes my shoulder once more, then leans back in his seat and grins, as casual as if we were driving down to the Outer Banks for the weekend.

"Now *fly*."

EIGHTEEN

WE SLIDE TO A STOP at Brenn's garage and hop
out of the aircar at a dead run. I'm fairly sure we lost
the cops on the outskirts of town, but I'd rather not wait
around and find out. I hope I can channel some more of
Malik's confidence, because with this next part, Asra's
family hangs in the balance.

Zee, Rion, and Brenn are waiting for us at the base of
the *Kick*'s boarding ramp, and the crash of relief I feel at
the sight of them takes me by surprise. I pull Rion into a
tight hug the second I'm close enough, burying my nose
in his uninjured shoulder, and reach out to grab Zee's
hand. Rion smells like dog, but I'm too relieved to care,
and it reminds me a bit of home, anyway.

"Everyone on board," I say, waving them all ahead.
"We gotta go. Is the dog already inside? Do we need anything else?"

Brenn and Malik lock eyes, and Malik turns to me,
arms folded and shoulders tense. "We're not coming with
you."

My heart clenches. "What? You have to, Malik, we never found the other device, it could—"

"Yes, it could, but we have friends and other family here, Nax. We have to get them to safety too. You go, do what you have to do. We'll be right behind you."

Then he pulls me into a hug.

My arms don't know how to respond at first, stunned still, limp at my sides. We haven't hugged since before the accident. It's been years.

But he's my brother.

My arms come up, and I clutch handfuls of his jacket, fight back the catch in my throat.

When he pulls back, he meets my eyes dead-on. "I meant what I said. You've changed. You're not the person who got in that wreck. Those people"—he gestured up the ramp—"they trust you with their lives. And so do I. You can handle this."

I have to look down and blink rapidly to chase away the pressure behind my eyes. My voice comes out ragged when I finally speak.

"If you think that, then why did you leave?"

Malik runs a hand through his hair and huffs a sigh.

"You couldn't even look at me after the accident, Nax. You cut me off like I never existed. And it was shitty, okay? I was pissed at you for that, but that's not why I left."

"Why then?" I hold my breath for the answer, an answer to a question I've been asking myself for years.

Malik smiles, subdued.

"You needed space to figure stuff out for yourself without me always hovering. Sometimes the best way to help is to just . . . back off. So I did. But it wasn't supposed to be forever."

His eyes shift to something over my shoulder, and I turn to see Zee beckoning me up the ramp.

It's time to go.

Malik backs away and takes Brenn's hand. "We'll talk more when this is all over. Promise."

"Be safe," I say.

"We will," Brenn replies. "Now, I worked hard on that ship, so don't go getting her shot out of the sky."

My chest gives a painful stab at that, but I force a smile that probably looks more like a grimace and shake her hand. "I'll do my best. Pleasure working with you."

"Likewise," she says, stepping back to let us leave. "You make it out of this okay, bring her back, and we'll finish the full job."

With a tiny smile, she tugs Malik away, and they run to a safe distance to watch us go. I raise a hand in one last wave good-bye, then head inside and bring up the ramp. Time to fly.

On the bridge, I squeeze Rion's good shoulder as I pass and throw myself into the pilot's chair, flicking a dozen switches to get us ready. As soon as I get a green light for the mag coils, I thumb a trickle of power into them, signaling to Brenn's ground crew that we're ready to go. A ground crewman waves us forward, guiding us out of the enormous garage doors and onto the tarmac beyond. I follow the painted markings out to the landing pad and, as soon as the ground crew have cleared off, hit the ignition to get the engines warming.

"Everything operating at peak efficiency," Case says, swiping through screen after screen of diagnostics. "The engines are well tuned, performing five percent better, actually." She frowns, tapping a few times. "I can't find Tau'ri in the nav database, though."

"It's unregistered," Asra says, waving her tab in front of the console's wireless data transfer point. "And not terribly friendly or talkative, either. They're a perfect target. Unregulated colonies don't get courier ships or goods shipments, and they don't show up on stock maps, so it could be days before anyone notices something happened to them." Her voice goes ragged at the end. "To them," she said. To her mother and sister. Zee reaches over and takes Asra's hand, a silent comfort.

"Nothing's going to happen to them," I snarl, kicking us off the ground and into the sky. "Because we're going to get there first."

"The weapon," Case says. "Best I can tell from the scans I took, it receives a trigger signal, then fires up the repeater and adds a little rider of code to the message. But I have no idea why. All I can tell you from the schematics

I pulled is that the device has an incredible power source, and the receiver is made from really expensive components."

"Let me see that code," Asra demands. Case angles her hip so Asra can get to the pocket where her tab is stowed, her eyes never leaving the control console.

Brenn's compound shrinks in the distance as we charge toward orbit, deadly silent but for the vibration of the engines and Asra's frenzied muttering. I hope we're not too late. I don't know if I can stand to see Asra's heart shatter, or see firsthand what will happen to Malik if we don't find a way to stop these attacks.

"Okay, okay, here," Asra says, flapping one hand to get our attention. "This little rider of code you spotted, yes, it instructs every device receiving the signal to repeat, too. It tells every tab, satellite, and computerized anything on the planet to spread the signal throughout its entire network, creates a giant digital echo chamber for this signal."

"What's the point of that?" Zee asks.

Rion braces a hand on the back of my seat and leans forward. "It must be weaponized in some way. There's no other explanation."

"Wait, what?" I glance over my shoulder; Asra has zoomed in on a little section of code and is following a section with her finger.

"It doesn't just repeat a digital signal. Here. If the device has external speakers, then set volume to max minus one, probably to account for distortion . . . and then it feeds a portion of the signal out through the speakers."

Rion swears. "A sonic weapon of some kind. The military back on Earth has been researching them for over two hundred years."

Zee hums in realization. "Yes, and the concept has been proven in several wars since. There are frequencies to disrupt vision, burst eardrums, induce nausea, bring on cardiac arrest, and there were even rumors they'd figured out one to cause brain aneurysms. It has to be very loud, though."

Case sends the final calculations for the jump to my screen, then leans around her seat back to face Zee. "I don't think that'll be a problem. Most modern small speakers can reach a hundred and forty decibels, and with all of them going at once? Even our damn toilets have speakers now, to tell us when they need cleaning. If every speaker in a house activated, and they all played the kill signal at max volume . . ."

"They could kill off most of the population all at once," Rion says. As if it needed to be explicitly stated.

"Not going to happen," I say again. We're nearly at the jump point. "Asra, are you going to be okay?"

Her smile is tight and grim. "I'm ready."

We climb through hazy cloud cover into the starry night sky, my gut churning harder with every second that passes. Asra said just under an hour. It's only been about forty minutes. We'll be there in five. We'll warn them, and everything will be fine. Completely fine.

No beautiful views of the planet for us this time. The dark of night swallows all the blue-green beauty that greeted us earlier today. Was it only a few hours ago? Brenn must have had her entire crew working on the *Kick* to get her ready so fast. It's amazing work, though; the controls feel a little tighter, more responsive as I hold us to our exit vector, and 50 percent engine speed feels a bit hotter than it did before. Not complaining.

Then the shooting starts.

Now I'm complaining.

Bullets pound against our shields, taking them down by nearly a quarter before I can juke out of the way. My heart leaps into my throat, strangling me as I try to yell for—

"Case!"

"Working on it!" she snaps before I can even give her the order. Data spills onto my HUD; flight trajectories, shield status messages, and an angry red dot closing in on our position. Fast.

Okay. Have to focus. I can do this. Asra's family needs us.

"Rion, Zee, get to the guns, see if you can get visual on it. Tell us if you see any identifying marks, then shoot it out of the sky, got it?" I throw the ship into an aggressive climb, weaving as little as possible for the sake of gaining speed and distance. The ship's vibration changes, and I hope it's not because a bullet has hit some vital exposed part. We just got the ship back, and if we've already broken it, I'm going to be very unhappy.

"I am so tired of this," I say, yanking us over as another volley flies past our portside wing. "Isn't this getting old? I think it's old."

"Got visual!" Rion calls over the intercom from the starboard turret. "It's a Ford Galaxy X4. I can't see all the details, but I'm pretty sure it's got that Earth First circle-logo thing on the side. Looks like they've come to finish the cover-up job in person."

"Of course they have. *Of freaking course*, because that has been our luck since we all met. Who's the bad-luck charm? Is it me?" I throw the ship into a sharp roll when the HUD shrieks. Under my feet, the ship vibrates in time with the clatter of the guns.

"Their shields are eating it up, Nax," Zee says, then pauses to fire again. "I'm not sure we'll be able to punch through before it's time to jump. How long do we have?"

Case tries to pull up our ETA to the jump point, but I have to jerk back on the stick to avoid a missile, and her arms go flying. She gets her hands back on the displays quickly, though, and calls, "Thirty seconds to break atmo, three minutes to jump distance at max speed."

"Give it all you got, people," I say, my eyes glued to

the tactical data scrolling across the display. "If we can hit them enough times to make them cautious, that'll give us the space we need to get to the jump zone."

My instruments shriek as the enemy ship gets a missile lock, and I cut the throttle and slam the stick over, tipping us up on our side. Maneuvering in atmo like this is eating up our fuel, but we're well stocked now, so we can deal. I refuse to be shot down again.

Ahead of us, the sky becomes wispy as the haze of the atmosphere fades around us. Three of the colony's moons are in this sector of space, and an army of satellites race along in low orbit. Behind us, the pursuing ship shows no signs of slowing. Rion and Zee are doing their best, calling back and forth to each other over the ship's intercom, working to trap the ship in a pattern of fire, but it's no use. Then I have an idea.

"Rion, Zee, listen. On my mark, I'm going to cut directly in front of the ship and pull back on the throttle. Be ready."

"Got it."

"Ready."

I weave my way through the space junk in lower orbit, one eye on the HUD, and blow out a breath. I hope this isn't a completely terrible idea.

I keep my hand light on the stick, my thumb on the throttle control. "Here we go. Three . . . two . . . one . . . MARK!"

I park the *Kick*'s ass straight in the other ship's path and dial back the throttle, cutting our speed sharply. Both guns go off at the same time, spitting bullets at the ship hurtling straight for us. The HUD scrolls off the distance between us and the target—way too close, too fast. I have to get us going again, and they've recovered enough to shoot back, our shields are dropping, 65 percent now—

I push the throttle wide open and we leap forward just as a shock wave rocks the ship, nearly knocking us into a satellite. Tiny fragments of the enemy ship's hull rain across our shields, too small now to do any real harm. Two whoops of triumph echo from the turrets, one low and throaty, the other higher and more subdued. We all join in, and I flop back in my chair. That was way too close.

"Great job, y'all!" I clap my hands for them over the intercom; they deserve some damned applause. "Now let's get to Tau'ri and—"

An explosion rocks the boat, a big one that takes out over half our shield power in one hit. Fifteen percent.

"What the fu—" Case starts, but I cut her off with a hard maneuver. I swerve close to one of the satellites, glancing at my readouts when I have half a second.

"What the hell hit us?" I ask, throwing the ship into a random weaving pattern through the space junk and satellites.

"Missile," Case says, her voice oddly quiet, considering the situation.

"Where the hell did it come from?" We blew the pursuing ship out of the sky. I saw it disappear from the HUD. Did they have—?

A new voice breaks into the channel, low and authoritative.

"Good afternoon, Mr. Hall," it says, just as my HUD lights up with another four ships, then eight, twelve total, as Case identifies and tags them as foes. Twelve fighters. Tiger Squadron, again. "This is Captain Thomas, and it'll be my pleasure to shoot you out of the sky today. It's a shame about the ship, but Mr. Pearson won't be needing it for long, now, will he?"

Yeah, because he's probably already lounging back on Ellis Station, safe from the death trap he helped fund. What a scumbag.

"The rest of the squadron is nearly in weapons range!" Case snaps. "We can't deal with twelve fighters, Nax. What are we—?"

"Power from the guns," I say, interrupting with a sharp gesture. "Like we did before."

She understands immediately, shifting all the power from the guns to the engines. A wave of lights flare on my console, warnings about engine heat and exhaust and a million other things, but it'll have to hold together. We're only thirty seconds out from the jump zone. We can make it. We have to make it. I have to do this. My hand hovers over the control to rev up the jump drive.

The comm crackles.

"It's been a pleasure chasing you, Mr. Hall. You're an excellent pilot. Bit of a waste, but Earth First—"

And that's all the time I give him. I punch the throttle, hard, don't bother weaving around, just point us straight for the border, giving them a good look at our aft as we rocket to the jump point. Bullets rain against our aft shields, their power draining steadily until the indicator light flickers red, but we're so close, so close. . . .

"You know we're just going to follow you," Captain Thomas snarls. "We know exactly where you're going, exactly what you hope to do, and we'll follow. Our people on the ground will be ready for you, and you'll never—"

We jump.

NINETEEN

THE SECOND WE POP BACK into normal space, I open the throttle wide and angle us toward Tau'ri, bringing the bold green arcing horizon into our front viewport. It's a breathtaking view, the sky spattered with bright points of stars, hazy with swirls of glowing gas pockets and glittering ice crystals, with Tau'ri's luminous form in the middle of it all.

It'll be even more breathtaking when I know it's not already full of dead people.

"We should be in communications range in about two and a half minutes," Case says, threading her fingers into her hair and squeezing. She mutters to herself under her breath for a moment, vaguely angry sounds, like she's scolding herself. My brows draw together in a frown.

"You okay?" I ask.

"Fine, I'm fine," she says, letting go and shoving her hair behind her ears. "My brain is being an asshole right now. I've got it under control."

Anxiety is the worst. I reach across the center console to

squeeze her shoulder. "Hey, you're amazing. I'm amazing. We've got this. Still maybe ten minutes to go before whatever is supposed to happen goes down. Plenty of time."

If I say it enough times, I might even believe it myself and convince my own heart to stop racing. I have a quick flash of déjà vu, of saying those exact words—"We've got this"—as we fist bumped in orbit around al-Rihla for the first time. Right before we crashed. Was it really only a few days ago? I sigh and rub a hand over my face, wincing at the rasp of stubble against my palm. I must look like a total mess. My blood sings in my veins, making my skin hypersensitive, my nerves electric. Every sense is on high alert, ready to be shot at again, ready to dodge, to run, to fight. Speaking of which . . .

"How are the shields recovering from the beating we took? Any lasting damage to the ship?"

Case blows out a breath and recenters herself, letting her hands fly with confidence over the navigator's console. "I've diverted the power from the guns to recharging the shields. We were at five percent when we jumped. Thirty percent and climbing now. We were lucky. They held just long enough for us to get to the jump point. No damage."

More of a lessening of panic than a true feeling of relief, but I'll take it. "Asra, do you have a message or something to send once we're in comm range?"

She hums an "I'm busy" noise in reply, the lightning-fast

taps of her fingers audible even over the rumbling of our engines. "I have a . . . data packet that . . . and I should be . . ."

She never does finish any of those sentences, but I assume they mean she has it under control. I don't entirely know what we could say in this instance that could really help. What will the people do, evacuate the whole planet in a matter of minutes? Conduct a planetwide raid for anything with the Earth First circle logo on it? What can we do, once we send our message?

"Comm range in three . . . two . . ." Case counts down, then flips a switch. The bridge is instantly filled with a cacophony of static and garbled voices, dozens of messages broadcast in the clear.

"Can't . . . whole area is . . . can you—?"

"—please repeat . . . our signal is—"

"—you try on . . . all frequen—s not our comm—"

"What the hell?" Case cranks the volume down with a lip curl of annoyance. "Why is everything so broken up?"

"My data packet won't go through, either," Asra says, her voice high and tight. Out of the corner of my eye, I catch her shaking her tablet in irritation, like that will help somehow. "Something must be—"

"Jamming," Case jumps in. "Kind of. There's a signal clogging up all the communication channels. I've tried every comm method we have, and even tight beam calls aren't working. Something's interfering with all communication planetwide."

I bang the armrest of my chair and let loose a frustrated growl. "Something like an endlessly repeated signal, maybe? Could that drown everything out?"

"Look. The same pattern," Asra says. She unhooks herself from her restraints and clings to the side of Case's chair, swiping through the data on Case's display. "It's still in the early phases, still working to get control over the whole network."

"This is the first step," Case says. "The prep work before the kill signal goes out. What do we do?"

Asra and Case bend their heads together, studying the signal patterns and muttering. I huff an exasperated sigh. Not fast enough. I feel like my bones want to crawl out of my skin, like I'm going to scream uncontrollably if we don't do something *right now*.

I take a deep breath and drum my fingers against my chair's armrests. We've come up on Tau'ri's outer orbit, so I slot us in with the other space junk, though no traffic controller has directed me to do so. Understandably, since they couldn't get through to us if they tried. "Do we have a plan yet?"

"We're tracing the source of the repeats," Case says, once again focused on the task at hand. "It has to be originating somewhere, but scans don't show it anywhere on this side of the planet. Can you take us into lower orbit and around to the other hemisphere?"

I take the controls, guiding us down into the maze of satellites racing along in their choreographed dance. The HUD lights up with warnings, then dims, then lights up, then dims—missile lock! No, just kidding. Ground guns! Actually . . .

"I think the signal is messing with their targeting, too. They're trying to lock on to us, but it keeps flickering—"

Then the HUD goes solid red with a missile lock warning, and I hesitate for the barest second before wrenching us out of low orbit and weaving around a satellite that nearly takes us out. Without restraints, Asra loses her footing at the sudden maneuver and tumbles across Case's lap, slamming her forehead into the center console with a dull crack. I risk a quick glance away from the front viewport—is that blood? I glance again: Case has Asra pinned to her lap with an arm around her waist while we level out, Asra's blood bright and shocking on Case's fingers. Another missile lock, damn it, and another juke nearly sends Asra flying again. I growl.

"Not to be a jerk, but will you please *sit the hell down*, Asra? What's happening out there, Case?"

Asra waves Case's hands away and staggers to her feet, clinging to Case's chair until she can throw herself back into her own seat and refasten her restraints. One by one, the blips on my HUD turn red as Case identifies and tags them. A midsize frigate sits on the edge of the system, and new blips spill from its position in pairs, some of which are already in weapons range. Probably Tiger Squadron again, coming after us as promised. Fuck those guys, seriously.

I toggle the intercom and leave the channel open. "Zee, Rion, can you see our company?"

"Only giving you one guess, Nax," Rion calls back.

"Please shoot some of them down before we leave," I beg, dancing around a glowing, jagged lump of space junk on my way around the planet. "We'll get the guns back online in just a sec."

I risk a glance at our current shield strength in the far corner of my display. Still only at 45 percent. Not great, but sometimes the best defense is lots of shooting.

"Case, reroute the power back to the guns, then get back on tracing that signal."

"I've already got the signal, kind of," Asra says. "We're not quite close enough to pinpoint yet, but it's definitely coming from somewhere in the capital city."

She grumbles; in my peripheral vision I see her leaning as far as she can in her restraints, holding her tab as close as possible to Case's console. "The signal is starting to interfere with my connection to the ship. I've gotta hardwire in. I'm gonna be useless here pretty soon otherwise."

Case keeps one hand on her display, manipulating the ship's power distribution even as she pries open a hatch underneath the console and tugs out a cable. With a snap of her wrist, she flicks it back to Asra, who clicks it into her tab's port with a relieved sigh.

The ship shudders as the power surges back into the guns and Zee and Rion exchange fire with the ships on our tail. The meter in the corner of my display begins to drain again: 43 percent, 41 percent.

This is bullshit.

I cut the throttle, shove the control stick forward, then dial the throttle back up to full, dropping us straight into Tau'ri's atmosphere. Shouts echo through the ship as we experience a brief moment of weightlessness before our inertial dampener can compensate for the sudden maneuver. And there it is, that feeling I've been chasing my whole life, the one that's got me in trouble so many times—pushed back in my seat, my stomach flipping with every twitch of the controls. This is what I was born to do. I *can* do this.

With an ecstatic whoop, I press the ship harder, faster, our nose glowing orange as we cut through the atmosphere. We have the advantage, for the moment; more weight and larger engines mean we can handle the entry better than a stunt fighter can, and before long the front viewport clears and the glorious waters of Tau'ri rise up to greet us.

The oceans, green with thick algae growth, give off a faint photo-luminescent glow in the dim evening light that fades as we fly into the day side of the planet. Overland, the terrain morphs into long plains of soft mossy groundcover interrupted by the occasional low treelike plant. The planet is largely untouched, being both an unsanctioned and fairly young colony, but as we draw closer to the founding city, scattered farms and homesteads begin to dot the fields and hillsides.

The fighters, four of them now, have no respect for the beauty of the planet. Their bullets shatter trees and splash into rivers, even slam into remote homesteads. I suppose they're planning to kill off the entire planet anyway, so they probably don't mind civilian casualties a few minutes early.

I *do* mind.

I take us in low, weaving between craggy mountains and taller trees where possible to obscure their line of fire, but the ship shudders with a few solid hits despite my best flying. I feel each shot from our guns as a short burst of vibration through my feet, in clusters and steady streams. Rion and Zee chatter back and forth to coordinate.

"Stay still, wanker! Let's focus on the one on to port."

"I'm fairly sure the goal is to *not* stay still."

"Okay, Miss Smartarse, you get him, then!"

An explosion rocks the boat.

"All right. Fair enough."

I take us back up above the mountains and point us toward the main city, squinting against the light of Tau'ri's sun. It's brighter than Earth's, and it pierces through the light cloud cover in golden rays that stand out against the vivid cyan of the sky. The cheery light and jewel-toned beauty spills over a smudge in the distance that slowly resolves into a knot of human-built structures. And of course, the people of Tau'ri seem to have a thing for building up rather than out; the city is a cluster of soaring spires and high rises, gleaming and bright. I would think it was beautiful any other time. Right now, all I see is how much of a bitch it's gonna be to fly through.

"Two more fighters coming in behind, Nax," Zee calls, just as Rion nails another one.

Case swears under her breath. "And it looks like the rest of the squadron has looped around to meet us. They're coming up on the city now from the opposite side."

I groan. "Asra, you have that signal yet?"

"The signal has *us*," she says, slamming her tab down on her lap and swiping irritably at the trickling blood beside her eye. "I'm blocking each pulse of signal as it comes in, but it's too much. Case, you'll have to finish the signal trace, and you have to be ready to disable our transmitter completely, or we'll die along with the settlers here."

"Sure, I can absolutely do ten thousand things at once, no problem!" she spits, her fingers flying over the console. "Nax, can you give me a quick spin over the city? I've almost got the signal's origin."

You mean, can I dodge ten skilled fighter pilots while weaving through a spikey death forest of buildings in a

300

ship that's really too big for this job? Probably not, no, but I guess I'm gonna try. I swallow down my terror and summon up every ounce of cocky striker attitude I have, then dial the throttle back and drop us down among the spires of the city. Proximity warnings drill into my skull, a constant blaring alarm that I finally cut off altogether so I can hear myself think. We have to finish this. I'm going to run out of luck eventually.

"Zee, keep firing enough to keep them cautious, but try not to hit them, okay? We don't want any civilian casualties when they crash. Rion, you're our best gunner—I need you to be ready to take out this receiver thing once we figure out where it is. We're doing a flyby now. Keep your eyes open."

No more talking—this is the trickiest flying I've ever done, even counting simulators. I settle back in my seat, keep my hand light on the control stick, and force my muscles to unclench, stay loose and reactive, keep my movements as small as possible. An overcorrection right now will kill us all, and Tau'ri with it.

"There!" Case shouts, stabbing a finger at her display. "The signal is originating from the spaceport on the edge of the city. Getting you a marker . . . now!"

My HUD lights up with a glowing green dot. I pull up sharply, taking us out of the spires to fly the most direct route, right as a fighter screams through the space we just occupied. Bullets slam into one of the metal-and-glass

301

towers, and the fighter doesn't pull up fast enough; it smashes into the same tower, glittering shards and fiery wreckage raining down into the city streets. A sharp pang of regret stabs in my chest, for both the pilot and the innocent bystanders, but I have to focus. No time to dwell. The whole planet is at stake. Asra's family. All our families, ultimately.

Asra sucks in a breath behind me. "Case, I can't keep up with this anymore. The network is almost completely overwhelmed."

Without a word, Case slips out of her restraints and crawls under the console. A few clicks later, she chucks a metal panel across the cockpit. The noise over the comms surges—then cuts off completely. Case crawls out slowly, bracing herself to avoid a head injury like Asra's, and manages to get back into her seat. Her hands tremble over her console, but she gets right back to work without a word.

We come up on the spaceport fast, its winking beacons guiding us in toward vast flat rooftops and brightly painted runways. And there—something on one of the raised landing pads, something out of place, with a bright splash of paint on the side. Blue and green.

Surrounded by several sprawled, still figures.

"Rion, do you—?"

"I see it, Nax, swing around for another pass!"

We're going too fast to make the turn. I blow past and cut our speed to tighten the angle—just in time to see all the fighters break off and make for atmosphere, their engines flaring bright. Fleeing.

Oh no.

"It's gonna happen. The weapon's about to go off, Rion—"

"Shut up and fly, Captain!" he snaps.

A wave of calm washes over me. My hands fly over the controls, adjusting throttle, leveling out the tilt of the wings, bringing our nose in line. Gotta give Rion the clearest, easiest shot I can, but it's still a mess—I can't go any slower than this or we'll fall out of the sky, and the spires are everywhere, reaching up to snatch us out of the sky, scrape our underside, claw out our guts, and Rion's shots are going just barely too wide because I can't give him the angle he needs, eating up the platform around the device, but not close enough, and any second, any second it's gonna—

A bullet slams into the device dead-on, right through the center of the circle logo, punching out the other side, then more, and more, shredding its innards. Case immediately throws herself back under the console and reactivates the *Kick*'s transmitter. The open comm channel gives a blast of static, then a sudden clamor of voices.

"—reporting heavy casualties in Center City—"

"Can anyone get in contact with New Chatham?"

"The fighters are on an outbound vector—"

"Has anyone IDed that ship?"

"At least a hundred dead out in Sharpsburg—"

"Please return to private channels and—"

Oh god, no.

Asra sucks in a shuddering breath as I yank back on the stick and send us soaring into the sky, up and away from the city of spires. Heavy casualties. Death tolls. Whole towns out of contact.

"I'm sorry," Rion says over the intercom. "If I'd made the shot sooner—"

I cut him off. "That was an impossible target and you nailed it. You saved a lot of lives."

The rest goes unspoken. But not all of them. Not enough of them.

With her tab finally working again, Asra opens a comm channel for wide broadcast. "If anyone out there is wondering what just happened, see the documents I'm sending you and destroy everything you find with the Earth First logo on it. Ground all flights and don't let anyone leave." She hesitates. "Except us. We have to make sure this can't happen anywhere else. Good luck."

A double beep indicates a channel swap, then Asra's voice changes, faster, breathier. "Ammu? Farah? Are you there?"

Silence.

"Mazneen, is that you?"

A choked-off sob answers. "Yes, yes, it's me, you're

alive, Alhamdulillah! I don't have time to talk right now, but you're okay?"

"I'm fine, Mamuni, but Farah was visiting a friend and I can't reach her, and three of our neighbors just dropped dead. That sound was excruciating, then it was just gone. What happened?"

Asra squeezes her eyes shut, and tears spill heavy over her cheeks, soaking in where her hijab meets her face. "You'll know soon. It should be over. But it's going to happen on the other planets and we have to stop it. I'll pray for Farah, but I can't stay right now. I'm so sorry, Ammu. I'll be back as soon as I can. I love you."

She cuts the comm off before her mother can reply and wipes her eyes on her sleeve.

"I'm sorry, I had to check."

"Understandable," I say. "I hope your sister is okay. But now what?"

Asra's face goes hard and determined.

"Now we take out this signal at its source." She unbuckles again, leans over to Case's console, and swipes back to the signal data. "You're not going to believe this."

Case leans in, eyebrows knitted, then sits back suddenly. "No. There's no way. It's impossible, the technology doesn't exist!"

"It does now, apparently," Asra says. "And what better way to coordinate simultaneous attacks throughout the entire galaxy than with a trigger signal from one fixed point?"

"What point?" I ask, though I have a feeling I know the answer already.

Case gives me a grim smile. "Ellis Station."

I blow out a long breath. "Back to the beginning, then. How long do we have until the zero hour from the memo?"

"Twelve hours," Case replies. "But I don't think that's going to matter. Those fighters are docking with their transport, and if they jump back to the station and report what happened, they'll know their secrecy has been blown. And they know their weapon works now. No reason to delay."

Damn, she's right; what's left of Tiger Squadron is disappearing two fighters at a time into the transport that brought them to this system. If we don't keep them from leaving, they'll beat us back to the Academy, tell them to send the trigger signal to all the other colonies, and it'll all be over. Can't let that happen. I open the all-ship comm again.

"Case, reroute all power to engines!" I snap, my finger resting on the switch for the afterburner.

"All of it?"

"Shields, life support, guns, everything! We'll need to cut it back in as soon as we're in firing range. Rion, Zee, the engines are your target. We *have* to beat them back to the station."

The flurry of blinking warning lights doesn't even faze me this time. The second the power is diverted, I kick in the afterburner and we rocket toward the transport, angling toward their aft, where the twin engines glow with a faint blue light. Two fighters are left, awaiting their clearance to land, but we blow straight past them, the *Kick* shuddering violently as Case reroutes all the power back where it belongs.

The rhythmic shots start up immediately, both guns focused tightly on the same spot of the closest engine. Their shields flare, the bullets slowly eating away at their strength, but not fast enough—the first of the two remaining fighters makes for the landing bay, while the second swings around, coming right for us.

"Rion, incoming! Zee, keep at that engine!" I call. It takes all my strength to leave the ship exactly where it is, a sitting duck, but it won't matter anyway if we can't take out this ship. They'll warn the station, they'll know we're coming, shoot us down as soon as we get in-system—

"No dancing this time, Mr. Hall?" the familiar voice of Captain Thomas asks over the comm. "Ah well. It's been fun."

"Ooh!" Case blurts, sounding . . . excited? "I found a new toy Brenn had installed. Wait for this . . ."

A targeting reticle appears on my HUD, and a tiny red button lights up on my control stick.

"Missiles?" I ask.

"Missile, singular," she replies. "A big one. Make it count."

Oh yes.

"Quick changeup!" I call to Rion and Zee. "Focus on the fighter for a minute, then switch back to the engine. You'll know when."

A hail of bullets slams into our shields as I finally roll away, out of Captain Thomas's line of fire. A quick turnaround, gun the engines, line up the shot, thumb over the button—and there's an explosion, a flash, a rain of debris.

But I never launched the missile.

"Yes, got the fighter!" Rion says with a whoop. "Point us back at the ship, Captain, let us at it."

But my heart is a lump of cold dread, heavy in my chest.

The transport ship is gone. Jumped away.

We saved a few people on Tau'ri—but we may have killed everyone else in the process.

"Case, jump to Ellis Station. Right now."

She obeys without hesitation, the jump vector appearing on my HUD barely a second later. I swallow a painful lump in my throat, steady my breath as I make the run up to the jump point.

I never thought I'd be heading back to Earth space

ever again. Once all this goes down, we'll almost certainly be arrested for violating the no-return rule. We'll be prosecuted, executed, all our dreams of life in the colonies, of piloting, gone.

But if we don't, we give a death sentence to every single colonist. Including Malik.

It's no choice at all.

"This is it," I say, steadying my hands on the controls. A grim smile tugs at the corner of my mouth.

"It's time to show the Academy why they never should have kicked us out."

TWENTY

EARTH.

We pop back into normal space, and it's the first thing I see—gorgeous ocean blue swirled with wispy white clouds, dancing through the black with its sole moon in orbit. Achingly familiar. And forbidden. If I get us too close to the planet itself, the automated orbital guns will take us out and rain our debris over our distant, untouchable families and friends. We may never be this close to them again.

Then I catch a glint of light off metal and kick the throttle up to full.

"Case, is that the transport?"

"Yes, and they're about fifteen seconds from comm range with Ellis Station. There's no way we'll catch them, even at full power. They'll know we're on to them and set off the weapon as soon as they're able."

I slam my hand on the center console, spitting every swear word I can think of as my heart plummets into my stomach. After everything, this is how it ends? It's bullshit.

"Look, this doesn't change anything," Asra says, getting her calm back, though she winces as swipes the back of her hand over her still-bleeding forehead. "Even assuming they hit the go button right now, it was about fifteen minutes from the start of the communication takeover to when they sent the signal on Tau'ri. And that transmitter must take an enormous amount of power to be able to send a signal over that distance, through A-space or however it works. It probably takes them time to recharge. We could still take out their transmitter before then. We have to try."

Her words restore a modicum of calm to my screaming brain. "Okay, probably right, but still, we can't just knock on the front door. How do we get through their shields and land on the station?"

"I've been thinking about that," Rion says from behind me, and I jump. When did he come up from the turret? He smirks. "I have an idea to get us in there."

Rion types on his tab for a few seconds, then projects an image into the air over the center console. A structure of some kind, with huge tunnels extending out one side, Earth floating in the distant background.

"Remember how I thought they might have been hiding personnel in the old abandoned station near Ellis before the attack?"

He stops and looks up to blank stares all around. I remember the conversation, but I honestly have no idea what this has to do with anything. He raises an eyebrow and points to the image.

"The two stations are connected by the tunnels," he says, and I finally get it. I saw those tunnels out the viewport when I walked to the terminal to catch my fail ship home, before all this started.

"Is this image to scale? It looks big enough to—"

"Yes. We'll have to shoot our way into the tunnel, but it's big enough to fly through. We'll need vacuum suits."

"Go, then. Everyone get suited up. Case and I will follow as soon as we can." I take a steadying breath as Rion and Asra retreat to the cargo bay, hear them meet up with Zee over the turret intercom. I'm doing my best to not obsess over the two and a half minutes it took us to come up with our plan. We can still make it. "Case, transfer control of the guns to my console."

"All yours," she says with a few confident keystrokes. Another button illuminates on the control stick, and I press it, switching from missile to guns. "Any point in trying to be sneaky about this?" she asks.

I shrug, angling us toward the waypoint Case provides me. "Probably not, but power down everything you can, then go suit up."

A series of clicks, and Case slides out of her restraints as I start our final approach to the old station. She squeezes my shoulder, leans down to press a friendly peck to the side of my head, and is gone a second later.

The old station looms in the front viewport, a gargantuan tangle of buildings shrouded in darkness. Completely abandoned, from the looks of it. If Earth First ever used this place in the past, they obviously aren't using it now. The connecting tunnels are barely visible in the darkness, made of clear reinforced polycarbonate that disappears in the shadows. Hopefully they aren't bulletproof. I'm too worried about being spotted to turn on the external flood lamps, so a bit of reflected light from Earth is all I have to target by.

My finger tightens on the trigger as soon as I'm in range, raining bullets down on the lunar surface. A few go wide, kicking up clouds of white-gray moon soil that never settle back to the surface, but I adjust the approach until the bullets find their target. They slam into the curved top of the tunnel, and my throat tightens. Pockmarks appear in the surface, but the shots don't punch through. I throttle back, giving more time for more bullets, but it's starting to look hopeless, pointless, still no real damage—until a single crack finally appears, creeping along the length of the tunnel, then more, and more, until the whole top collapses in a shattering, glittering heap, leaving the tunnel wide open for me to thread the needle.

I hold my breath, too afraid to even blink as I kick in the mag coils and throttle back as far as I can, slipping the ship through the hole in the roof of the tunnel. I have to fly on instruments alone, which I always find completely nerve-racking. It's too dark to have a good visual sense of distance. I have no idea where the edges of the hole I made are, but I haven't heard any horrific screeches yet, so I take it as a good sign. My eyes are drying out from the lack of blinking, but I'll kill us all if I look away. The internal comm clicks.

"Nax," Case begins, "do you think—?"

"Not now," I snap, regretting the sharpness of my tone, but I don't have the extra brainpower to formulate an apology right now. I force the tension out of my shoulders and watch the altimeter carefully, making twitchy little micro-adjustments as needed to keep the ship from touching the ragged edges of the tunnel. Then we're through, the *Kick*'s mag coils catching the iron rails lining the bottom of the tunnel, and I throttle up as much as I dare in the darkness. One minute to the station at this speed.

"I wish I could turn on the lights, damn it," I mutter to myself, then raise my voice so Asra can hear me over the comms. "Any chatter from the station yet?"

"Nothing that concerns us," Asra replies, her voice calm and even. Good. I'm hoping they won't notice us until it's too late. How many minutes have passed? We're so close. Thirty seconds.

"Y'all might feel some vibrations back there," I say, thumbing the weapons back over to missiles. "I'm making us a door."

The tunnel curves slightly, and there's Ellis Station, straight ahead in the distance. I tweak our alignment, then, at twenty seconds out, pull the trigger again. Our only missile fires from underneath the *Kick*'s nose, rocketing forward and slamming into the vast cargo doors that connect the station to the tunnels. The doors evaporate, along with the next several rooms beyond, and there must be just enough stray atmosphere from the station to carry the sound, because a deafening *boom* reverberates through the ship, echoed by shouts of alarm from the others.

Holy shit. Case was right. Big missile.

I bring the ship to a smooth stop right outside the destruction and tear off my restraints, flipping switches as I go. Out the door, down the central hallway, and into the cargo bay, where the others wait, mostly suited up and ready to go. Zee dabs at the gash on Asra's forehead with careful precision, tapping down the edges of a small butterfly bandage, then steps back to let Asra wipe at her fresh tears and put on her helmet. Rion holds my suit out for me, helps me step into it and zips the front from navel to neck, then fits the slim helmet over my head and fastens it to the suit. Case shoves my tab in a pocket, already synced to the helmet comm, and presses a chem gun into my gloved hand with a grim smile. Asra sets the ship to lock after us, and it's time.

"Ready?" I ask, raising my gun in salute.

Four affirmative responses. Everyone fidgets in their own way, betraying their nerves at going back to the place that rejected us. We have to do this, though. We have to.

I lead the group down the ramp and into the demolished cargo area, my steps clunky in the magnetized boots that keep us from floating off in the low lunar gravity. The edges of the metal still glow red in some spots, and I can feel the heat radiating even through the thick vacuum suit. The landscape around us is cold and desolate by comparison, all gray rocky sand. I gently kick a tiny rock and watch its lazy trajectory as it goes tumbling through space. Weird.

"Is it strange," Zee asks, "that we've been to three different planets in the past week, but our own moon is the one that feels the most alien?"

"I was just thinking the same," Rion says, his voice tinny through the helm speakers. I have to agree. The trees and sunlight might be different colors on the other worlds, but at least they had . . . something. This barren landscape feels forbidding. Even with our mag boots gripping the ground and the wrecked structure all around it, it still feels like I could go flying off into space at any second, like I'm closer to the void. A shiver runs up my spine, but I force my mind to the task at hand. We're about to come upon an interior door that wasn't blown away by the missile. This is where it begins for real.

"Okay, listen up," I say. "They're probably sending people to investigate the explosion, so we should expect shooting almost immediately. Rion and I will take point. Case can navigate for us. Asra, stick with her in case there's security in our way. Zee, watch our six, and shoot or kick anything that moves."

I blow out a breath and will my heart to stop jackhammering. "Any questions? Comments? Last-minute genius ideas? Prayers, hymns, interpretive dances?"

Asra shrugs and gives me a watery smile. "Lā hawla wa lā quwwata illā billāh."

My ammi used to say that every time she left the house for a patrol shift. "There is no power or strength save in Allah." A bit of protection. A little slice of home. I return Asra's smile and nod an acknowledgment. We'll have to go back to check on her sister as soon as this is over. It must be eating her alive inside.

I check the chamber on my chem gun and flick off the safety, then deactivate the mag grip in my boots. Case bumps her shoulder against mine as we approach the door, singing a few bars of a peaceful little tune under her breath. Something about a blue boat. I raise an eyebrow at her, and she grins.

"It's my favorite hymn. Bit hard to believe in the 'inherent worth and dignity of all people' when some of those people insist on committing genocide. I thought it might inspire me." She shrugs and goes back to her song, the whispered notes echoing off the inside of her helmet as she taps at her tablet while we walk. When we're a few steps away, she spins around and projects the publicly available map of the station into the air between us.

"I've got a trace on a large energy signature that looks to be right about here." She points, and a blip appears on the map. "It's one of the server rooms, so that would make sense. Beyond this door are maintenance hallways I don't have a map for, though, so I'll guide us as best I can."

I take a deep breath. "Okay. Once we find and disable the transmitter, we should find a computer terminal where Asra can pull up information about where the devices have been sent. We send it and all the other data we've pulled to the GCC, post it publicly on the web, send it to news outlets, transmit it as far and wide as we can on Earth, and repeatedly. Just in case the devices can somehow still be activated in person."

Case nods. "And . . ." She pauses, swallows. "Maybe we can sign our names to the communications. Make sure it's known that we're the ones who did it. Maybe they'll drop the charges against us if we do."

Rion snorts. "Assuming we live long enough to get arrested in the first place. Let's face it—our plan is to walk in and start shooting. No problem, yeah? Back in time for tea."

And just like that, the tension breaks and we all collapse into nervous giggles. This is truly, completely cracked. Ah well.

Zee claps a hand on my shoulder. "Seriously, hotshot," she says, her grin fading, "It's been a strange couple of days, but you got us here. Thanks for leading us, Captain."

"Yeah," Case agrees. "Thanks, Cap'n."

Asra gives me a loose salute with her trademark sly smile, and Rion yanks me into a one-armed, space-suited hug. I'm horrified to feel wetness pricking in the corners of my eyes, and I pull Rion closer for a minute to give myself a chance to blink it away. The tightness in my throat eases, and I manage to grind out a quick "Thanks."

We've come a long way. I'm really gonna miss these faces when this is all over. Watching everyone go their separate ways is going to eat me alive—assuming I *am* alive after this.

Part of me is weirded out by how quickly this kind of super-dangerous, hastily constructed plan has become business as usual. Part of me is ready to vomit my guts out. But the part that surprises me, that's growing fast now that we're here, is what I could almost call . . . brave. Determined.

No, scratch that. Fucking pissed. These are the murdering assholes who killed off an entire station of people. Who ruined Case's, Rion's, and Zee's plans to serve on the colonies. Who executed half a planet of innocent people, maybe Asra's sister, and they'll do the same to my brother, all because they disagree with settling the stars. Disgusting. Now I wish that missile had been bigger.

Time to move. I take a slow, deep breath, then nod.

"All right, rejects. Let's blow this thing and go home."

TWENTY-ONE

ON THE OTHER SIDE OF the door, our touchy-feely share-time feelings fade away behind masks of forced calm. Despite the brave face I put on for the others, the paranoia is running deep. I'm afraid to breathe too loudly, lest the station's inhabitants discover that the rats in the walls are actually vigilantes with a collective death wish. Alarms blare through the hallways: decompression warnings, intruder alerts . . . and a request for all available reinforcements to report to deck AA23.

"Case? Are we—?"

She nods. "AA23. Time to go."

The air quality analysis readout in my helmet is green, so I retract the face shield and take a deep breath in. The smell of the Academy's recycled air gives me an immediate rush of sense memory: I'm back at my interview, standing flat backed before the panel of officers, my dress slacks stiff against my legs. Sweating bullets and so full of naive hope. Feels like years ago.

Case guides us quickly and quietly through the dimly

lit corridors, Rion and I on either side of her with guns at the ready. Case, Zee, and I each brought some of the chem grenades we stole from Jace's warehouse, not willing to risk the traditional kind with the vacuum of space pressing in, but "all available reinforcements" makes me feel like a few little grenades won't be enough.

The lights overhead flicker, then dim by half, throwing the hallway into dancing shadows. I hold my breath as a live announcement interrupts the blaring alarms: "Power has been temporarily rerouted for charging. Three minutes to transmission."

Oh god, it's happening.

Bang! Something whizzes past my ear, and I hit the ground on pure instinct, scrambling to face our attackers.

"They're here!" a man shouts over his shoulder, around a corner. Footsteps echo up the corridor; more coming, and the man has taken cover, is lifting his gun, aiming at Zee, can't let it happen—

I pull the pin from my chem grenade and chuck it down the hallway, bouncing it off the wall behind the man and down the side hallway. A shout, then it explodes with a bang and a wet splatter of sleep chem. A bit of the green liquid sprays into the main hallway, and the man who shot at us slumps over. No more footsteps come from that direction.

I want to relieve the man of his gun, but there's no time. Less than three minutes. Gotta find that transmitter.

Case has already set off down the hallway again, running full tilt this time, her tablet stashed away, a grenade in one hand and a chem gun in the other. She must know exactly where we're going now. Around the first corner, all clear. Next corner, grenade, turn. Around the next corner, clear. Around—shit!

I slam into the chest of a man at least six inches taller and broader than me and see Rion do the same out of the corner of my eye. The man's enormous tree-trunk arms pin my elbows to my sides so I can't aim my gun, can't hit him, can't do fucking anything—except go dead weight and slip straight down through the circle of his embrace.

My ass hits the floor, and I swing my gun up, squeezing the trigger, releasing a steady stream of chem pods. Most soak harmlessly into the man's clothing, but all it takes is one. A single pod splatters against his forearm as he aims his own gun at my forehead. His finger tightens on the trigger, his mouth hard with determination—then his eyes slide shut, and he staggers forward. I roll out of the way just in time as he comes crashing down gun first, his head hitting the deck with a loud crack.

Adrenaline blasts through my system; my hands shake as Rion helps me to my feet, and my fingers refuse my brain's command to let go once I'm up. He clutches my hand right back as we step over the bodies of the two men, following Case's lead down another branching hallway.

"Ninety seconds to transmission. Prepare for a power surge."

Rion's eyes meet mine, wide and fearful. This is it. This is—

Case skids to a stop in front of an unmarked door. A keypad next to it glows red. Asra curses under her breath and presses her tablet to the wireless maintenance interface, swiping and tapping with incredible speed.

"The door will open the second this works," she breathes, her words nearly silent. "Be ready."

I motion for Rion and Case to stand to one side of the door, while Zee and I crouch on the other side. I slip a new canister into my gun, and Zee hefts our last remaining grenade. My heart flutters in my chest, fast as a rabbit's panicked heartbeat, and my head spins with the dizzying cocktail of urgency, frustration, sheer terror. The others look just as bad off: shallow breaths, flushed faces, nervous twitches.

Asra inhales sharply, and that's all the warning we get. The door slides open, and on the other side, they're ready for us.

Zee rolls the grenade over the threshold the second the gap is wide enough, the small explosion sounding more ferocious in the enclosed space. I peek around Asra—four people in tech coveralls sprawl over consoles. No movement, except for the digital countdown visible on one of the displays: thirty seconds. Twenty-nine, twenty-eight . . .

I'm really gonna throw up this time.

The room is a mess of computer consoles, wires, and long, thin tubes feeding through a hole in the ceiling. My chest is cracking open with the panic, my breath loud and hard. There's so much shit in here, how are we supposed to find the transmitter? Twenty-three, twenty-two—Asra taps frantically at the display next to the countdown. More shouts from back the way we came, damn it. I slap the door control and lock it, though I doubt that will stop anyone with proper clearance. Zee throws open an access panel full of breakers and starts flipping them three at a time, nothing, nothing.

Rion, Case, and I look on helplessly as the clock ticks down, eighteen, seventeen—*there*. In the corner, a huge boxy structure, newer than everything else in the room, slightly different shade of paint. I tear off the front panel, and inside, at waist height, buried among a rat's nest of wires, is a circuit board with a familiar tiny blue-and-green logo. The transmitter.

"Here!" I shout, my voice ragged and panicky even to my own ears. The board is screwed in; I can't get my fingers around it, so I tear at the surrounding wires instead, but nothing stops the timer as it ticks on and on. Ten, nine . . .

"Back!" Zee orders, roughly shoving me away from the console. She takes a step back and swings her leg high, snapping the toe of her boot into the board once, twice, then shifting her hips to slam the heel of her boot in a final resounding crack.

The countdown stops at four seconds, then is replaced with a blinking error message.

HARDWARE FAILURE.

My cheeks are wet. My mouth tightens—then breaks into a grin. I look around at the others: Rion, Case, and Asra openly weep, arms limp at their sides as the adrenaline drains. Zee, on the other hand, looks positively delighted. She rolls her head from side to side, cracking her neck, then her knuckles, then shaking out her legs one at a time.

"That was surprisingly therapeutic," she says with the biggest smile I've ever seen from her.

"I bet." Rion laughs. "I'm almost jealous!"

I snort, but a quick glance at Case's face sobers me up quick. She looks nervous as hell, bouncing on the balls of her feet.

"Okay everyone, time for part two," I say, reining everyone back in before we get too drunk on our victory. "We still have to live through this and get out of here. Asra, can you use the terminal in here to reach Earth?"

She tries two different terminals before shaking her head. "We wrecked or shut down too much vital stuff in here. We'll have to find another terminal somewhere."

Case and Asra bend their heads together, examining the layout on Case's tab, muttering back and forth.

"The medbay, I think," Asra says finally, and Case nods with her.

"It's close, and the only people in there are noncombatants or already injured, theoretically," Case says. "Shall we?"

"Lead the way."

Then the door behind us crashes open, and bullets slam into the wall behind me.

A hot point of fire drills through my left arm, and I fall back against the wall, everything blurring together for several long seconds. The arm of my vac suit locks down around my bicep, sealing off the wound, and the tight pressure snaps me back to awareness in time to see two silhouettes in the doorway collapse backward into a third. Zee drops into a crouch beside me, yanking my wounded arm none too gently around for her to see. The pain makes her voice hazy and distant.

"It's just a graze, Nax. You'll be okay," she says, hauling me up by my other arm. "I'll wrap it as soon as we get to the medbay, but we need you and your gun to help us get there. Now. Are you with me, Captain?"

I bite my lip and take several long breaths through my nose, then nod. The flooding heat starts to ebb away, replaced by a dull throbbing pain, but I step over the bodies in the doorway and follow Case as ordered. Can't slow everyone down. Gotta keep moving. There will be more reinforcements coming. Besides, Rion actually got shot, not just grazed, when we were stealing the *Kick*; I can't faint now or I'll never live it down. Some captain I'd be.

Another bullet zings past my head, and Rion and Zee return fire behind me. The motion of the security cameras catches my eye as we turn a corner, so in the next hallway I take aim and fire at one of them; no damage, but at least the gelatinous chemical goop will obscure their view. God, I hope we're almost there; I'm leaving a helpful trail of blood drips in our wake that practically invites the Earth First assholes to shoot us in the back.

We turn one last corner and come face-to-face with a door painted with a giant red cross. The medbay. I shoulder Asra out of the way, meet Rion's gaze, and slam the door controls with the elbow of my good arm. We don't bother looking, just fire at anything vaguely human shaped, and bodies go down over hospital beds and computer consoles before anyone has a chance to react. Case and Zee squeeze off a few more shots down the hallway behind us, then duck through the door. Asra hits the controls and locks everything from the inside.

"We have maybe thirty seconds before they override the door controls. We need . . ." She scans the room for a few long seconds, then darts over to a console in the far corner. "Can you keep them off my back for a few minutes?" she asks, already working to establish the link.

"Let's set up shop, y'all," I say.

Case grabs the mattress off the nearest rolling hospital bed and kicks it onto its side, then rolls another bed in front of it, providing some small amount of cover. There's a snarl, and I whirl as Zee sends a chem blast into the face of a patient, the man's hand half curled around a surgical knife. She swaps the gun to her opposite hand as she rifles through a cabinet and emerges with a can of the same spray-on bandage she used on me after our shuttle crash.

"No time for anything more. Sorry," she says, dropping down beside me and yanking my bad arm to her. I consider making a crack about her bedside manner, but it's probably not a good time. Besides, the door controls are making unhappy chiming sounds as the murdering assholes work to override the lock, so I'm willing to forgive some finger-shaped bruises for the sake of expediency.

Rion pulls the gun from my hand and slips a fresh chem cartridge in for me, then repeats the process for Case. His diplomat mask is in place, and his hands are steady, but his fingers linger on mine when he presses the gun back into my hands. I catch his eye and try on a reassuring smile, but it must come out more like a grimace. His expression is pained as he looks away. No good. Time to rally the troops.

"Okay, seriously," I say in my best Nax Hall, Professional Bullshitter, voice. "Asra said thirty seconds until they hacked the door, but it's been at least a full minute.

They tried to shoot me, but I've gotten mosquito bites bigger than this back home. How exactly did these geniuses manage to take over the station and launch an evil plan for interstellar genocide?"

Not my best material, but the others dissolve into snorting relief giggles anyway, just as the door finally gives a satisfied chime. Back to the shooting it is.

Except they have grenades now.

"FIRE IN THE HOLE!" I shout as an egg-shaped explosive sails over our hospital bed fort. My middle-school baseball instincts kick in—I catch it and hurl it back the way it came, then drop down on top of Case, Rion, and Zee. Only after the grenade explodes a second later with a deafening *CRACK* do I process how colossally bad that could have been. Game over with one little explodey egg thing. No time for panic, though.

I roll off the others and bring my gun up, sighting on the door through the gap between the hospital beds. Charred body parts litter the floor in front of the entrance. I drop back down, hot bile surging into my throat. I'm shocked at myself; I don't feel guilty in the slightest, though the sight is nauseating. But over it all is the sick knowledge that it could have been Case's burned arm, Rion's bloody torso. Get it together, Hall.

Then a voice comes over the room's comm system. "Earth First personnel, Mr. Pearson requests that you spare his stepdaughter if possible. He is on his way to collect her. You have your orders for the rest. Make it quick." It's the headmistress, Dr. Herrera. The one who made this whole thing possible, who took the thousands of lives in her care and snuffed them all out. Vile.

"I'm sorry, guys," Asra says over her shoulder, voice tight and clipped, somehow never looking up through all the chaos. "This is taking too long. I have the info, and I've gotten the message out on every major social media outlet, but someone's blocking my connection every time I try to establish a link with the GCC headquarters on Earth. It's taking time to work around them. Can you—?"

Her voice breaks in a way I've never heard it do before. Not when we stole the ship, not when her brother shot at us, not on Tau'ri . . . never. She takes a deep breath, another, and tries again. "Can you hold for just a little longer? Are we okay?"

I duck as another wave of people pours in through the door, their guns peppering the hospital beds with bullets. No grenades this time—guess they learned that lesson.

"We'll do our best, Asra. Just focus. We'll keep you safe," I say. And god, I hope it's true.

Pop up, fire a few shots, duck down, move. Repeat. It's not working. I can't look long enough to sight a target and aim, much less hit anything. More people push their way into the room, working to set up crossfire, and shit, this is going to hell really fast.

I press myself against our cover and look around our

330

half of the room. There has to be something we can use to our advantage, anything. There's a cabinet with a glass door, shattered and filled with toppled pill bottles, an emergency exit, a door marked PLUMBING AND VEN-TILATION, a biohazard disposal container, a row of chemical tanks, a large suspended machine for . . .

Wait.

Oh no, I have the worst plan *ever*.

The frantic chatter of automatic weapons joins the fray, the rain of bullets ripping our mattress barricade to shreds. Must be actual soldiers responding to the situation now. I rub a hand down my face, collect my courage, and nod.

"Case, follow me."

To her credit, she doesn't hesitate for a second. "With you, Captain."

I count to three to psych myself up, then lean out and fire wildly, managing to bull's-eye one person in the fore-head and send the rest diving for cover. My rollout from behind the hospital beds is so far past graceful, but it gets me behind the next table with a minimum of damage to my messed-up arm, so I can't complain. Case is so close on my heels that she rolls straight over me, and we flail in a tangle of limbs for a moment until I can get oriented again. The chemicals, the chemicals . . . yes, there, four giant canisters that come up to my waist marked N_2O—nitrous oxide.

"Everyone seal your helmets and turn on your O_2 flow, now!" I say into my helm mic. "Incoming, ten seconds!" My helmet shield snaps into place, and I get a hit of fresh oxygen mix, then glance over at Case. She's already good to go, so I wave her over to the first canister and motion for her to grab her side of the valve wheel. I hate putting her in the line of fire with me, but my left arm is useless right now, and I need the help.

"Hope you're all set, 'cause this might be my worst idea yet," I say, and heave the valve wheel to the left. Case throws all her strength into it, and it turns, slowly at first . . . then releases all at once. The gas comes gushing out into the medbay with a sound like a fire extinguisher. I grab the top and yank it toward me, lowering it gently to the ground with Case's help, then push it across the floor until it's out from behind cover.

The second my head pokes around the corner, a blast of gunfire nearly takes my face off. I throw myself back behind the chemical storage locker, peek out one more time—and lock eyes with none other than Jace Pearson, here to finish us himself. I duck back as a hail of bullets strikes my cover, and take one deep, calming breath. This can still work.

"Zee!" I call over the comms, then wave a hand at the billowing gas canister, inviting her to do the honors. She sketches a tiny bow, then drops to the floor behind the tank, leans back, and slams into it with both feet, sending it rolling straight toward our attackers. She leaps back just as the gunfire concentrates on her location . . . then the shots begin to taper off. Rion's marksman ability has put a good dent in their numbers, but it's the tank of gas pouring directly into the assholes' faces that ends the resistance completely.

And the laughing starts.

I risk a look around the corner, and I'm so glad I did.

The Earth First soldiers who were shooting at us, the vicious assholes who were part of a plot to kill off half the population of the galaxy, are leaning all over one another in fits of giggles, drooling and grinning like little kids. The best, though, is Asra's stepdad, who drops his gun to bat at invisible somethings around his face with a puzzled expression. I probably look like I got a dose myself; a goofy grin stretches across my face as a wave of cool relief pours through every vein.

Could this really be almost over?

"Laughing gas, Nax?" Rion says, standing up from his cover. "Seriously?"

I sent a mental thanks to Tucker Fineman, wherever he may be. Asshole he may have been, but if he hadn't gotten high on N_2O that one time, I would never have thought of this. This one's for you, Tucker.

And there's still one step left: eliminating the reinforcements.

"Yes, Rion, laughing gas, and we're not done yet," I

say. "Zee and Rion, stay and cover Asra in case we get new visitors. Case, I need your engineer brain over here." The door to the plumbing and ventilation room opens without a fuss, and Case catches on right away, rolling another N_2O canister inside. She immediately sets to work rigging it up to dump into the ventilation system, which is great, because I wouldn't have the slightest clue where to start. Instead, I grab another tank of gas and roll it in behind the other one.

We repeat the process twice more, emptying each tank fully into the system until all four of them are kicked, then gently guide the high-off-their-asses soldiers—and Jace—out into the hallway. Case rigs the door once again, but takes her time to really rip the guts out of the maintenance access panel this time. No one will be getting in unless we let them.

"Oh, you guys are going to love this," Asra calls from across the room with a wicked grin. She beckons us over, and oh good god, it is golden. She has the security camera footage from the mess hall, main office, and the headmaster's quarters up on screen, where people are sprawled out on the tables, grinning from ear to ear or dancing in slow, lazy circles. The headmaster, Dr. Herrera, who recorded our wanted notices and signed the orders to kick us out of the Academy, looks like she's doing a solo waltz in her office. And in the hallway directly outside the medbay, Jace continues his invisible-fairy-catching dance. Asra aims her tab at the video screen and records a short clip of it with a satisfied smile.

"Mission accomplished, by the way," Asra says. "Command is now in possession of all of Earth First's files and plans, along with the message we wrote. Just in case they aren't paying attention, though, I took the liberty of transmitting a live stream of this footage down to Earth. If nothing else, the generals at GCC HQ will notice this for sure."

As if on cue, the comm system sounds an incoming call tone. Rion leans over and taps the receive button with a jaunty little flourish, barking a laugh as a round-cheeked man appears on the screen. He looks positively livid.

"What in god's name is going on up there?" the man roars, the mic distorting from his volume. "Who the hell are you?"

Everyone crowds around me, getting into view of the camera. Asra waves. Case salutes. Zee crosses her arms, and Rion shoots the man two fingers. Not very diplomatic, that. The fist that's been squeezing my heart in a stranglehold for the past four days finally fades away, and a grin tugs at the corner of my mouth. I throw my arms around my friends and look straight into the camera.

"Nax Hall, captain of the *Swift Kick*, at your service," I say with a little bow of my head. "And before you say anything else: you're welcome."

TWENTY-TWO

MY QUARTERS ABOARD THE *KICK* feel almost homey now. Brand-new sheets, a little magnetic growing pot with a cheerful mint plant, and my old tablet from home sitting on the bedside table. Some of my old clothes from Earth live in the drawers now, and the chevra mix from my parents' care package is stashed in my newly designated snack drawer. But despite it all, it's hard to shake the feeling that the world is going to fall out from under me at any second. My brain and body can't seem to get the message that it's over.

It's over.

It sure was nice of the GCC to fall all over themselves to apologize to us. They sent up packages from our families within twelve hours of the whole ordeal, then transferred documents clearing us of wrongdoing, along with a hefty sum of reward money. There was some vague grumbling at the start when they tried getting us to admit to stealing the *Kick*, but we said nothing, and they can't prove it. We have documents showing our legal ownership now, so they can't do a damn thing about it.

My only punishment in this? They nailed me for, of all things, piloting without an interstellar license. Blow me. I'll pay the fine out of my beautiful reward cash, thank you very much. After what I've been through, the piloting exam was an utter cakewalk.

My parents are . . . less than happy with me, I think. We only got to talk for a minute before the GCC shut us down—something about the integrity of the investigation—and we had to leave Earth orbit to get the *Kick* back to Brenn's for repair soon after. But it sounded like my parents were forced to deal with all of my extended family's judgments and opinions once the wanted notices came out. Grammy was clutching her Southern lady pearls, and Pa and my dad's brothers were right pissed. Same with my aunties and uncles on my ammi's side. Turns out I started quite the family scandal.

Again.

I am actually kind of sorry for that.

They recorded a message for me on my old tab before they sent it up, though I haven't watched it yet. I don't really know what to expect. Never contact us again? You never should have left? Why are you such a screwup? Don't forget to wash your underwear?

I flop onto the bed and throw an arm over my eyes, the tab on the table beside me silently judgmental.

It can wait. I need a nap.

Or not.

A knock comes on my open door. I crack one eye open to see Malik standing there, arms folded, leaning in the doorway.

"Have you watched it yet?" he asks.

I fight down the automatic wave of annoyance at his nagging. I'm trying to be better about that. Trying to make things better between us.

"No." I hesitate, then opt for honesty. "I'm afraid they hate me."

Malik chuckles. "I got a message from them this morning. They definitely don't hate you." He uncrosses his arms and backs into the hallway. "Watch the video, then Brenn wants to meet you all in the mess hall. Five minutes, okay?"

"Okay."

He closes the door behind him, and I'm grateful for the privacy. Guess I have to get this over with.

My old tab is cool and familiar in my hands as I tap the message to open it. The video loads up right away, with a view of my parents sitting in their dining room, the refrigerator and door to the spice kitchen behind them. They look at each other for a moment, a silent conversation passing between them, then they face the camera.

"Hello, Nax," my ammi says, her voice solid and confident, but with an edge of sweetness that I've always associated with her. I've been hearing that voice in my head all week, every time I touched the ships' controls, reminding me of our piloting lessons. Hearing it for real is . . . nice. In her typical way, she launches right into things, direct and honest. "First of all, erase every awful thing you think we're about to say from your brain. You should really know us better than that by now."

My dad clears his throat, a faint blush staining his fair cheeks. He always did get embarrassed at emotional discussions. "We know that part of why you left home was because you felt like you made trouble for us. And I know by the end we weren't all on the best of terms. I won't lie, son, it wasn't always easy, and there were times where I wanted to punch your uncle Ronnie in the face for the things he said—"

Ammi elbows him sharply in the side, and he coughs, grins weakly. "But now that you've stopped a galactic terrorist attack, he can eat it, so thanks for that."

"We just wanted you to have a stable career of some sort, but I suppose all of this . . . heroic stuff will do," Ammi adds with a vague hand wave.

My dad starts to make a terrible lawyer joke to defuse the mushy feelings, but he's silenced by an all-too-familiar look from my mother, the look that melts criminals and cracks witnesses. I feel a rush of affection for them, the familiarity of their banter. The desperation to escape to the Academy and leave my childhood home in the dust feels so far away now. It was what I needed, and I still think it was the right decision, but I can't help missing them now. I wish we had left it on better terms, though, wish I'd been kinder to them in those last few minutes. Or at least that I'd hugged them or something, instead of storming off in silence.

"Well," my dad continues, "at least you're doing better than Uncle Ronnie's son. That child is a train wreck waiting to happen, let me tell you. But the point is, we're sorry if we ever made you feel unwelcome. And we're proud of you."

"And we're so glad you and Malik have finally worked things out," my ammi says, wiping her eyes. "I always hated that the accident drove such a wedge between you two, especially right before he left home. You always looked up to him so much."

My cheeks heat, and my eyes burn in the corners. Trust my dad to know my reaction and save the day, though.

"*Anyway*, we know we can't expect to see you face-to-face anytime soon. The nice man from the GCC told us that even though your circumstances are unusual and you were technically given clearance to return to Earth when you were, uh, denied enrollment, that the no-return rule is still in effect for you since you traveled beyond Ellis Station."

It's like a punch to the gut all over again, and I can tell they feel it the same way. It feels more real in this moment, looking at their faces, than it has through all of the explosions and fancy flying and evading arrest. I can never go back, and my heart *hurts* with it.

"And it's fine, we're sure that's the way you wanted it anyway," Ammi cuts in. "The cows and goats may miss you desperately, but I'm sure you haven't missed them one bit." Her bright eyes dance with good humor, like I know they will when I tell her about the Goat Incident. She'll love it. "We've always known you wouldn't stay here a moment longer than you had to. Always with your head in the stars. We don't take it personally."

"Well, your mother doesn't," Dad says, "but she's always been the better half."

They share a smile that makes my heart ache for a minute, then turn back to the camera. "The point is, Nax," my ammi adds, "we're thinking maybe one day we'll retire out there, once your grammy and pa are gone and your cousins get their heads out of—well, we still have hope for them. But we hope to see you again one day, beta."

"And until then," my dad commands, "if you don't send us regular messages and return to Earth orbit at least twice per year for video calls, I will send your mother out after you. She made senior detective this week, so be afraid!"

I thumb a bit of wetness from my cheeks as I laugh, nodding even though they can't see me. "Got it, Dad."

The light catches on the tiny jeweled stud in her nose as Ammi leans forward to press a kiss to her tab screen.

"Love you, Nax," she says.

And it's over.

I'm tempted to lie here a while longer, play it again, but I shouldn't. I have to put on my captain face and go to this meeting. Truth told, I've been avoiding the others since we came down from the high of our victory and jumped back to Valen. I spent a night at my brother's house, played with his dog, got to know Brenn a bit, because I know they'll be around and it turns out that Brenn is pretty great when she's not being scary. The others? Who knows. They'll probably be going their separate ways once they've had some downtime.

I make my way down the hall to find Asra huddled in the corner of the rec room, listening to her sister's latest message, while Case and Zee sprawl across the giant bed and watch the news projected on the far wall.

". . . appeared to be a sonic weapon that would affect the entire population as the signal was propagated across each planet. The technology, including the high-powered transmitter, is being studied by Earth-based scientists as we speak. The last of the so-called Earth First terrorists who had infiltrated the station were apprehended late last night. Efforts are under way to discover the full extent of the corruption, though experts believe it will be some time before all collaborators throughout the colonies can be identified and charged. Citizens of all worlds are asked to come forward with information that may assist local and interstellar law enforcement in making the arrests. An all-systems bulletin has also been posted for Dr. Maia

Herrera, former headmaster of the academy at Ellis Station, who managed to flee before—"

"Bullshit!" Case sputters. Zee shushes her with a hand on her shoulder.

"—and is believed to have been assisted in her escape by a law enforcement officer sympathetic to the Earth First cause. Jace Pearson, a prominent al-Rihla politician who coordinated Earth First efforts on the colony and is believed to have funded much of the campaign, has also disappeared. Meanwhile, memorials and vigils are being held on Earth and all colony worlds in memory of the thousands who lost their lives on Ellis Station and the previously unknown colony of Tau'ri. The death toll is still rising as investigation continues. The five youth responsible for bringing the—"

Case taps the tab screen to silence the video, obviously as sick to death as I am of reporters playing the same footage over and over again: our call back to the GCC, our reactions to the official pardon, our group statement (written and delivered by Rion, of course). We've been famous for all of three days, and I'm already sick of it. With a roll of my eyes, I push off the doorjamb and clear my throat.

"Meeting in the mess hall," I say. "Coming?"

Case shuts down the projection and scrambles off the bed, then takes Asra's hand and pulls her up. Zee does a graceful leap off the bed and lands on the balls of her feet, bouncing.

"We'll see you there in a minute," she says. And I'm alone again. I blow out a slow breath for this next one.

When I get to Rion's door, I poke my head in and wince at the sight of him reading on his bed. It's hard to look at him right now, knowing he'll be gone soon.

"Meeting time. You in?" I ask.

He smiles. "Hey, there you are. Thought you'd disappeared on us again."

He gets up from his desk and walks over to me, hands in his pocket, the air between us growing more tense with each step closer. I wrestle with myself for a long moment, my eyes locked on his, pulse hammering in my ears.

I could. I *want* to. The tension stretches, tightens—

I take a step back.

"The others are waiting," I whisper, though the corner of his mouth is lifted in a regretful smile. I back into the hallway, Rion right behind me, and every cell in my body screams to forget the others, make them wait, just *go for it*.

But I'm not about to start something only to have it end tomorrow. He's probably leaving. Why torture myself with a taste of what I can't have?

We walk together in near silence, our shoulders brushing in the narrow hallway. I wish I'd gotten to take that nap; I'm pretty sure I could fall asleep right on top of the mess table. Except we round the corner and find the others drawing on it. In permanent marker.

"Are you defacing our table?" I ask, incredulous.

"Nope," Asra says, sketching a stylized, blocky number four. "Just personalizing a bit." She finishes with a flourish and leans back, revealing a date—today's date, sketched out in Universal Time Code: 17|08|2194. The name VSS *Swift Kick* arcs above it in looping script. She signs *Asra Haque* below it, then taps the marker against the table as I sit beside her, Rion sliding onto the bench next to me. Brenn and Malik walk in a moment later and take their seats, so I grab the pepper shaker from the center of the table and bang it gently against the shining metal.

"I call this meeting of rejects to order. I hope everyone's most recent round of interrogations with the GCC went well?" Groans, eye rolls, sighs. About what I expected. "Yeah, mine was great too. Glad it's over. Brenn, you had news?"

She nods and pulls out her tab. "Just wanted to give you an update on the repair work. The *Kick* was in pretty rough shape when you got here, but we've managed to finish most of the bodywork already. I've left a few scars in place that I personally think give her a bit of a rakish flair, but we're happy to fix those for you too, if you want."

She projects a list of critical systems onto the wall with notes next to each. "The shield batteries took some serious stress, so those have to go, but the engines held up incredibly well. We're reloading your ammo and missile tube, and we've already repaired the shrapnel damage to the starboard-side gun. I've got a few more toys I might slide under the hood if time allows, too. But there's one critically important decision that still needs to be made. Your paint job."

She stands, claps a hand on my shoulder. "You drive a hard bargain, Captain Hall. For your near-insulting negotiated price, I couldn't *totally* control my designer. Mind of her own, that one, quite something to rein in. But I think you'll be happy with her choices all the same."

She walks back to her seat and taps her tab, and a perfect 3D scan of the *Kick* appears, spinning slowly. But rather than the disassembled, battle-scarred thing she is now, this *Swift Kick* is utterly gorgeous.

Her long, sleek lines are even more pronounced, the pinstripes flowing along the curves of the ship and accenting her natural lines. If Brenn's painters can pull that off, they're true artists. Instead of her former dusky blue-black, she glows in a white-gold metallic paint, like a small sun. Flecks of silver dance where simulated light bounces off the paint.

And just in front of the engines, her name is painted in strong, looping script: VSS *SWIFT KICK*, with some kind of design below it. Brenn zooms in on the spot, then folds her arms and gives me her smuggest smile.

Under the arc of the name are two human silhouettes. One person's leg is lifted in a high, strong kick. The outlined foot is buried between the legs of the other silhouette. A swift kick to the balls.

"Oh my god," Case says through a laugh, and Rion collapses forward onto the table beside me with an undignified snort.

"Brenn, you truly know us well," I say over the crew's middle-school giggles. "It's perfect. Thank you."

"Pleased you like it, 'cause that's what you're getting." She plays it stern, but her eyes betray her humor. She waves her tablet near Asra's and transfers the design file, and Asra immediately projects it back up on the wall. Brenn and Malik stand and make their way to the door.

"Y'all come by for dinner at Brenn's tonight, okay? I'm cooking," Malik says, a bit of our shared accent creeping back in. My stomach growls in anticipation.

"We'll be there," I say. He nods, and Brenn puts a hand at the small of his back to guide him out. I spread my hands and look to the others. "More news? Anything that can top that?"

Asra grins. "Well, not so much news as digital spoils of war. Once you pulled your laughing-gas trick, I had plenty of time to play around in the Academy's databases until they cut me off, so I thought I'd pull some goodies for you all. Here," she says, hitting a few buttons on her tab screen, "are all of your Academy records, including forms filled out after your entrance exams. I didn't read them," she adds quickly. "I know there's a lot of private information in there. But I thought you might want to read what they wrote about you before you make your decision."

"Decision about what?" I ask. I don't bother opening up the file; the malicious comments and awful memories aren't going anywhere. They'll keep.

Silence falls over the group. Some kind of significant eyebrow gesture passes between Case and Rion, and Rion sighs.

"Guess you didn't check your messages. We just got word a few hours ago," he says. "The new interim headmaster at the Academy has unrejected us. We can start next week, if we want."

A hollow pit opens up in my stomach. I knew they'd all be leaving eventually, but I hoped we'd have a few weeks together, at least. Gotta breathe, gotta say something, be supportive—

"Well, that's awesome. I'm really happy for all of you. You'll have to let Asra and I drop by to visit you all once you get your assignments. And the *Kick* is always yours if you need transport somewhere. Free of charge, of course."

Zee snorts in the awkward silence. "I appreciate the sentiment, Nax," she says, folding her arms on the table in front of her. "But I was hoping you would have need of a medic for the *Kick*. I would be happy to offer my services."

My heart gives a little leap. "Of course! I mean . . . right, Asra?"

Asra grins. "I'll leave personnel decisions up to the captain, though I believe Zee's track record speaks for itself.

I already have our first cargo-hauling job lined up, and though it should be perfectly tame, you never know when you might need a mend or a swift kick to someone's . . . head. And hey, the ship is kind of named for her."

Zee nods. "It's true. I would be happy to kick many more things in this ship's service, if you'll have me."

"God, is this even a question? Of course you're welcome to stay. I'm sure Asra and I will be glad for the company, and you might even get to kick Jace when we go back for him." I offer my hand to Zee across the table, and she gives it a firm shake. It's a deal, then.

"Yeah, I'm staying too. And no, that's not up for a vote," Rion says, leaning his shoulder against mine. Under the table, his hand lands on my knee and squeezes—and stays there, his thumb brushing back and forth. My breath catches in my throat at the warmth in his eyes. "We got shot together. Can't just abandon you after that. Besides, if you're flying around the galaxy taking jobs and making deals, you'll need someone who can talk a game without putting a foot in his mouth."

A laugh bursts out of me, and I feel like my chest is cracking open—but in a good way, for once.

"Fair enough. We can definitely use your skills in that area." I let my fingers drift against his under the table, savoring the tiny thrill in my stomach. His smile is stunning. I'm regretting that opportunity I passed up in the hall earlier, but I'll be making up for it the second we're alone again. I can feel it already, my hand bunched in his shirt, his lips against mine, warm and confident like his voice, and . . .

Rion smirks, as if reading my thoughts, and my cheeks grow hot. It takes me a moment to catch my breath before I can turn to Case and prepare myself for her verdict. We all know what's coming, and I smile to make it easier for her.

She fixes her eyes on me and shrugs.

"I already sent a message back to the Academy."

There was never any chance of the entire crew sticking around. They're all so smart and capable, with tons of talents they can put to use anywhere in the colonies. They all came to the Academy in the first place with ideas about what their life out here would look like. The tiny bit of hope I'd held on to crumbles. I can't be selfish. I have Asra, Zee, and Rion, at least for now. Case deserves this. I hold out my hand for her like I did for Zee, and give it a firm shake.

"Well, congratulations," I say, and my voice even sounds mostly steady. "I'm really happy for you."

"I deferred," she says.

I blink.

"What?"

She smiles, a slow, sly thing that creeps onto her lips bit by bit. "Under the Academy's charter, students can defer enrollment after preliminary acceptance for up to one year without penalty. I deferred my decision. So," she says with a little kick under the table, "if you'll have me, I'd like to stick with you all for a while. Train up a new copilot, at least. Gotta make sure you don't fly yourselves into a sun or something, right?"

"God, yes!" I say with a disbelieving laugh. "Yes, please, I'd love for you to prevent our inevitable fiery deaths."

Rion reaches his unoccupied hand across the table to bump knuckles with Case, and Zee plucks the permanent marker from Asra's hands. She writes for a moment, then passes it to Case, then to Rion. They each sign their full name below Asra's signature:

Asra Haque
Zinaida Ivanova Rozhkova
Casandra "Case" Hwang-Torres
Rion William Kwesi Turner

It's perfect. The crew of the *Swift Kick. My* crew. My friends.

Rion presses the marker into my hand, tangling our fingers together and bringing them to his lips. "Last but never least, Captain. Finish it off."

I take the marker and lean over the table, adding my own messy scrawl to the end of the list.

Nasir Alexander Hall, Captain

Then, with a wicked smirk, I sketch our new ball-kicking logo at the bottom.

Yeah, I know. I'm a bit of a disaster. But hey, aren't we all?

Doesn't mean we can't fly.

Acknowledgments

This book was secretly built from the affectionate frustration, patience, and hard work of an entire space station's worth of people who I dragged on this wild space adventure with me. Y'all are the best.

First thanks always go to my parents: my mom, who took me to the library, indulged me at Waldenbooks in the mall, and kept my feet on the ground; and my dad, who taught me all about space and rockets and Isaac Asimov, took me to work with him at United Space Alliance, and made me dream of stars. Thanks to you both for teaching me courage, passion, and work ethic, and for letting me be myself—a giant weirdo.

To my amazing/scary/fabulous agent, Barbara Poelle, who wooed me with Sherlock gifs, endured my anxiety, and made everything possible. I have the world's fiercest warrior agent on my side! Thanks for making dreams come true and all that mushy crap.

To Abby Ranger, who first acquired this book; Abby's smart assistant, Rose (who I know only by her clever comments on this manuscript); Emilia Rhodes, who brought wisdom and polish to the final drafts; and Stephanie Stein, who saw *The Disasters* through to the end: thanks for believing in my book, for sharing your vision for these space nerds with me, and for bringing me into the HarperCollins fold. Everyone involved in this process, from copyeditors to designers to typesetters to publicists and many more: thanks for making this book shiny. I appreciate you all and look forward to our next project together.

In my librarian life: thanks first to Maureen Frank, who told me I was a good writer once and had no idea it was exactly what I needed to hear at exactly the right time. To all my lovely coworkers, especially Hayley, who put up with my utter spaciness and fluctuating stress levels—thanks/sorry! And, of course, to my teens in both AC and Virginia: you are all over these pages in small ways because you inspire me every day. You're amazing people, I adore you all, and I can't wait to see who you become.

Fandom friends, both new and old: Rachel, Dara, LeighAnne, Leslie, Darcy, Heather, Lesley, Cait, Christine, Catherine, Anya, Dante, Misty, and the whole trash crew, too many wonderful people to name. You give me life, you beta read my fic, you answer my weird questions (because we have every specialty covered in our group chat), and you listen to me scream about literally everything. Thanks.

I had an army of readers who worked hard to keep me from embarrassing myself. All remaining mistakes are on me! Lemon and Kerri, agent sisters extraordinaire, who gave this book its first true ass-kicking way back in 2015. Please, miss, I'd like some more. Clara, who read my first terrible book and made me think that maybe I could do this thing. The incomparable Sheba Karim for her guidance, including catching plot holes you could fly a spaceship through. Rania B. and Mey Valdivia Rude, for giving me important things to think about and being enthusiastic cheerleaders. You were all essential to this process and you have my gratitude.

The whole Pitch Wars organization played a huge role in bringing this book to print. Thank you to Brenda Drake and her tireless crew for the immense amount of work it takes to make Pitch Wars happen. Sarah, thanks for being my guide to the publishing process and introducing me to the group that would become my writing family. The Pitch Wars class of 2015 is an incredible group of talented and kind souls. You're all so important to me. A few in particular:

Mike, who is far wiser than me and always managed to be there right when I needed to be pulled off a ledge. Cindy, my HarperCollins sister: your generosity and strength astound me. Retreat friends Monica and Steph: may we always be there to save each other from spiders. Everyone who's ever responded to one of my frantic pleas to read a chapter (which I swear is half the group at this point, but definitely Jenny, Kate, Anissa, Isabel, Maria, and probably a dozen others): you rock, I appreciate you, and I owe you one! Leigh the character genius, who endures my lengthy rambles while I talk out book ideas: thanks for always being there for a good G-chat scream or writing date. And my dearest Jamie: What would I do without you? My reader, my friend, my partner-in-potato—you are incredible, you are strong, and you deserve all the wonderful things. I'm gonna go mail you some toilet paper now.

(. . . and I actually did. You're welcome.)

To the Electric Eighteens: thanks for being my support system and sharing your wisdom through this wild ride of a debut year. Special shout-out to my SFF buddies!

Lisen: How do I even thank you? You literally sat across from me and shared my wasabi peas as I wrote this book in 2014, and I had no idea that would become one of the most important moments—and friendships—in my life. Thanks for reading this book a thousand times, and for being my lovely writing wife and fellow overambitious take-charger. Spacegoats forever!

Miscellaneous thanks: to my English teachers over the years, especially Ms. Todd and Ms. Davidson. Even though I didn't actually get the confidence to write until many years later, I never forgot that you told me I should. To Dave, my favorite DM, who feeds my need for gaming: many book and character ideas were born at your table. Thanks for being a constant source of inspiration and taking me to Disney so I can chill tf out. To New Jersey Sarah, who let me talk their ear off about queer things, library stuff, and Sherlock: many thanks. You got this.

And last but never least, my partner, Nathan, whose contributions to this book are too numerous to be contained here. Endurer of my brainstorm ranting, listener of my crappy first drafts, cleaner of my messes, preparer of my sustenance, and guardian of the endless scraps of random receipts and envelopes that actually contain critical plot information and character arcs and I will die if you throw them away. I would never have made it this far without you.

I've surely forgotten many people. To everyone who has supported me along the way: please accept my gratitude for your help in getting me here.

And to everyone who has read this far: thanks to you, too. Be kind to one another.

Keep reading for a sneak peek at
M. K. England's next book:
Spellhacker

ONE

I DON'T KNOW WHY I thought the cops wouldn't follow me onto the roof.

Honestly, most of the time it's true. When I go up, the cops stay down, and I'm home free a minute later. Ninety-nine jobs out of a hundred are in, steal, out, profit.

It figures that this, our crew's last job ever, would be the one fiery exception.

"Dispatch, this is 21-501. I have the suspect cornered on the roof of the Ivon Building. Requesting backup and air support."

Cornered? Please. She knows I'm up here, but she doesn't know *where*. It's only a matter of time, though. And isn't air support a bit overkill? The officer sweeps her gaze over the rooftop, pulling threads of glowing fire between her fingers as she glances right over the nook I've crammed myself into. The low concrete wall at my back bleeds evening chill through my hoodie, and my thighs burn with the exhaustion of holding still in a crouch after running for a mile straight. I clutch my bag tighter, as if that will somehow erase the vials of stolen maz inside.

This is fine. Totally under control.

Ania is probably close by, near enough to cook me up a distraction of some kind if I ask. I sneak a hand slowly into my back pocket and click the button to turn my deck back on. It gives a slight vibration in response. I turned it off earlier so I wouldn't get distracted by messages and calls while I was busy, you know, *not getting arrested*, and about a billion missed notifications flood my vision as soon as the interface pops up in my contact lenses.

Epic Group Chat: LAST JOB EVER Edition
Jaesin: Remi and I are almost home
Ania: I'm still waiting on Diz at the meet point
Dizzzzzzzz
WHERE ARE YOU
The client is getting pissed
He says if you bring cops down on him he'll make sure we're blacklisted
Jaesin: Good thing this is our last job anyway
Remi: you ok, diz?
don't make me come after you dizzy I will fight
Jaesin: She probably found some shiny new building to climb
DIDN'T YOU DIZ

Your vital signs for the hour: Average pulse rate, 98; Blood pressure . . .

(private) Remi: diz?

Kyrkarta weather update: Scattered showers beginning at
3:30 a.m., with . . .

(private) Jaesin: Don't be an ass, call Remi
They're kind of panicking right now
(private) Ania: Okay, we're really worried

Sera Shortner followed you. Follow them back?

(private) Davon: You decided about the job offer yet?
I sent you a little something for graduation
It's fine, I know I'm the best cousin ever, you don't have to say
(private) Ania: Diz, I'm seriousssssssssssss.
(private) Jaesin: Do we need to turn around and come back?

I double-blink to clear the clutter from my vision, then
give the deck a silent command to bring up a map. The tiny
sensors that read the movement of my throat have been
messing up *all the time* lately, though, so I get my bank app,
a word game, and a half-read fanfic before I actually get the
map I asked for. Ania's dot blinks on the map at the drop
point, about two blocks from my location. Definitely close
enough to create some kind of diversion for me. I start to
subvocalize a message to the group chat, hesitate . . . then
delete the whole thing and close the map.

They'll all be gone in a week. Literally moving on with their lives, to a whole new city. College, jobs, all that.

I'm not going anywhere. Besides, I know this city better than anyone. If anyone can figure a way out of this, it's me. I need to do this myself.

I let my head fall back against the wall and try to visualize the roof. In the half dozen times I've been up here before, I've used the maintenance ladder, the staff exit, or the breezeway over to the next building. This cop is between me and all of them. I ease myself up slowly, just high enough to see over the wall at my back and past the hulking air-conditioning unit behind it to the roof's nearest edge. Against the inky black sky, two faint curves are backlit by the glow of the neon signs from the street below. A fire-escape ladder.

In the distance, the whine of aircar engines and sirens grows louder.

Well. No time like the present.

As soon as the cop turns her back to me, I vault over the low wall and sprint for the ladder. Her shout goes up barely a second later—"Halt!"—which is about a second longer than I expected to have, honestly. I dive to one side, tumbling over a two-foot-wide pipe with the bag held tight against my stomach. A bright flash of orange maz blasts the metal just beside my hand, turning it red-hot in a flash. Seriously, she's just gonna sling firaz around? She

4

doesn't know what's in these pipes. What if they explode?

Apparently, she doesn't care. Another fireball blasts at my heels, leaving a black scorch on the concrete.

Point taken.

I grab the top of the ladder where it connects with the roof and swing myself over the edge, dangling by one hand for half a terrifying second until my feet find the rungs. My shoulder screams in brief protest, but it's used to this kind of abuse by now. A quick glance below, and I spot a landing about two stories down, where the ladder turns to stairs. Perfect.

Another blast of fire connects with the top of the ladder, then two more in quick succession. Then more. What the hell is she doing? What a waste of maz. I guess when the city's paying for it, you can use as much as you want, though.

Then the ladder starts to heat up under my hands, and I understand.

Shit.

I need to hurry, outclimb the warming metal under my palms. I risk another glance down. The landing is closer, at least; less than one story to go. Above me, the cop pokes her head over the side and winds up for another blast.

I let go.

For one brief second, my chest fills with the weightless

thrill of falling, falling.

Then I look down, soften my knees to absorb the shock, and exhale as I land on the balls of my feet and guide myself into a forward tumble. Perfect form, way to stick the landing, self.

Unfortunately, the platform is slightly shorter than I anticipated, and I roll straight past the edge of the landing and onto the first staircase. Behind me, the landing rattles with another blast of firaz, then another, closer. A message pops up in my vision:

(private) Ania: Our client is getting ready to murder me, therefore I'm getting ready to murder YOU

Our client can eat one thousand bees for all I care. I subvocalize a message back that thankfully translates correctly.

(private) you: Kindly FUCK OFF when your best friend is being chased by the cops

Perfect. Good rule for life.

I use my unintended momentum to swing myself over the railing onto the next set of stairs, then the next, the bag full of stolen maz thumping against the small of my back with each landing. If I were at all talented with maz, I could have sacrificed one of the vials (and a bit of our

6

pay) to fight back. Maz is not my thing, though. You want your ex's social media profiles hacked so they look like an ass? I'm on it. With maz, I'm useless.

Well, except for the stealing-and-selling-it thing.

Far above me, the staircase rattles as the cop makes her way down in the more traditional manner, but as soon as my feet hit the asphalt, I may as well be invisible. I'm gone, around a corner, over a fence, through a narrow alley—

—and onto an empty street with another officer at either end.

Seriously?

Both cops charge at me, but before I can find yet another alternate route, an arm darts out from the alley I just came from and yanks me back, then behind a dumpster. I'm all but thrown against the cold stone wall—by Ania. Thank the stars.

"Our client actually let you leave to rescue me?" I ask through gasping breaths.

"Kindly *fuck off* while your best friend is trying to save your ass."

I bite back a grin. Ania *never* swears like that. I'm proud to be responsible for it.

Between us, her fingers fly as she weaves together a quick and simple concealment spell. Plum-colored strands of obscuraz pour from her fingertip implants, coming together in a tightly knit pattern. She ties it off with a

7

quick yank, then rips it in half and shoves half of it into my hands, keeping half for herself.

"Stay absolutely still," she murmurs.

The spell crumbles into faintly glowing sparks as it takes effect, and I press back against the alley wall and breathe as shallowly as I can. Ania does the same, taking my hand and holding tight as all three cops converge on the alley. The woman who chased me across the rooftops does a slow scan of the entire alley, sharp eyes looking for any sign of our whereabouts. She takes a step closer to the dumpster, squinting at something on the ground, then peeking around behind the thing until she's looking right through us.

One of the other cops calls out to her, and I flinch, my shoe making the faintest scuffing sound . . . but she pulls away and turns back to her counterparts, meeting them back in the middle of the alley. They talk too quietly for me to hear well, but it sounds like they're trying to assign blame for losing me. Just as I'm starting to go light-headed from the lack of breath, they turn to leave, disappearing back in the direction I ran from.

Once they've been gone for two full minutes, I shake off Ania's hand and step away to get some space, taking a few deep breaths.

"Thanks," I say, still keeping an eye on the mouth of the alley. "Let's get to Mattie's. I want this maz off my

8

back and those credits in our account."

Ania nods vaguely, zoned out in that way that means she's doing something on her lenses, her slim legs crossed at the ankles, where expensive skinny jeans and low boots let a strip of warm brown skin peek out. The yellowy light from the streetlamp shines through her hazy cloud of curls, wrapping each dark strand in threads of gold. We seriously just left the sewers forty-five minutes ago—how the *hell* does she look so put together? She must have ditched her sewage-covered rain boots somewhere.

Ania snaps back to reality and dodges my gaze in a way that I know means she was just messaging Jaesin about me. She turns to lead the way back to our drop point, and I scowl at the back of her head, dashing off a quick message to Remi as I follow.

(private) you: Hey, sorry, ran into some trouble. It's fine now. Heading to the drop point.
(private) Remi: GOOD because I have something that will make you die
DIZZY LOOK

The next message is a link to a news article: "Tifa and the Flower Girls to Play Two Surprise Shows in Kyrkarta on Aeraday and Firaday." A photo quickly follows: Remi with their hands pressed to their cheeks, screaming at the camera.

(private) Remi: WE ARE GOING
I'm heckin serious I don't care what Jaesin and Ania say

I bite my lip and clear the notification away, swallowing down the knot in my throat. Of course we'll go. One last chance to dance with Remi before they leave, the bass pounding in our chests, singing in our blood. I start to reply, then delete it.

Later. I'll deal with it later.

We cross the block to the next intersection, moving slowly to take advantage of any lingering effects from the concealment spell. It won't do any good if we run screaming down the street, but if we're chill, it might help an errant gaze or two slide past us. A few minutes of tense silence later, we arrive at a nondescript elevator that takes us up twenty levels.

A quick walk across one of the thousands of breezeways connecting the buildings of Kyrkarta, and we come to a darkened flower shop with loud, busy arrangements filling the front window. The CLOSED message glows bright in one corner, but the door opens anyway, held by a guy a few years older than us with tawny skin and *way* more piercings than me. Mattie, our client for this job. He's got a siphoning crew of his own, but they couldn't

10

get it together in time to pull off this job for whatever reason, so they contracted it out to us. Their loss.

It's a big haul, and the particular combo of maz strains they requested took us to a part of the city we'd never hit before. Maz Management Corporation's system looks the same no matter where you are, though: pipes in sewers, hiking through sludge, Ania and Jaesin watching our backs while I hack the security and Remi draws out the maz in manageable quantities. We got it done, despite the trouble at the end.

"Where's the goods?" Mattie asks as he leads us into the back. His sweet old mother who owns the shop would skin him alive if she knew that "staying late to clean the shop" actually meant "conducting illegal business in the stockroom." I let the pack slip down my arms and swing it up onto a work top littered with trimmed stems, wilting leaves, and shed petals.

"I didn't realize I was supposed to walk in juggling the vials for all to see," I say with an eyeroll, pulling a hard plastic case from the bag. I click the latches open and lift the top to reveal five clear vials nestled in their foam padded spots. Each one glows with contained threads of maz, coiled as tight as each strain allows. Our very last haul. Thick bronze terraz, sparking green vitaz, some of the same hazy purple obscuraz Ania used earlier.

Mattie picks up each one and inspects them all carefully, like he's some kind of master maz connoisseur. I bite the inside of my lip to hold in a sigh of annoyance. A less obnoxious client would have been a much nicer way to end our siphoning career together. So much for going out in a grand blaze of glory, walking off into the sunset with our riches as a team, the latest overplayed graduation anthem seeing us off.

Then again, this group has always been a mess, and I'm pretty sure it's my fault.

Epic Group Chat: LAST JOB EVER Edition
Remi: Are you dead, Dizzy?
Ania, are they killing her?
Ania: Remains to be seen. She's getting fussy. Will report back.

Fussy? I burn a hole in the side of Ania's face with my glare. I'm actually going to be forced to murder her.

Jaesin: I call dibs on her deck
Remi: Please, she probably has that thing programmed to self-destruct if she dies
You know what she's got on there
Jaesin: No, I don't
and I don't want to

The corner of my mouth pulls up in a half smile. I quite enjoy this reputation of mine, at least partially deserved. My files are largely boring records of which public officials are breaking their spousal agreements, local celebrities' secret dating profiles, and the internet search histories of Kyrkarta's most prominent business leaders. I suppose some people might find it valuable information, but gathering it all is just a way to keep myself entertained when I can't sleep.

"Oi, what's with this one?" Mattie snaps, pulling my attention away from the group chat. He holds one of the vials of obscuraz between his thumb and middle finger, tilting it this way and that to let the light filter through the strands. I see what he means. It's a notably different shade than the other vials of the same maz, like a few of the threads have turned a brighter violet-purple.

"Did you bring me contaminated maz?" he says, shoving the vial in my face. My stomach turns, and I jerk away, putting the table between us.

"That's what came out of the tap point, Mattie," I shoot back, working to keep my expression under control. "We went where you told us. MMC's pipes are clean. It's not contaminated."

Even as I say it, as I *know* it's true, the worry begins to boil in my stomach. Remi is the only one who ever has contact with the maz we siphon off from MMC's pipes, and they were diagnosed with the spellplague when they were eight. Would they even know if the maz was contaminated? It's not like you can get infected again if you're already ill.

Mattie growls and puts the vial down with the others. "I'm only paying half for that one, and if it *is* contaminated, I'll put the word out, believe it."

Ania meets my gaze, then looks at the ceiling, her subtle way of rolling her eyes among company. We're never working a job again *period*, no matter how much I might want to, so he can shove his empty threats.

"Fine, yes, half for that one vial," I say. "Can we please close this deal now? We've got places to be."

Mattie scowls but pulls out his deck and sets to work on the credit transfer. A moment later, a transaction notification pops up on my lenses. Payment cleared. Our bank account once again has more than two digits.

"Pleasure doing business," I say, throwing the vial case back in my bag and walking away, Ania on my heels, before Mattie can find another excuse to complain. As I reach the elevator, I bring the group chat back on-lens with a grin.

Epic Group Chat: LAST JOB EVER Edition
you: Against everyone's better judgment, he did not kill me. We have our money
Remi: DIZZY YESSSSSSS
SHE LIVES
Jaesin: Thank god, now we can CELEBRATE
Ania: Let the Grand Farewell Tour commence!
you: You all were in mortal peril today too, you know

14

Ania: Yeah, but *we* don't inspire murdery feelings in everyone we meet
Remi: Yikes, shots fired

I shove Ania's shoulder, and the elevator fills with our laughter. I can't wait to get home, even as I feel a weird sort of nostalgia for those little vials of maz we just left behind. Ten years of friendship, two years running jobs together, and now it's over. The others are understandably ecstatic, brimming over with the thrill of getting away with one last haul and looking forward to their shiny futures. Futures that require moving away.

In seven days.

Hence our Grand Farewell Tour of Kyrkarta: seven nights, seven locations, one amazing last hurrah before we go our separate ways.

Before they all move away and abandon me here, more like.

Ania startles me out of my mood with a quick excited double clap.

"I have a surprise for you," she says, throwing an arm around me and leaning down to rest her head against the top of mine. I cringe but endure her cuddling. Might as well take it while I can.

"I hate surprises," I say. "What is it?"

She grins and holds up one hand, waggling her fingers as the elevator stops and the doors slide open. Her

15

wrist and the inside of each finger are lined with thin metal, unassuming, but actually packed with bend sensors, accelerometers, and other techy bits. The tip of each finger ends in a small implanted extruder that, by her command, releases threads of whatever maz she had loaded into the chambers strapped to the underside of her wrist. She doesn't have the natural ability to work maz with her bare hands, like Remi does, but she's good with her hardware. She's had her maz license since the day she turned eighteen—not that the lack of a license stopped her before. Not with me as a friend. I may not be able to work with maz myself, but I can build ware better than anything her mommy and daddy can find in an overpriced shop. Her ware is a Dizmon Hela original, and I'm proud of my work.

"This is a fun surprise, promise," she says, flipping her hand over to glance at her nails instead. "I went in for an A-level maz certification practice test today, and I think I pushed it a little too hard. The fifth position flow was kinda weird and uneven during our job. Wanna fix it before we go out tonight?"

I perk right up, then narrow my eyes. "You know I do, but don't think this gets you off my list. *Fussy?* Are you serious?"

"I love you, Dizzard Lizard," she sings, syrupy sweet, and I fight down an unexpected surge of anger. She obviously doesn't love me enough to *not leave*. None of them do. I want to sink in to that anger, to let its talons grip tight and pierce and fill my veins with heat. It's right there under the surface, all the time, just waiting for the wrong turn of phrase, the wrong change of subject.

But if I say anything, I'll only lose them all sooner.

My shoulders slump, and I take three long, deep breaths, one for each word.

Let. It. Go.

"Come on, then," I say, beckoning her forward. "Let's see what poison Jaesin has on the cooker tonight, and I'll take a look at that mix sensor before we go out. You didn't notice it until we were already in the middle of the job?"

She hums in agreement but doesn't elaborate as we cross into the crowded intersection at Four Bridges, where the three rivers converge at the business sector. Too many voices clamoring for airspace, and Ania hates to shout. We pass glowing storefronts nestled in the bottom floors of bulky office buildings, offering everything from maz tech to spellweaving services, rare foods to custom aesthetic implants. We don't need any of it, of course, and I wouldn't be caught dead paying business-sector prices even if we did. We already have Ania for a techwitch, and Remi the spellweaving prodigy, and I have all our hardware needs covered. Jaesin rounds out the group with most of the mundie skills, like keeping us from starving to death. And hitting people. But only sometimes.

We pass into the slightly more run-down part of town

I call home a few minutes later, and the Cliffs, the dorm complex I live in, comes into view. With the chaos of business behind us, Ania finally answers my question.

"Yeah, I had some magnaz loaded in fifth position, and by the time I finished setting up our wards at the draw point, it wasn't flowing as easily as the rest. I was having to force it a little more than normal, and I can't stop thinking I'm gonna pull on that thread so hard I'll blow my own hand off."

"Nah, I'll take care of that. If it's not the sensor, it's the extruder, and both are easy enough to fix. Should be no problem to finish it before we go out tonight."

Out to one of Ania's fancy clubs, where we've been begging her to take us for ages, for night one of seven. The beginning of the end. My stomach sours.

Then the ground . . . shivers.

Ania and I stop dead. Wait, absolutely still.

Another tremble, longer. Definitely not imagined. Our eyes meet as the ground shifts under our feet, harder this time, a threat.

A promise.

Another earthquake.

We run.